PENGUIN BOOKS

DOUBLE VISION

'Complex, deeply engaging, wholly engrossing. A story that is both terrifying and fascinating' *New York Times*

'Precisely realized [with] unflinching intelligence and dry humour' *Independent on Sunday*

'Complex, absorbing, suspenseful. An unflinching exploration of difficult and topical territory' *Boston Globe*

'Barker poses interesting questions. She is an immensely skilled writer and this is a powerful book' *Literary Review*

'Excellent' *New York Sun*

'Barker writes superbly, with a lovely talent for darting images. The reader is drawn on, from page to page . . . it leaves one pondering on the difficult uncertainties she raises' *Economist*

'Complex, deeply engaging . . . a book of ideas' *International Herald Tribune*

'Sinewy, absorbing, exceptionally satisfying' *Metro*

'Eerily gorgeous' *Philadelphia Enquirer*

'Hard to put down . . . we want to go on reading' *New Statesman*

'Brilliant prose, clear-sighted unsentimentality. Lucid and rich with hope' *Image*

'Absorbing and strangely reassuring' *Harpers & Queen*

D0311019

ABOUT THE AUTHOR

Pat Barker was born in Thornaby-on-Tees in 1943. She was educated at the London School of Economics and has been a teacher of history and politics. Her books include *Union Street*, winner of the 1983 Fawcett Prize, which has been filmed as *Stanley and Iris*, *Blow Your House Down*, *Liza's England*, formerly *The Century's Daughter*, and the following published by Penguin: *The Man Who Wasn't There*, the highly acclaimed *Regeneration* trilogy, comprising *Regeneration*, *The Eye in the Door*, winner of the 1993 *Guardian* Fiction Prize, and *The Ghost Road*, winner of the 1995 Booker Prize for Fiction; *Another World*; *Border Crossing*; and *Double Vision*.

Pat Barker is married and lives in Durham.

Double Vision

PAT BARKER

PENGUIN BOOKS

PENGUIN BOOKS

Published by the Penguin Group
Penguin Books Ltd, 80 Strand, London WC2R ORL, England
Penguin Group (USA) Inc., 375 Hudson Street, New York, New York 10014, USA
Penguin Books Australia Ltd, 250 Camberwell Road, Camberwell, Victoria 3124, Australia
Penguin Books Canada Ltd, 10 Alcorn Avenue, Toronto, Ontario, Canada M4V 3B2
Penguin Books India (P) Ltd, 11 Community Centre, Panchsheel Park, New Delhi – 110 017, India
Penguin Group (NZ), cnr Airborne and Rosedale Roads, Albany, Auckland 1310, New Zealand
Penguin Books (South Africa) (Pty) Ltd, 24 Sturdee Avenue, Rosebank 2196, South Africa

Penguin Books Ltd, Registered Offices: 80 Strand, London WC2R ORL, England

www.penguin.com

Published by Hamish Hamilton 2003
Published in Penguin Books 2004
6

Copyright © Pat Barker, 2003

All rights reserved
The moral right of the author has been asserted

Typeset by Rowland Phototypesetting Ltd, Bury St Edmunds, Suffolk
Printed in England by Clays Ltd, St Ives plc

Except in the United States of America, this book is sold subject
to the condition that it shall not, by way of trade or otherwise, be lent,
re-sold, hired out, or otherwise circulated without the publisher's
prior consent in any form of binding or cover other than that in
which it is published and without a similar condition including this
condition being imposed on the subsequent purchaser

for David

No se puede mirar. One cannot look at this.
Yo lo vi. I saw it. *Esto es lo verdadero*. This is the truth.

– Francisco Goya

One

Christmas was over. Feeling a slightly shamefaced pleasure in the restoration of normality, Kate stripped the tree of lights and decorations, cut off the main branches and dragged the trunk down to the compost heap at the bottom of the garden. There she stood looking back at the house, empty again now – her mother and sister had left the morning after Boxing Day – seeing the lighted windows and reflected firelight almost as if she were a stranger, shut out. A few specks of cold rain found her eyelids and mouth. All around her the forest waited, humped in silence. Shivering, she ran back up the lawn.

Gradually she re-established her routine. Up early, across to the studio by eight, five hours' unbroken work that generally left her knackered for the rest of the day, though she forced herself to walk for an hour or two in the afternoons.

The weather turned colder, until one day, returning from her walk, she noticed that the big puddle immediately outside her front gate was filmed with ice, like a cataract dulling the pupil of an eye. She heated a bowl of soup, built up the fire and huddled over it, while outside the temperature dropped, steadily, hour by hour, until a solitary brown oak leaf detaching itself from the tree fell on to the frost-hard ground with a crackle that echoed through the whole forest.

People had glutted themselves on food and sociability over Christmas and New Year and wanted their own firesides, so the first few evenings of January were spent alone. But then Lorna and Michael Bradley asked her to their anniversary party and, though she was enjoying the almost monastic rhythm of her present life, she accepted. Since Ben's death that had been her only rule: to refuse no invitation, to acknowledge and return any small act of kindness – and it was working, she was getting through, she was surviving.

Once there, she enjoyed the evening, in spite of having restricted herself to just two glasses of wine, and by eleven was driving back along the forest road, her headlights revealing the pale trunks of beech trees, muscled like athletes stripped off for a race. She was leaving a stretch of deciduous forest and entering Forestry Commission land, acres of closely planted trees, rank upon rank of them, a green army marching down the hill. Her headlights scarcely pierced the darkness between the pines, though here and there she glimpsed a tangle of dead wood and debris on the forest floor. She kept the windows closed, a fug of warmth and music sealing her off from the outside world. The lighted car travelled along the road between the thickly crowding trees like a blood corpuscle passing along a vein. Somewhere in the heart of the wood an antlered head turned to watch her pass. Almost no traffic – she overtook a white van near the crossroads, but after that saw no other cars. The road dipped and rose, and then, no more than 400 yards from her home, where a stream overflowing in the recent heavy rains had run across the road forming a slick of black ice, the car left the road.

There was no time to think. Trees loomed up, leapt towards her, branches shattered the windscreen, clawed at her eyes and throat. A crash and tearing of metal, then silence, except for the tinny beat of the music that kept on playing. One headlight shone at a strange angle, probing the thick resin-smelling branches that had caught and netted the car.

She lay, drifting in and out of consciousness, aware that she mustn't try to move her head and neck. She knew she was injured, perhaps seriously, though she felt little pain as long as she kept still. Saliva dribbled from the corner of her mouth, blood settled in one eye.

After what seemed a long time she heard the noise of an engine. Her own wrecked car filled with shifting parallelograms of light and shade as the other car's headlights swept across it. The engine was switched off, footsteps rang clear on the road, slurred across the grass verge, and then a figure appeared at the window. A headless figure was all she could see, since he didn't bend to look in. She tried to speak, but only a croak came out. He didn't move, didn't open the door, didn't check to see how she was, didn't ring or go for help. Just stood there, breathing.

She tried to lift her head, but a spasm of pain shot down her spine and she knew she mustn't move. Slowly she slipped into unconsciousness, fighting all the way, then battled her way back to the surface, where now there were other voices, frightened voices – frightened of her, of what she'd become.

'Ambulance,' she heard. 'Police.'

Then the familiar sound of somebody thumbing numbers into a mobile phone, and at last she was able to let go and accept the dark.

In something too high, too tight, for a bed. White sheets pinned her legs down. Walls the colour of putty. Mum's voice, then Alice's, but she knew they couldn't be here, they'd left the day after Boxing Day, and so she refused to acknowledge them, these phantom relatives, and concentrated instead on getting some spit going in her mouth. Her tongue felt swollen, and was so dry it stuck to the roof of her mouth.

'Look,' said Alice. 'She wants a drink.'

Her mother's head came between her and the light. 'Dead to the world. Can't hear a word you're saying.'

'Oh, I don't know. They always say, don't they, "Keep talking"? You never know how much gets through.'

Was she dying? Couldn't persuade herself it mattered much.

Water . . .

Alice's scent, sharp and sweet. A spout pushed between her lips, jarred her teeth. Water, too much water, gagged, choked, spout pulled away, reinserted, gentler now, and she glugged, once, twice. Dribbles ran down the side of her neck, were dabbed away on a cold flannel. She stared at the cracks in the ceiling, only to find them replaced, almost immediately, by her mother's and her sister's heads.

'Do you think she can hear us?' Mum said.

She has been somewhere else. She remembers the trees, the dark road, the branches pushing through broken glass, the man by the window, breathing. But then it all begins to fade.

She tried to turn her head and couldn't. Some kind of brace round her neck stopped her moving. Her right arm was swaddled against her side by the tight sheet. She could feel her arms, and her legs, and her toes. She wiggled them to make sure, remembering how her father, right at the end of his long illness, after the stroke, had hated the arm he couldn't feel and kept pushing it away from him. At least she wasn't like that. It all still belonged to her, this barren plain she looked down on from the height of her raised head, this fenland under its covering of snow.

She started to drift off again, heard her mother say, 'We're only tiring her. I think we'd better go and let her sleep.'

Somebody had sent roses. She opened her eyes and there they were, tight, formal, dark red buds, like drops of blood in the white room, but her eyelids were too heavy to go on looking, and when she opened them again the roses were gone.

*

As soon as she could support herself, they got her out of bed and made her sit in the armchair beside it. Her feet were cold. She was depressed, worried about the work she wasn't doing. She'd taken on a big commission, a huge Christ for the cathedral, it should have been well on the way by now, and yet here she was, stuck in an armchair like an old woman, unable to move, helpless.

The physiotherapist came to see her, and then she started regular sessions in the physiotherapy room, where she stared in the floor-to-ceiling mirrors at the neckless creature she'd become. 'Very good,' the uniformed girls kept saying. 'Very good.' She hadn't been spoken to in such jolly, patronizing tones since she was in nappies. She smiled, desperation simmering under the surface.

Back on the ward, she set off down the corridor clinging to the rail, forcing herself to keep walking, though each step sent twinges of pain up her spine. Now and then she met another patient, similarly handicapped, head on, and then they'd pause, assess the extent of each other's disability, and decide, silently, which of them was better able to let go of the rail and stand unsupported while the other shuffled past. So much courage. So much decency. She was humbled by it.

But then it was back to the ward. Her room overlooked a courtyard where even evergreen plants, deprived of light, sickened and died.

'I've got to get out of here,' she said, when Alec

Braithewaite, the local vicar and also a friend, came to see her.

He took a step backwards, raising his hands, pretending to be knocked over by her urgency. 'Good morning, Kate.'

She sighed, accepting the reproof. 'Good morning, Alec.'

'How are you?'

'Going mad.'

He came and sat beside the bed. 'Nobody likes hospitals. The main thing is to get better.'

'The "main thing" is the Christ.'

He smiled. 'I'm pleased to hear you say so.'

'You know what I mean, Alec. *My* Christ.'

'Can you lift your arm?'

She tried, as she tried a hundred times a day. 'No.'

'When does it have to be finished?'

'May. In time for Founders' and Benefactors' Day.'

'That's not too bad.'

'Alec, it's a massive figure. It's barely enough time if I were all right.'

'Can't you negotiate another date?'

'I've never missed a deadline in my life.'

She sat brooding, her chin sunk into the padded collar. She looked broken, Alec thought, as he'd never seen her before, not even in the first weeks after Ben's death. 'Then you're going to need help.'

'I don't want an assistant.'

'Other sculptors use them, don't they?'

'Yes.'

He leaned forward. 'So what don't you like about them?'

'Where to start? For one thing, they're always art students, and they keep on asking questions. "Why did you do that? Why didn't you do the other?" And even if they don't ask, you can hear them thinking it. Nine times out of ten it just turns into a tutorial. I know it sounds terribly ungenerous, and I do – I do actually like teaching, but I don't want to do it when I'm working.'

'Does it have to be an art student?'

'It's the obvious pot to dip into.'

He shrugged. 'Depends what you want.'

'All I want is somebody strong enough to lift, who isn't . . . too interested in what I'm doing.'

'Hmm,' he said. 'Bit of bored beefcake?'

She refused to rise to him. 'Doesn't have to be a man. I do all the lifting normally.'

'Do you remember the lad who used to do the churchyard after we lost the sheep?'

A hazy memory of a young man wielding a scythe in the long grass between the headstones. 'Vaguely.'

'He's very reliable, and he builds patios and walls and things like that, so he must be fairly good with his hands. And I shouldn't think he's got a lot of work on at the moment. I know he was hoping to get a job in the timber yard, but I think that fell through. They're very quiet at the moment. Shall I see if he's available?'

'That's not a bad idea, actually. What's his name?'

'Peter Wingrave. I'll give him a ring, shall I?'

He looked down at her, noticing the lines of tension

around her eyes and mouth. What he thought she needed at this moment was faith, but he couldn't say that. She'd come to church once or twice after Ben's funeral, but only to show her appreciation of a difficult job well done. A youngish man, a violent death. It's not easy in such circumstances to know what to say, particularly to a congregation of atheists and agnostics up from London on cheap day-returns. Kate made no secret of her lack of belief. He did wonder what she'd be able to make of this commission, but then he thought that the risen Christ was, among many other things, a half-naked man in his early thirties, and Kate did male nudes very well indeed.

'How's Justine?' Kate asked, making an effort to set her own problems aside.

Alec's face brightened, as it always did at any mention of his daughter. 'Much better.'

Justine had been due to go to Cambridge last October, but in September had gone down with glandular fever and had to ask for her place to be deferred for a year. She'd been at a loose end ever since, mooching round the house, lonely and depressed. Alec had been quite worried about her, but now, he said, she'd got herself a little job as an au pair, twenty hours a week, and that gave her some pocket-money, and, even more important, a framework for the day. 'The Sharkeys. You know them? Their little boy.'

'Oh, yes. Adam, isn't it?'

'Anyway,' he said, hearing the rattle of cutlery in the corridor outside, 'I think I'd better be off and leave you to your lunch.' He bent to kiss her, and she grasped his hand. 'I'll have a word with Peter as soon as I can.'

The doors swinging shut behind him let in a smell of hot gravy and custard. She never felt hungry, though when food was put in front of her she ate it all. She knew she had to build up her strength. As she ate, she thought about Alec, who was an odd person to find in charge of a rural parish. He'd written several books on ethical issues raised by modern genetics and by developments in reproductive medicine, including one on therapeutic cloning that Robert Sharkey described as the most level-headed discussion of the topic he'd encountered. And he did a lot of work with released prisoners, battered wives, drug addicts, even converting part of his own house to give them somewhere to stay. No, he was a good man, though she didn't personally see that his goodness had much to do with his religion. And he had another claim on her affection: Ben had always liked him.

After the pudding – apple crumble indistinguishable from cement – she heaved herself out of the chair and started again on the long walk to the top of the corridor.

Winter sunshine streaming in through the tall windows created a grainy shadow that almost seemed to mock her efforts as she edged and shuffled along. Her walking was getting better, but she'd gladly have crawled around on her bum for the rest of her days if only she'd been able to raise her right arm above her head.

At night she lies awake, worrying about the Christ,

her fingers aching for the scarred handle of her mallet, as her body aches for Ben, a cold hollow inside. She tucks her knees up to her chin, consciously foetal, but the position puts too much pressure on her back and she has to straighten out again and lie on her back like an effigy. She remembers going into the church at Chillingham with Ben, turning the corner into a side chapel, finding Lord and Lady Grey together on their slab. Holding hands? Side by side, anyway, in a silence that still, after five centuries, feels companionable. And that extraordinary domestic detail: the fireplace in the wall opposite their tomb. As once there must have been a fireplace in their bedroom. Firelight on sweaty bodies, the first time they made love, firelight on the cold alabaster of their effigies. And then her mind drifts to Ben's grave in the churchyard here, backed by a low stone wall, dry blond grasses waving in the field beyond. And again she stretches out her legs, hears the rattle of the trolley bringing tea, and realizes that at some point in all this, surely, she must have slept.

A nurse crashes through the swing doors, red-faced, cheerful, rotund, rustling in her plastic apron, squeaking on rubber-soled shoes.

'Physio today, Mrs Frobisher,' she says, pouring beige tea into a cup.

Physio every bloody day.

When they'd done everything they could to get her mobile, they let her go, though she had to return to the hospital twice a week for more physiotherapy.

In the car, being driven home by her friend Angela Mowbray, Kate felt optimistic. She'd been managing better the last few days, and she knew the physiotherapist was pleased with her. Another fortnight and she'd be all right, perhaps even well enough to do without the bloody assistant. Alec still hadn't got back to her on that.

Angela looked sideways at Kate, thinking the surgical collar looked a bit like a ruff, reflecting light on to her face, emphasizing the lines of tiredness, the blue shadows underneath her eyes. Kate said she hadn't been sleeping well in hospital, but then nobody could. Footsteps squeaking up and down the ward, blinds on the corridor side left up because you had to be observed all the time, and then there were admissions, sometimes in the middle of the night. The memories of her hysterectomy were fresh in Angela's mind. Poor Kate, she thought, and such a bad patient.

They were approaching the scene of the crash. Angela slowed down – had to, it was a dangerous bend – though, imagining what Kate must be feeling, she would have preferred to pick up speed and get past as soon as possible.

'Do you mind if we stop here?' Kate said.

Surprised, Angela pulled over on to the grass verge. Kate got out. It was a struggle and Angela came round the car to help, but by the time she got there Kate was shakily standing up.

'Why do you want to stop?'

'I just want to see where it happened.'

Kate walked along the verge, thinking she might not recognize the spot, but there was no danger of that. Skidding off the road, the car had left scars, flattened bracken, made tyre tracks in the mud, smashed stripling trees – and then her nemesis: the tree whose branches, broken by the impact, had reached through the shattered windscreen to get at her. She had a flash of it happening again and closed her eyes. The trunk had proved solid, though the roots had been disturbed. She looked down and saw how they'd been prised loose from the earth. At that moment a light wind started to blow between the trees, a current of air moving at ground level, quickening the forest floor. Dead leaves rose up and formed twisters, little coils and spurts of turbulence, and the shadows of branches danced and shook on the snow-stippled ground.

Then it was over and the wood was as quiet and still as it had been before.

Kate was aware of her breathing, the sound, the movement of her ribs, and the sight of it too, furls of mist escaping from her lips to whiten the air.

Angela shifted behind her. Coughed. She thinks I'm being eccentric, Kate thought. Well, *she* can talk.

There was something else, something she needed to get clear, a memory that bulged above the surface, showed its back and then, in a burst of foam, turned and sank again. It was the sound of her breathing that had summoned it. She groped after memories that dissolved even as she tried to grasp them. She had a sense of missing time. The minutes – how many minutes? – she'd drifted in and out of consciousness, while somebody had stood by the car, breathing, watching, not calling for help.

But all her memories were confused, and for large stretches of time she had no memory at all. Nothing about the ambulance journey or the arrival in hospital, nothing about the emergency treatment, the fitting of the back brace and the surgical collar, nothing about that. Nothing, in fact, until she woke the following morning to find her mother and Alice by the bed. So probably her memory of the man who'd stood and watched her was a distortion. A symptom of concussion.

Two days after the crash a young woman doctor had sat by her bed for half an hour, asking her questions about what time it was, who she was, where she was, why she was there, and, although she hadn't felt confused or uncertain of the answers, she'd got most of them wrong.

It was a relief to turn and see Angela's worried face.

She made herself smile. 'Lucky escape.' She was thinking of another road, in Afghanistan, the road Ben had died on. For a moment she felt a deep affinity with him, a closeness, and then it vanished, and the loneliness rushed back, worse than before. She raised her hand to her neck and touched Ben's amulet, feeling the disc cold under her fingertips, rasping it along the chain. 'That's that, then,' she said. 'Come on, let's go.'

Two

Back home, Angela bustled around quite as if the place belonged to her. Kate would have liked to make herself something to eat, but Angela had brought stacks of home-made food from her freezer. Feeling useless and too tired to protest, Kate sat in her armchair and let Angela get on with it.

The fire was already laid and only needed a match put to it. Angela propped a newspaper up against the hearth, and a photograph of burning cars was sucked into the draught. The paper darkened, grew crisp and thin. An orange glow began at the centre of the page, which blackened round the edges until, at the last second, Angela whisked it away, filling the room with a spurt of acrid smoke.

This is like old age, Kate thought, looking round the room. Shadows leapt across the walls, tentative flakes of snow fumbled at the window pane and were whirled upwards out of sight. Watching them, she tried to trace the progress of a single flake, but her eyelids were heavy, and when she opened them again Angela was putting a tray with pâté and warm bread rolls on to the table beside her chair. She watched Angela's faded English-rose face turn pink again from the warmth of the fire. A strange girl – though she shouldn't say girl, Angela was forty-five if she was a day, but girlish still in many ways, gushing, giggly, inclined to develop crushes on people. Also stoical, unassuming, brave.

And a trial at times, Kate thought guiltily, wanting to be alone. All those times when Kate had tried to talk about her grief for Ben, and Angela had gently, but firmly, reminded her that *she* had lost Thomas and William and Rufus and Harry. Yes, Kate had wanted to say, but Ben was my husband, and they were like, well, . . . SHEEP?

She'd always managed not to say it, remembering the time she'd switched the television on to watch the six o'clock news and seen Angela rolling around on the muddy ground, displaying her knickers to the whole nation, as she defied the men from the Ministry of Agriculture who'd come to kill her 'boys'. It had taken three policemen to hold her down. And anyway who was she to quantify somebody else's love or decide how much grief was reasonable? She remembered watching Angela feed them, how they'd all stopped cropping the grass and answered her with their plaintive cries when she called their names.

Kate ate and drank and drifted off to sleep again. When she woke, Angela was putting on her coat. 'You sure you'll be all right now?'

'Quite sure. Thanks. I'll just sit over the fire a bit longer.'

'I'll be in again tomorrow first thing. Ring if you need anything.'

After she'd gone, Kate stood for a long time by the window, listening to the minute creaks the house made – wood and stone still settling after five hundred years – and watched the snow, falling more thickly now, cover the ground. Darkness seemed to rise in a blue vapour from the snow. She went back to the fire, wondering how she should spend the next few hours. Having slept, she supposed, for an hour or an hour and a half, she now felt too awake to go to bed.

In the hospital, with its unchanging routines, she'd been protected from the urgency of time passing, but now she counted the days lost since her accident – nineteen. She was tempted to go across to the studio, but knew she mustn't. The desolate expanse of floor, the tall windows open to the night sky, no, she wasn't ready to face that yet, and anyway there was nothing she could do. By now there should have been a roughly carved figure standing there. Instead there was nothing, not even an armature, and it would take five to eight days of hard work to produce that.

And she couldn't do it. She couldn't work at all without an assistant, and even the best assistant would leave normal working hours curtailed. She regularly started at five or six o'clock when things were going well. That would have to change, and not only that. The way she worked. Everything.

She hobbled back to her chair, missing the other patients whose slow progress back to mobility had mirrored her own. Round about now the visitors would be leaving. The nurses would be stuffing flowers into vases, drawing the blinds, settling people down for the night – and her solitary, shuffling progress suddenly seemed lonely and pathetic. Sometimes the only cure for feeling sorry for yourself is a good long sleep. She would make herself stay up till ten o'clock, make a few calls, watch television, have a couple of stiff whiskies and go to bed.

She was just about to switch on the television when she heard a car approaching. The forest road at night was not much frequented even in good weather, and she wondered who it might be, and hoped it wasn't Lorna or Beth or Alec come to see how she was. The car slowed to take the bend. She pictured the unknown driver spotting the damage to the trees and wincing – though by now the snow would have covered the tyre marks on the verge. She waited for it to pick up speed again, but it slowed still further, crawling along, looking for the entrance. A shifting skein of light drifted across the wall and stopped as the car stopped. Going to the window, she opened it slightly and heard the crunch of approaching footsteps, but could see nothing. The drive was thickly lined with rhododendrons that in winter formed a long dark tunnel. The footsteps grew louder. A young man with bent head, his dark hair stringy with melted snow, emerged from between the bushes. The security light flicked on as he broke the beam, and flung his shadow behind him up the wall of thick green rubbery leaves.

The door bell rang.

She almost knew who it was. The name was on the

tip of her tongue, but to be on the safe side she put the chain on before she opened the door and peered through the crack.

'Hello?'

'I believe you're looking for an assistant.'

'Ye-es.'

'Alec Braithewaite sent me. I used to do the church-yard last summer, do you remember?'

'Yes, of course.' She released the chain and opened the door. Light streamed on to the path, catching his glasses so that for a moment he looked blind. 'Come in.'

He stepped over the threshold, bringing with him a smell of wet hair and wool, and began stamping his snow-clogged boots on the mat, shaking off thick curds of white. Snowflakes caught in his hair and on his shoulders dissolved as she gazed.

'I didn't realize it was still snowing.'

'It's not.' He smiled. 'I knocked a branch and got a shower. I think I'd better take my coat off. I'm only going to drip all over your carpet. And these,' he said, looking down at his feet.

'I'm afraid I don't know your name.'

'Peter Wingrave. Look, would you like to ring Alec and check?'

'No, it's all right. He did mention you.'

She was thinking it was no wonder she hadn't recog-nized him. Last time she saw him he'd been suntanned, stripped to the waist, wielding a scythe on the long grasses between the headstones. She'd bumped into him once or twice as she was walking across the church-yard on her way to the shops, and they'd exchanged a few words about the cull. 'Isn't it awful?' they'd said in passing, as people did who weren't directly involved. There was no ignoring it. Clouds of oily black smoke from the pyres dominated the skyline. The smell of burning carcasses had hung over the village for weeks.

The cull was the reason for his presence. Until last summer the grass had been cropped by sheep imported for the purpose. Black sheep – she suspected Alec of a clerical joke. They kept the grass down and their droppings, even when deposited on a grave, were not too offensive – or at least nobody had complained. 'Cows, now,' Alec had said, 'I don't think we could go as far as cows.' The great thing was they fed themselves and didn't need to be paid. But then the men from the Ministry came and carted them off to be killed. Peter was more expensive than the sheep, but also, she couldn't help thinking, more decorative. She remembered him clearly now, sweat glistening on his arms and chest, his jeans slipping further and further down his hips as he swung and turned. As a young single woman, she'd have been seriously tempted. Even as a happily married middle-aged woman, she'd paused to admire the view.

He stood up, flushed from the effort of getting his boots off, wriggling his toes in their damp socks. The boots were old and obviously leaked.

'Come through,' she said, hobbling ahead of him into the living room.

'Oh, a real fire. That's nice.'

An educated voice, deep, pleasant. She wondered how he'd ended up doing unskilled jobs – but that was his business. And anyway, she thought, gardening isn't unskilled – it's just badly paid. He'd shown plenty of skill with that scythe. 'Do you know, I think you're the only person I've seen using a scythe.'

A small shrug. 'I grew up in the country.'

'Oh, whereabouts?'

'Yorkshire. My grandfather used to use one. But you're right, I think he was the only person I ever saw doing it. Though it's not difficult, once you get the rhythm.'

'Would you like a drink?'

'Yes, please.' He looked around for clues and spotted the whisky bottle on the table. 'Whisky'll do fine.'

She poured two large glasses. 'Well,' she said, lowering herself cautiously into the armchair, feeling like a frail old lady in contrast with his obvious strength and vigour. 'Alec said he was going to have a word with you.'

'Yes, he rang a couple of days ago. I left a message on your answering machine, asking if I could call round.'

'I'm afraid I haven't got to the answering machine yet. I only came out of hospital this afternoon. So you're a gardener?'

'Mainly, yes.'

'Must be pretty lean pickings at this time of year?'

'Awful. Basically it's dead between November and March. There's very little.'

'So how do you manage?'

'Do a bit of tree surgery. And I'm trying to specialize in water gardening, because actually this is the best time of year to dig ponds. If you leave it till Easter, you've missed half the season. And then if it gets too bad, I give in and get a job in a restaurant.'

'Cooking?'

'No. Chopping veg and loading dishes.'

'Sounds pretty dire.'

'It is, yes, but it's only for a few months. As soon as the grass grows the phone rings.'

He had a charming smile.

'Did you train as a gardener?'

'No.' A pause. 'No, I read English.' He raised the glass quickly to his mouth, hiding his lips.

All right, she thought, no personal questions. Well, that suited her. The last thing she wanted in the studio was chatter.

'I can give you references. People I've worked for.'

He fished in his pocket and produced a sheet of paper, folded twice and slightly damp. Five people were listed on it, four of whom she knew fairly well. 'Fred Henderson. He's got that big place just outside Alnwick, hasn't he?'

'Yes, that's right. I did his water garden. He went in for it in a big way when he retired. In fact I think it's the biggest job I've ever done.' He smiled. 'What can I say? The patio's level. The ponds don't leak. The waterfalls work. And the stream's full of fish.'

She smiled back at him. It was impossible not to like

him. 'Shall I tell you what I want first? Then you can judge for yourself if you can fit in with it.'

He nodded, watching her intently, rocking the whisky from side to side in the glass, amber lights darting across his fingers. He had big hands.

She sensed he was desperate for work, that chopping veg and loading dishes might be looming, so she didn't bother making the hours attractive. Eight till four, five days a week. Saturday mornings would be great if he could manage it. 'And I'll pay whatever Fred paid. Is that all right?'

'Fine.' He looked at her – perhaps he sensed desperation too. 'You haven't said what you want me to do.'

'Driving, lifting, making an armature . . .' She waited.

'I know what it is. I've never made one.'

'I'll show you.' It hurt her to say it, to think of other hands on her work. 'I can't do it.'

'Alec said it's a statue of Christ. How big?'

'Fifteen feet.'

'*Fifteen?*'

'Yep.'

He was looking at her, assessing the extent of her disability. 'How high can you raise your arm?'

She pulled a face. 'Shoulder height.'

'You'll need a scaffold. I can't see you shinning up a stepladder' – he nodded at her stick – 'with that.'

'Could you make one?'

'Yeah, it's not difficult.'

'You're sure?'

'Yeah, no problem. Anyway, I'll bounce up and down

on it first, so if anybody breaks their neck it'll be me.'

'Might be as well.' She smiled. 'I don't think my neck could take any more.'

'How long do you have to wear the collar?'

'Another month at least.'

'But you will get the mobility back?'

'So they say.'

A pause. 'So how shall we leave it?' he asked. 'Do you want to check with Fred first?'

'No, I need to get started. How about tomorrow?'

'Are you sure you're well enough?'

'I've got to be.'

'Well, if you don't feel up to doing much, I can always be making a start on the scaffolding.'

She felt relieved beyond measure. It had all happened so quickly, so easily. Her first job tomorrow morning must be to ring Alec and thank him. It was a bit late tonight, she thought, glancing at her watch.

Immediately, Peter put his glass on the table and stood up. 'No, don't get up,' he said, seeing her reach for her stick. 'I can let myself out.'

She heard him pulling on his boots, grunting with the effort, and then went to the window to watch him go. The security light flicked on again as he crossed the beam. He seemed to sense her watching and without turning round raised his hand as he disappeared into the dark tunnel of rhododendrons.

A moment later she heard the car start. The noise was distorted, as every noise here was, by the wall of trees. He reversed, turned, and then she heard the hum of the engine diminishing into the distance before being swallowed up by night and silence. Then there were only the trees, and a few flakes of snow shuddering on the black air.

Three

The following morning, after seeing Peter start work on the scaffold, Kate accepted Angela's offer of a lift into the village and went to see Alec Braithewaite.

It was a cold, clear day, the grass around the head-stones rimed with frost. A trail of muddy, trampled snow led up to the rectory door. She rang the bell and heard it clang deep inside the house, a vast, draughty Georgian mausoleum of a place. She wondered why Alec didn't protest to the bishop and insist on being given somewhere more sensible to live. Justine was only left at home because the wretched glandular fever had kept her back for an extra year, and Kate found it impossible to imagine what it would be like for one person living here alone.

Justine's mother, Victoria, had left eight years ago, in a scandal that rocked the parish, though as far as Kate knew no other man had been involved. Alec, pursuing her down the garden path, was supposed to have asked, as she heaved her suitcases into the waiting taxi, 'Is there anybody else?'

'Yes!' Victoria had roared, at the top of her voice for the whole village to hear. '*Me.*'

Angela deplored this behaviour, which she regarded as unforgivably selfish. Kate secretly applauded. Everybody had thought that Alec would leave the parish as soon as another living could be found, but he'd elected to stay, mainly for Justine's sake – the local girls' high school had an excellent reputation and Justine had been very happy there. But she'd now left school, and Alec still showed no inclination to move on, though he often talked wistfully about his desire to do more obviously valuable work in some inner-city parish. Like opening his door in the middle of the night to kids off their heads on crack, Kate thought. He was probably safer here. She rang the bell again. The last time she'd spoken to him about his plans he'd seemed to feel guilty that his life had settled into an undemanding groove, ministering to the spiritual needs of what Angela called 'green-wellie Christians' – weekenders who wouldn't have dreamt of attending church in the city, but who in the country dropped in to morning service on their way to the Rose and Crown, as if – Angela again – God was thrown in as a job lot with Labradors and waxed jackets.

There were the locals, of course, but they turned up only two or three times a year: Easter, perhaps, Harvest Festival and the Christmas carol service. All dates at or near the main pagan festivals, as Alec cheerfully pointed out. She rang the bell again, thinking she might as well be waiting for some little Victorian maid ninety years dead to get up from her grave and answer the door.

Instead she heard the slap of bare feet on lino. A disgruntled voice called, 'All right. I'm coming.'

The door opened and there was Justine, flushed from

27

sleep, big-breasted inside a too-tight Snoopy T-shirt, yawning, showing the pink cavernous interior of her mouth as uninhibitedly as a cat. 'Dad's in the church, I think. Do you want to come in and wait?'

Looking at Justine's bare feet on the coconut mat, Kate said, 'No, it's OK, thanks. I'll have a walk across.'

She trod carefully across the cattle grid at the entrance to the churchyard – put in, at some expense, to contain the sheep – clinging to the railings because there was nowhere to put her stick. She missed the mournful clanking of the sheep's bells as they moved between the graves. Slowly, carefully, up the path, one step at a time. It was a struggle to turn the iron ring and push the heavy door open. That didn't bode well – she must be weaker than she thought. She shuffled, in her new three-legged state, into the cold, hassock-smelling interior, with its fugitive glints of multicoloured light on the stone flags.

Alec was kneeling at the altar rail. He didn't look round as she closed the door quietly behind her.

A sulky central-heating system, just turned off after Holy Communion, distributed the smell of warm dust evenly around the church, without making any notice-able difference to the temperature. Shivering, she looked up at the crucifix above the chancel arch and beyond that at the rose window: Christ in Majesty, surrounded by concentric circles of apostles, angels, prophets, patriarchs and saints. At the moment she hated all representations of Christ, impartially and with great venom. If they were good, they underlined the folly of her thinking that she had anything new to contribute to a tradition that had lasted 2,000 years. If they were bad – like the painting in the Lady Chapel of Christ in a chiffon nightie, its diaphanous folds failing to hide the fact that there was nothing to hide – they seemed to invite her mockingly to add to their number.

She tiptoed down the aisle, away from Alec, who had still not looked up, and concentrated on the engravings of Green Men that decorated the roof bosses. What faces: savage, angry, tormented, desperate, sly, desolate. She'd noticed them first at Ben's funeral and had been paying them regular visits ever since. Images of the Green Man were everywhere these days. A secular world sifting through pagan images, like a rag-and-bone man grubbing about for something – anything – of value. A symbol of renewal, people said, but only because they didn't look. Some of these heads were so emaciated they were hardly more than skulls. Others vomited leaves, their eyes staring, panic-stricken above the choking mouth. No, she thought, wincing with pain as she craned to look at them, they were wonderfully done – some anonymous craftsman's masterwork – but they were figures of utter ruin.

Looking up like this made her go dizzy. The faces filled her whole field of vision, a horde of goblins. Alec came up behind her, and she was glad to hold on to him and close her eyes until the walls stopped spinning.

'Are you all right?'

'Fine. I just went a bit dizzy.'

'Oh, you were looking at the Green Men?'

'They're supposed to be symbols of rebirth, but actually if you look at them they're quite horrible.'

'I think it's part of the cult of the head. Did you know the Celts used to cut off the heads of their enemies and stuff the mouths with green leaves?'

'No, I didn't. Not particularly optimistic, then?'

'Not if it was your head.'

She smiled. 'I really only popped in to thank you for sending Peter Wingrave round.'

'Oh, he came to see you?'

'Yes, last night.'

'And you took him on?'

'My dear, I jumped at him. He's there now, putting up scaffolding.'

'That's good. You're looking a lot better, Kate.'

'I feel better.' They sat in the pew behind the hymn and prayer book stand. 'Have you known him long?'

'Quite a while. Seven years, something like that. But not continuously. He's travelled around quite a bit.' He seemed to be debating whether to say more. 'He's an interesting person. I think you'll like him.'

'Why gardening, though? I mean, he's got a degree.'

'Plenty of graduate gardeners, Kate.'

That wasn't fair. She wasn't being snobbish about gardeners, she was saying, Yes, but something's not right, something doesn't fit, and she felt Alec had understood that perfectly well and decided not to acknowledge it.

'We were very happy with him,' he said. 'The parish

council. If we can't get any more sheep, we'd certainly use him again.'

'That's not exactly a ringing endorsement. Second choice after the sheep?'

'We don't have to pay the sheep.'

'Do you think you will get some more?'

Alec shook his head. 'I just don't know. You notice the farmers aren't restocking?'

Kate remembered men in white decontamination suits chasing squealing sheep around the graveyard. They'd been sent to the pyre at Ravenscroft Farm. Kate had stood with Angela, whose precious boys had been destroyed in the same cull, on a hill not far away from the farm and watched the fire burn. Clouds of foul-smelling black smoke had obscured the setting sun. The pitiful legs of cows and sheep stuck up from the mound of corpses and rubber tyres. A stench of rotting flesh drifted towards them over the valley, scraps of burnt hair and skin whirled into the air. Kate put her arm around Angela's shoulders and was trying to persuade her to leave, when a flake of singed cowhide landed on her lower lip, and she spat and clawed at her mouth to get the taste away.

Alec was staring at her. She realized she must have been silent for too long. 'I was thinking about Angela's boys.'

'Oh, yes. Thomas, William, Rufus . . .'

'And Harry.'

'And Harry. I knew there was another.'

'I wish she'd get herself some more.'

Alec raised his eyebrows. 'You think she needs sheep?'

'You can't buy people.'

'You don't need to buy people.'

They were getting into one of those conversations that threatened to become pastoral, and as always Kate avoided going any further. 'I'd better be going. Angela'll be wondering where I've got to.'

The door creaked open, letting a shaft of sunlight fall across the stone floor, and Angela appeared. She blushed when she saw Alec, though she saw him at every service – Holy Communion, Matins, Evensong, she was never away. The three of them chatted for a while, then Kate thanked him again and watched him walk down the aisle, genuflect in front of the altar – a bit more of an effort these days, she noticed, he held on to a choir stall to lever himself up again – and stride off into the vestry.

Angela went ahead to get the car. She'd parked outside the chemist's, she said, and that was too far for Kate to walk. Kate followed more slowly, testing the rubber tip of her stick on patches of ice. Alec hadn't been particularly informative about Peter, but in a way she didn't mind that. The closer Peter came to being simply a pair of hands, the better she'd be pleased.

At the gate she turned and looked across to Ben's grave. The air was iron cold and still. She would never, never, never be able to accept his death, and she didn't try. This wasn't an illness she would recover from; it was an amputation she had to learn to live with. There was a great and surprising peace in acknowledging this.

She took a deep breath, wondering if she could possibly walk as far as the grave, but then Angela called her name, and she limped across the cattle grid and down the grass verge to the car.

Four

On Stephen Sharkey's last night in London he went to the leaving party he hadn't wanted to have, and ended up getting thoroughly drunk.

He woke at five the next morning with a mouth like a dustbin, and had to ferret around with his tongue to work up some spit before he felt human enough to stagger into the bathroom. One look in the mirror said it all. Lids crusted, eyelashes matted, the whites of his eyes criss-crossed with red veins, a Martian landscape. Contact lenses left in. After several painful attempts he managed to get them out.

He forced himself through washing and shaving, made coffee, ate two slices of dry toast for breakfast, then started to pack. He had a busy morning ahead of him, seeing his solicitor, then his publisher, and he couldn't possibly do either looking like this.

On his way to the first appointment he stopped at a chemist's, bought eyedrops and selected one of the few pairs of sunglasses they had in the shop. He looked, he thought, peering at himself in the mirror above the display stand, like a soon-to-be divorced, almost middle-aged man, sweaty, frightened, uncool and desperate to prove he could still pull. Which, he informed his reflection waspishly, is exactly what you are.

By two o'clock he was on the train to Newcastle. He slept intermittently, woke, watched the backs of other people's houses rush past, then travelled two hours through a rain-sodden landscape. Ploughed fields with flooded furrows like striations of sky. Once they stopped in the middle of nowhere, and a herd of cows came trudging over to the fence and stared at the train, chewing, in a mist of their own breath.

At the station he lugged his cases on to the platform and stood with them, one on either side, like inverted commas, he thought, drawing attention to the possible invalidity of the statement they enclose. Invalid, or invalid, whichever way you cared to pronounce it, that was how he felt. A man who'd sacrificed his marriage to his career, and, now that the marriage was over, had turned his back on the career as well. Stop beating yourself up, he told himself, shifting from foot to foot, but it was hard not to. He felt anxious, but that was partly the drink. If this cottage turned out to be too claustrophobic – too close to Robert, in other words – he could easily find somewhere else to live. And he wasn't going to starve. He had a network of contacts. If the book took longer than three months to write, he could keep himself going on freelance work.

No sign of Robert. Just as Stephen was thinking he'd have to find a phone – he'd forgotten to charge his mobile just as he'd forgotten to take his contact lenses out – he caught sight of him, threading his way across the crowded concourse with that hospital doctor's disguised run of his.

Striding towards Stephen, Robert opened his arms. They embraced, awkwardly, their preconceptions of each other failing to accommodate the reality of muscle and bone.

Robert held him at arm's length, wincing and throwing his head back – a comment on the sunglasses.

Stephen took them off and ogled him.

'Oh, my God, you look like a terrorist.' He picked up one of the cases. 'I'm parked just outside.'

Stephen followed him out of the station, head down into an icy wind that snatched the breath from his mouth. His trousers, too thin for the weather, flattened against his shins.

'What you going to do for a car while you're here?' Robert asked, as he unlocked his own.

'Buy one.'

'Nerys got yours?'

'Yup. To be fair she used it more than I did.'

Robert settled himself into the driving seat, hauling the belt across his chest. 'How are you?'

'Tired.'

'Hung over.'

'*And* tired.'

Robert turned the heater on, and within a few seconds Stephen felt himself start to grow drowsy. Blinking hard, he opened the window and gulped the moist air.

'So that's it, then?' Robert said.

'Yeah, that's it. Last assignment.'

'And you actually mean it this time?'

'I've handed in my resignation.'

'Because last time –'

'It's the same as any other business, Robert. You get typecast. When I got back from Afghanistan, I said, Right, that's it, finished. I don't want to do it any more. And everybody said, Right, fine. No problem. And the next thing I knew I was being measured for another flak jacket.'

Robert was smiling. 'You could've refused.'

'Yeah, if I didn't mind not working.'

'And where's the flak jacket now?'

'I don't know. On a peg somewhere.'

'Waiting to be worn.'

'*No.*' Stephen's face felt numb as if he'd just come out of the dentist's. He rubbed his cheeks and shivered inside the too-thin jacket. 'How's the family?'

'Fine. Beth's a lot happier now she's got somebody reliable to look after Adam.' He braked, drove slowly through a huge puddle, water curling up on either side of the car. 'God help us if this lot freezes.'

Looking out over the sodden fields, Stephen was aware of winter in a way that he almost never was in London. There was a rhythmic squeal as the windscreen wipers swept to and fro, creating triangles on the mud-spattered glass. Robert pulled out to overtake, and for a second the windscreen was blind, marbled with flung spray. Stephen made himself keep quiet, remembering how competitive they'd been as boys, how furious Robert had been when Stephen passed his driving test first time. Robert had managed it only at the second attempt.

'So you're definitely out of it?'

Why did everybody find it so hard to believe? 'Yeah.'

'How do you feel?'

'Fine. It's the right time.' Actually, he thought, not fine. More like an unshelled nut lying on the ground, any hope of future germination a lot less convincing than the prospect of being snuffled up by a passing pig. 'Anyway, that's enough about me and my problems. How are you?'

'Fine.'

He hoped Robert's 'fines' were a bit more honest than his, otherwise the whole bloody family was up the creek. But Robert was all right, of course he was. You only had to look at him – happiness and success oozing from every pore.

'I've just applied for a research grant of three million pounds.'

'What for?'

'Possible treatments for Parkinson's and dementia.'

When Stephen didn't immediately reply, he added, with a slight edge, 'I'm afraid my line of work's a bit less glamorous than yours.'

Stephen was wondering if Robert had as many doubts about the coming weeks of proximity as he had himself. They'd never been close, even as boys, and since their mother's death had met only at weddings and funerals. And yet, when he had rung Robert and told him his marriage was over and he needed somewhere to live, Robert offered the cottage, immediately, without hesitation. Shared genes, Robert would have said. The biological basis for altruism.

They were driving by the side of a lake, its water pockmarked by falling rain. A moorhen picked its way across the boggy ground and disappeared into the shadow of some willows whose bare branches over-hung the water. Beyond the lake an immense dark stain of forest spread over the hillside. As they came closer, he could see that it was already dark beneath the trees, and would have been darkish even at noon. No life on the forest floor, or none that he could discern, though a sign warned of deer crossing. At intervals along the road there were small, crushed bundles of flesh and fur: rabbits, mainly, but here and there the gleaming iridescent plumage of a pheasant.

'Carnage,' Robert said. 'The speed people drive through here. They've only got to hit a deer and it'd be the end of them.'

Robert's house lay between the village and the forest. As they came out of the shadow of the trees, Stephen saw a grey stone farmhouse, appearing and disappearing with each bend in the road, fitting in so seamlessly with the surrounding fields that it scarcely seemed to have been made with human hands, but rather to have been thrown up by some natural process, like the granite boulders that littered the valley floor, left behind by a retreating glacier of the last Ice Age. Certainly it was less obviously a human artefact than the forest that crept over the hills towards it.

Robert turned up the drive and stopped in front of the house. Stephen got out, feeling surprisingly stiff, and stood awkwardly as his ten-year-old nephew, Adam, hurled himself over the threshold to hug his father. He didn't seem to know when to stop, but simply crashed headlong into Robert's chest. 'Dad, Dad, I've found a badger.'

'A dead one? Where?'

'On the forest road.'

'And you pulled him all the way back?'

'I put him on a bin liner and dragged him.' He was tugging at Robert's sleeve to make him come and look.

'Hey, hey. Say hello to Uncle Stephen.'

'Hello,' Adam said, but he was too shy to make eye contact and seemed to be hoping that if he didn't look at Stephen he might disappear. 'Dad.'

Robert let himself be tugged around the corner of the house and, not knowing what else to do, Stephen followed. A path led by the vegetable patch, where last year's yellowing cabbage stalks stuck out of the muddy ground, white and flabby and marked at intervals with leaf scars like ringworm. A whiff of decay, which Stephen held his breath to avoid encountering, and then they were out on to a long sloping lawn that led down to a stand of trees – conifers of some kind, an advance guard of the invading forest.

The badger was sprawled on his back, legs splayed, a trickle of black blood running down from one side of his mouth. His fangs were bared, snarling at the car he'd seen too late. Bending over him, Stephen had the feeling that if you looked long enough into those golden eyes you'd see headlights on a road at night, just as earlier generations believed that a murderer's image was preserved on the victim's retina.

Robert knelt down on the grass and touched the pads of the front paw. 'He's still warm.' He ran his hands across the thick pelt, frost-tipped hairs flattened by his hand springing up again as soon as it passed over them, as if they, at least, were still alive. 'Poor old thing.'

Adam stood behind his shoulder, breathing heavily through his open mouth, excitement and the pride of discovery struggling with a sorrow he hadn't known that he felt till now.

The January day was closing in. Stephen was intensely aware of them as three figures, three related figures, in a winter landscape, with the blank windows of the farmhouse behind them. Something to do with Robert's hand resting on the badger's pelt. His hand. Their father's hand.

Even in this weather a column of ants was moving purposefully towards the trickle of blood.

'He'll keep overnight,' Robert said, standing up.

'Can you cut his head off, Dad?'

'I don't think so. It's not that easy, cutting off heads. The neck ligaments are very strong.'

A machete would do it easily enough, Stephen thought, blinking the images away. Suddenly he wanted to be indoors, somewhere safe, away from the memories of long grass and the skulls you trip over in the dark.

'Can't we boil it?'

'I think Mum might have something to say about that.'

Adam was squatting down, stroking the head. Stephen could see him lusting after the strong secret white structure underneath.

'Let's go and have tea, Adam,' Robert said. 'And I'll see what I can do in the morning.'

He got Adam firmly by the shoulder and pushed him towards the house. But Stephen lingered for a moment, looking down at the badger, feeding off the raw power. Then, seeing Robert and Adam waiting for him by the patio door, he hurried up the lawn after them.

Beth was in the kitchen, beating oil and vinegar together in a bowl. She hadn't so much aged since Stephen last saw her, as faded. Her features had blurred as if somebody had rubbed one of those enormous, squishy artist's erasers across her face.

'Hello, Stephen,' she said briskly, offering her cheek to be kissed. 'Have you seen the badger?'

'Yes,' Adam said.

Beth and Robert exchanged a glance above his head, the intimate, conspiratorial look of co-creators.

Robert said, 'I think you'd better wash your hands, young man.' He put a hand on Adam's shoulder and steered him towards the door.

The adults stood around chatting, while Beth put the finishing touches to the meal. Odd, these meetings with relatives, Stephen thought. The long past stretching out behind you and yet, on the surface, a lack of things to talk about, the daily flotsam of life not available for picking over and comment. They talked about the spate of accidents on the railways, train delays, the foot-and-mouth epidemic that had devastated the local economy ... And then, closer to home, how Beth was coping with her new job as a full-time hospital administrator. She'd only ever worked part time before, and she was finding the new job a strain. It took over an hour to get home in the evenings, so somebody had to collect Adam from school and stay with him till she got back.

'It's been better since Justine arrived. Mrs Todd just pulled out, no warning, and then Adam went down with chicken pox and of course I was going frantic, but then Robert remembered Justine.' Beth dipped a ladle into the soup, her face open-pored and steamy in the heat. 'And she's been great, hasn't she? Doesn't do much housework, but frankly as long as Adam's happy, I couldn't care less about the housework. I can do that at the weekends.'

'She's very good with Adam,' Robert said, taking the plates from under the grill where they'd been warming. 'And he's not easy.'

'He's not difficult,' Beth said. She turned to Stephen. 'Adam is a very, *very* rewarding child.'

Say no more, Stephen thought. He'd been a very, *very* rewarding child himself, in his day.

Beth served the soup. As they sat down at the table, Stephen asked, 'Do you know Kate Frobisher?'

'Yes,' Robert said. 'She was one of the judges for the Sci-Art competition, so I saw quite a bit of her for a while.'

'What's she like?'

Robert shrugged. 'Cheerful. Down to earth. Loves her house. Of course, this was all before Ben died.'

'That house is enormous,' Beth said. 'And she's on her own now. I'd be terrified if it were me.' She handed the bread round. 'You knew Ben, didn't you?'

'Yes, quite well.'

'I'm surprised you don't know her, then.'

'Ben didn't spend all that much time in London. I have met her once or twice. But I'd like to use some of his photographs for the book, so I'll need to go and see her.'

'She lives, what, about five miles away?' Robert said.

'About that,' Beth said. 'Oh, and I think you might find her in a surgical collar. She had quite a nasty accident a bit back.'

'But she's all right?'

'As far as we know,' Robert said.

'She is,' Beth said. 'I bumped into her in the hospital. She comes in for physiotherapy twice a week.'

All this time Adam had been sitting quietly, dipping hunks of bread into his soup but not eating much. He kept pulling at his ears like a much younger child, and clawing at his arms where a few chicken-pox scabs still lingered.

'He's tired,' Beth said, following the direction of Stephen's gaze.

44

'No, I'm not.'

'So you like animals?' Stephen asked.

Not looking at him, Adam wriggled acknowledgement.

'What kind do you like best?'

Adam thought. 'Dead ones.'

'He collects bones,' Robert put in quickly. 'Going to be an orthopaedic surgeon, I expect.'

Or a serial killer. 'What's the best one you've got?'

'Human femurs. Dad gave them to me, didn't you, Dad?'

Robert smiled. 'Do you remember, Dad had them up in the attic? It's amazing, isn't it? You couldn't be that casual today.'

'I remember we used to play pirates with them.'

Even this shared memory brought with it a slight constraint. Robert had followed their father into medicine, whereas he'd gone off at a tangent, pursuing a career that nobody in the family had much respected.

'You could show Stephen your collection,' Beth said. 'After tea.'

Adam nodded, scratching inside his T-shirt.

'Don't do that, you'll break the skin,' Robert said.

Adam kept still, until the adults started talking again, and then, out of the corner of his eye, Stephen saw him slide his hand inside the T-shirt and rub at his skin again. Poor kid.

After coffee, Beth went upstairs with Adam to put some kind of soothing ointment on the scabs. After she'd gone, Robert raised his eyebrows at Stephen. 'Do you know, I think I might have a drink. Would you like one?'

'If you don't mind,' he said awkwardly, 'I think I'd rather have a bath and settle in.'

'Yes, of course.'

Since Stephen had brought two suitcases and a laptop, Robert drove the short distance down the lane to the cottage. Frost glittered on every twig of the hawthorn hedge that enclosed the small front garden. Stephen stamped his feet, breath pluming round his face, while Robert bent to unlock the door. Above their heads, bare branches netted a shoal of stars.

'You haven't brought much with you,' Robert said, looking at the cases.

'No, well, I didn't leave home with much. Nerys's storing most of it.'

'Oh, so it's pretty amicable, then?'

'Huh! I don't know about that.'

They went into the hall. 'You'll find a few basic things in the cupboards. The fire's been on all day, so it should be warmed through.'

A low door led into the living room, so low that even Robert, who was a couple of inches shorter than Stephen, had to duck to get through. Stephen bent his head and followed.

A stone fireplace, a huge fire blazing in the grate, logs piled high in baskets on either side.

'You can buy more logs,' Robert said. 'There's a sawmill just up the road, about three miles, but there's a coal-house round the side' – he gestured vaguely –

'and you'll find enough there for a couple of weeks.'

The log on the fire had burnt almost to ash, its side creased and cracked like elephant skin. Robert bent down and put another log on top of it. Sparks flew up, and for a moment his face became a bronze mask, and then, as the green wood spat and smoked, darkened to grey. He stood up, scuffing wood chips from his palms.

'This is ideal,' Stephen said, looking round.

'You should be able to work, at least. It's quiet enough.' He seemed to be debating whether to say anything more. At last he said, 'Stephen, are you all right?'

'I'm fine, Robert, honestly. Just a bit tired.'

They looked at each other, slightly awkward, aware of the silence, then somewhere at the back of the cottage an owl hooted. As if this were a signal, Robert said, 'I'll leave you to settle in.'

Five

As soon as Robert had gone, Stephen looked all over the cottage, feeling a surge of pleasure as he took in his surroundings. Despite the fire there was a chill in the air, but then the cottage had been standing empty for a year, the foot-and-mouth epidemic having destroyed the market for weekend breaks.

A small kitchen and, upstairs, a tiny bathroom. In the front bedroom there was a desk and chair, useless for writing, at least in their present position, because they were too close to the window. Flying glass. He'd always felt bizarrely safe in the Holiday Inn in Sarajevo because the glass in the windows was long gone. He would lie curled up, fingers thrust into his armpits, hoarding warmth, and listen to the pitter-patter of rain on the polythene sheets that divided him from the thudding sky, until the mingled sound of rain and small-arms fire became a lullaby. He missed it when he got home. Surrounded by leafy trees and the hum of London traffic, he'd found it impossible to sleep. At the time he'd preferred to regard this as a personal quirk rather than as a symptom of post-traumatic stress disorder. He still did.

The back bedroom was larger. He stood at the small, ivy-fringed window, looking out over the garden. A patch of lawn, shrubs, a path leading down to a gate and beyond that, on the crest of a hill, a copse of deciduous trees. Bare branches clotted with rooks' nests stood out against the smoky red of the sky.

He took off his trainers, shirt and jeans and stretched out on the bed, telling himself he couldn't possibly sleep, and, almost immediately, slept. Once, he jerked awake at a sudden sound – the creak of a floorboard perhaps? – but the sound wasn't repeated and he made himself relax. Somewhere near by an owl hooted, and he waited for the scream of a small creature finding dusk turn to night in the shadow of immense wings. Nothing. The owl hooted again. It must have a nest up there among the trees.

Drowsily, he tried to catch the words that were drifting through his brain. Something to do with owls being restless in a place where people had met violent deaths, but he couldn't remember, and anyway it was nonsense, nobody had died here, or only in their beds of sickness or old age. No violent deaths since the union of England and Scotland brought the long centuries of border raiding to a close. No skulls in the grass, no girls with splayed thighs and skirts around their waists revealing, even in the early stages of decomposition, what had been done to them before they died. No smell of decay clinging to the skin. Just a square of window fringed by dark leaves. He closed his eyes, and the window became a pattern floating on the inside of his lids, turning first to orange and then to purple before fading, at last, to black.

His sleep was threadbare, like cheap curtains letting in too much light. He woke, slept, turned over, slept again, and then woke finally with a cry in the blackness, disorientated, thinking he could hear the patter of rain on polythene.

But there was no sound of rain at the window, so the pattering must have come from his dream. Brutally awake now, he started to think about Ben, as he'd known he must sooner or later, coming here to Ben's home ground.

It had been raining that night in Sarajevo, heavy showers falling as sleet and blown across the road. The cold hit him as he came out of the television centre and stood, upright and exposed, on the steps leading down to the street. The snow was pockmarked under his feet. He took a deep breath, dragging cold into his lungs, and was about to step down into the road when he heard a sound behind him and turned round to see Ben Frobisher come out of the swing doors behind him.

'Do you mind if I tag along?'

Stephen did mind, but it was too late to say so. The armoured car had gone, and there was no other way of getting back to the hotel. He was secretly furious: the whole point of this walk was that he should do it alone.

They stepped out into a world so dark their faces and hands seemed to give off the only light. Far away on the horizon the flickering artillery rumbled. A flare went up, and, for one trembling second, the roofs were edged in blue, then darkness fell again, deeper than before.

Despite the cold, he started to sweat, raising his gloved hand to wipe his upper lip. The flak jacket and the body armour encumbered his movements, and he was aware of Ben walking in the same robotic way. They passed graffitied walls whose scribblings they couldn't read, and then a block of flats with all its windows shattered, shards of glass lying in the slush around the chained gates. Despite the chains, people still lived here. He was aware of eyes all round them, of ears straining to listen as their feet slithered through the slush. In places the snow covered pieces of rubble. He was intensely aware of Ben, of the gleam of his eyes and teeth, of his body as a source of heat in the cold dark, almost as if the brain, deprived of vision, developed a kind of thermal-imaging technique. Far away to the right, in the darkness, snipers waited for somebody desperate enough for heating, or water, or food, to break cover and step out into the road.

As they approached the crossroads, he turned in his lumbering moon walk to Ben and pointed him deeper into the shadow of the building. Scuffing their shoulders, they scaled along the wall, then stopped for breath, side by side now, leaning against a door while they nerved themselves to face the dash across the open road. For two or three seconds they would be dark shapes against the glimmering whiteness.

'Well?' Ben whispered.

Stephen nodded, and braced himself against the door, which gave way under his weight so that he staggered back into the stairwell of the building. Ben followed, stopping when he was safely inside to examine the lock that had been smashed.

A flight of stairs led up into the dark. A scuffle from above, a sense of pricked ears and eyes watching. Ben produced a torch from his pocket, cupped his hand around the light, and shone it over the walls, so that they saw the dank passage and threadbare carpet veiled in his blood. His fingers were dark shadows in the ruby skin, like an X-ray, Stephen thought, and that red glow spread over the walls. Splinters of glass lying on the stairs had been crunched to a fine powder in the centre of the treads. Upstairs, the scuffling started again.

'Up there,' Ben whispered, pointing. He started to move towards the stairs.

Stephen caught his arm. 'No, come on, leave it.'

Ben pressed on, not shaking him off, just quietly disengaging himself. Reluctantly, Stephen followed.

A smell of mould met them at the top of the first flight, and the red torchlight revealed fungus growing on a damp patch of plaster. Then other smells took over: the musty smell of old carpets covered in dog hairs, the burnt toast smell of dried urine on mattresses, and finally a smell Stephen fought against recognizing.

In a corner of the landing, away from the danger of flying glass, a girl huddled on a mattress. She didn't speak or cry out or try to get away. Ben swung the beam along the wall until it found her face. Eyes wide open, skirt bunched up around her waist, her splayed thighs enclosing a blackness of blood and pain.

Stephen fell on his knees beside her and pulled down

her skirt. A voice in his head said, Don't touch anything. This is a crime scene. And then he thought, Bugger it. The whole fucking city is a crime scene. He wanted to close the terrible eyes, but couldn't bring himself to touch her face.

He sat back on his heels. No way of telling whether this was a casual crime – a punter wanting his money back, a drug deal gone wrong – or a sectarian killing linked to the civil war. Increasingly crime and war shade into each other, Stephen thought. No difference to their victims, certainly, and not much either in the minds of the perpetrators. Patriot, soldier, revolutionary, freedom fighter, terrorist, murderer – cross-section their brains at the moment of killing and the differences might prove rather hard to find.

'What do we do?' he asked.

'Nothing. There's nothing we can do.'

The building felt empty – of people anyway. It must have been rats they heard moving. He could feel them now, waiting, and scanned the shadows outside the wavering circle of light. Ben glimpsed one – its naked tail trailing through dust – and let out a roar of anger. 'Don't –' Stephen had time to say before he hurled the torch. It hit the wall and fell, its single weak eye, yellowish now, picking out a blister in the wallpaper where damp had seeped through.

Then it went out. Darkness, except for a strip of moonlight that fell across the floor and reached the girl's eyes.

'Come on,' Ben said, getting hold of Stephen's arm and pulling him to his feet. Far away the rumble of gunfire started again. Stephen thought of black clouds over bright cornfields, the sheen of sweat on naked arms, lit by flickers of summer lightning.

Then he was back on the stinking landing with the girl and the rats.

'Come on,' Ben said again. 'There's nothing we can do.'

Ben went across the landing and Stephen followed, waiting while Ben picked up the torch, feeling the girl's eyes boring into the back of his neck. Sweat prickled in the roots of his hair. Ashamed of the state he was in, he made himself go downstairs first and peer through the crack of the door. The air struck cold on his eyeball as he scanned the street.

Behind him in the dark he heard the bustle of rats begin.

'All right?'

He turned to look at Ben, who nodded, braced. Stephen edged round the door, feeling the whole right side of his body cringe in expectation of the bullet that would come from that direction, if it came at all. His left side seemed almost relaxed, as if congratulating itself on its immunity. There was time to ponder this mad dislocation of awareness, to register it as a distinct sensation, before he hurled himself out of the shelter of the building into the white light of the crossroads. Ben's gasping breaths behind him, their joined shadow on the snow, then he reached the other side, blind with fear, burrowing into the wall, and turned to take Ben's full weight as he crashed into him. They stayed still for five minutes, their breathing becoming gradually less painful, their eyeballs less congested, fingertips no longer shaken by the beating of their hearts. Swallowing had become impossible. Stephen let his mouth hang open and panted like a dog.

Another hundred yards and they were home, bursting into the foyer to find the hotel in darkness. Candles on tables all around the bar illuminated the faces of people they knew well. Drink, food, conversation, laughter, but that night, while snow accumulated on the sagging polythene of his window, Stephen lay cramped and wakeful inside his sleeping bag, thinking about the girl, and the way her eyes had looked up at him, seeing nothing. Her head was beside his on the pillow, and when he rolled over on to his stomach, trying to get away from her, he found her body underneath him, as dry and insatiable as sand.

Nothing else had ever affected him in the same way, though he'd seen many worse things. She was waiting for him, that's the way it felt. She had something to say to him, but he'd never managed to listen, or not in the right way.

He was still groggy from sleep when a banging on the front door sent him stumbling downstairs. Feeling slightly sick, he opened the door and there on the step, blinking in the sudden light, was a young girl. He stared at her. She seemed at first to be part of the dream, but then the blast of cold air reminded him he was wearing only his underpants and socks, and he blinked.

She was smiling. Wide blue eyes, scrubbed face, a stocky, powerful body – she could have been any age from twelve to seventeen, though, since the baggy sweatshirt failed to hide surprisingly large breasts, seventeen was probably more like it.

She was carrying a stack of yellow towels in her arms.

'Beth sent these. She's just remembered she forgot to put any towels in the bathroom.'

'Oh, right. Come in.'

A man with no trousers on is never at his most confident, particularly if he's forgotten to take off his socks. All he needed now to look completely ridiculous was an erection, but fortunately he'd reached an age when these show up only when required, and not always then. She passed with averted eyes, and a giggle that suggested rather less innocence than he'd supposed.

'You'd better shut the door,' she said. 'You'll catch your death.'

Closing it, he saw a small car – a Metro, he thought, its colour uncertain in the dark – pulled up on the grass verge beyond the garden gate. He followed the girl into the living room, trying to remember her name. Beth had mentioned her. She looked like one of those flushed, pink, sturdy English girls who never make it past the first round of Wimbledon. 'You're just in time. I was going to have a shower.' He looked at his watch.

'No rush. Meal isn't on yet.'

'I was hoping for a drink.'

A flash of the blue eyes, but she went shy on him again.

'You must be Justine.'

'That's right. I look after Adam.'

And how's that? he wanted to ask, but felt he shouldn't. 'Were you with him when he found the badger?'

'No, thank God. I only do a couple of hours. Collect him from school, do a bit of housework, stay till Beth gets back. I'll just put these upstairs. You've found out where the airing cupboard is?'

'No.'

'On the landing.'

'Oh. Right.'

He was losing interest. He got a clean pair of jeans and a T-shirt from his suitcase and put them on. Robert had put his laptop on the table. He decided he would work in here, where he could enjoy an open fire, and began searching for the nearest plug. Tomorrow he'd get Robert to drop him in town so that he could buy a printer and start looking for a car. He could hear Justine moving around upstairs. Heavy footed.

When she came down, she said, 'Looks like work.'

'It is. Well, meant to be.'

'You writing a book?'

He guessed Beth had told her. 'That's the idea.'

'What's it about?'

'The way wars are represented.'

That was generally enough to discourage further questions, but Justine was made of sterner stuff. 'War photography?'

'Yeah – but not just that. Goya seems to be squatting

57

all over it at the moment.' He was too – like a monstrous jewelled toad.

Justine plonked herself down on the sofa.

'Don't you have to be getting back?'

'No, I'm finished for the – oh,' she said, flushing and jumping up again. 'I see what you mean.'

Regretting his churlishness, he said, 'No, it's OK, don't rush off. Do you want a cup of tea, or something?'

'I'll make it.'

'No, you won't. It'll do me good to find out where everything is.'

In the end they made the tea together, unearthing, as a final triumph, a bowl of sugar left behind, he suspected, by the last tenants – Beth would never have given houseroom to anything as unhealthy as sugar. It was caked to the sides of the dish and brown in the middle from careless dipping of wet spoons. As Justine raised the mug – it had a yellow duckling on the side, which suited her, he thought – she blew a wisp of ultra-fine blonde hair out of her eyes. She wasn't particularly attractive, not to him anyway – too fresh-faced, too wholesome – and yet when she lowered the mug and he saw her full, fleshy, pouting lips gleaming with wet he did feel a tweak of desire, impersonal but not exploitative. He wouldn't have dreamt of making a move, even if he could have convinced himself that a teenage girl might find a middle-aged man with white hairy legs and raging conjunctivitis irresistible. She made him feel positively decrepit – rumpled, just out of bed, smelling, no doubt, a bit stale. Only he liked her mouth.

It would repel lipstick, that mouth. No matter how carefully it was applied, she would never manage to retain more than a thin stain around the edges of her lips.

Good manners required that, after her questions about his book, he should show some reciprocal interest, so he set to work to draw her out, something that from long practice he found easy to do. She was nineteen, so older than she looked. She'd had a place at Cambridge – she was supposed to be there now, but she'd got glandular fever just after the A-level results came out, and had to ask for her place to be deferred.

What A-levels did she do? Biology, Physics, Chemistry, Psychology. She'd wanted to do Art as well, but the timetable clashed.

So: four A-levels. No mention of grades. Bright and modest, or so perfectionist that no grades were good enough? There was nothing sharp or quick about her, nothing obviously clever – she seemed, if anything, rather hesitant. Young for her age. Painfully young. He kept getting this sense of pain from her – and yet she sounded cheerful enough.

'Still,' he said, 'you're only missing a year.'

'Yeah, but I'll be twenty by the time I get there.'

'Oh, I shouldn't worry. I expect they have a lot of mature students.'

'I suppose so,' she said, not detecting irony.

He felt slightly ashamed, though he hadn't meant to be unkind. He pictured her there, jogging along the Backs – but why jogging? She didn't seem particularly athletic, perhaps it was the sweatshirt and the trainers

– one of the hundreds who pass through and make no impression, but years later can recall the precise sound of oars in rowlocks, hear the voices of the coaches yelling encouragement from the banks, smell wood smoke, see misty light around a street lamp and feel an obscure pain, a longing, thinking of a key that never turned properly in the lock, a door that might have opened but didn't.

Pain again. He must be projecting all these complex layers of pain and regret on to her, she didn't feel anything like that, how could she? She was just a young girl at a loose end because her friends had moved on and left her behind.

'Are you over the glandular fever now?'

'Yes. Though I still get a bit tired. I'm in bed by ten o'clock.'

Bored rigid, he thought, refusing to dwell on the thought of Justine in bed. 'Have you any friends still around here?'

'One or two in Newcastle. I see them at the week-ends, but round here, no. Well, one person, I suppose.'

Blue shadows had appeared in the thin skin under her eyes, and for the first time it was possible to believe that she had recently been quite seriously ill.

Boyfriend, he thought. Ex-boyfriend. Somebody who should have stayed around when she got ill and didn't.

'Where do you live normally?' she asked.

'London.'

'Why on earth did you come here?'

'Peace and quiet.'

'You'll get plenty of that.'

'I'm in the middle of a divorce,' he said, more honestly. 'I need somewhere cheap to live. And I've got to work my arse off.'

'You won't be disturbed here. You'll see graveyards with more life.'

Again that bitter, restless chafing. It made her interesting to him, and again he looked at her mouth, then raised his eyes to hers and found her watching him. Careful, he thought, replacing the mug on the kitchen table. 'I think I'd better have a shower.'

'I'm sorry I woke you up.'

'No, just as well. If I'd slept any longer I mightn't have slept tonight.'

He saw her to the door. Neither of them said anything about meeting again, because they knew they would. He closed the door as soon as she was safely through the gate. A moment later he heard the engine start and the car – borrowed from her mother? A present after A-levels? – drive away.

After she'd gone, he washed up the mugs, aware that his stocking-feet were leaving damp footprints on the tiles. God, he was disgusting. These days, without warning, he poured out this cold, clammy sweat. But it would pass. Exercise, rest, decent food, cut back on the booze – drastically – and within a few weeks he'd be back to normal. This was his main objection to the psychiatrist they'd insisted on his seeing: that the man had understood the symptoms perfectly well, but had underestimated Stephen's powers of recovery. He couldn't have done his job as long as he had without having the power to slough off exhaustion and the after-effects of shock. But now, at this moment, he needed, above all, to feel clean. He could tackle the rest later.

He got into the shower. The water was so hot he had to jump out again and readjust the settings. Already the small bathroom was full of steam. He got in a second time, more cautiously, and scrubbed every part of himself, washed his hair and rinsed it till it squeaked, then, deliberately, taking a deep breath, turned the shower to cold.

After the first yelp he took it in silence, letting the icy water plaster his hair flat against his skull until he was as mindless as animals seem to be in heavy rain, every sense subdued to the battering of the elements. Last, he raised his face and let the sheet of water, falling on his closed eyelids and into his open mouth, remove whatever he had left of feeling or thought.

He towelled himself dry in front of the fire, then hunted in his suitcase for clean socks and pants, before setting off, damp-haired and red-eyed but otherwise presentable, for his brother's house.

Justine's car had gone, he saw with a twinge of disappointment, but then remembered she'd said she was going home. He was faintly amused at himself, at how cheerful he suddenly felt. Nothing like lust to make you feel life's still worth living, even if the particular attraction is one that you absolutely do not intend to pursue.

Six

When Kate finally decided her state of dream-filled, dry-mouthed semi-consciousness no longer qualified as sleep, she levered herself up on one elbow and looked at the clock. Five fifteen. This was ludicrous. If she went on like this, day and night would be reversed.

She dressed quickly, pulling on her oldest work clothes, and went down to the kitchen, where she made coffee and drank it wandering round the kitchen table. Her eyelids were prickling so much from tiredness that she was tempted to go back to bed, but there was Peter to consider now. The rhythms of her working life had to adjust to this other person.

Chafing against the new dependency, she drank the first cup of coffee too hot and scalded her tongue. Her neck felt terrible, her back ached. Every morning there was this interval of pain and stiffness, while her vertebrae got reacquainted and resigned themselves to working as a team. It got better. Warmth helped. Exercise helped.

Muffled against the cold, sheathed in her own breath, she stepped across the glittering yard, crunching across iced-covered puddles and ruts to the studio. The hens were just coming out of the barn, scuffling and pecking at the mud, the cock strutting about with the sun's rays caught in his jiggling comb, light streaming off his feathers, burning purple, oily green and gold. The farmhouse roof kindled, as she watched, frost glittered for a moment more fiercely, then began a slow retreat.

In the studio, red-faced, fingers and toes tingling, she made another pot of coffee and then walked round, staring at rolls of hessian, piles of newspaper, coils of chicken wire, buckets of sawdust, wood chippings, bags of plaster, bundles of straw, a tray of builders' masks, mallets, pliers, chisels – all the materials and tools of her trade. She sighed, steam from the coffee rising into her eyes, and worked her arm round and round in its socket, wondering what, if anything, she could achieve before Peter arrived.

She hated having people in the studio while she worked, had never liked it, even back in art college, when it had been unavoidable. As a young woman she'd schemed and struggled to find her own place, initially a dank basement in Paddington, then, later, in Liverpool, a lock-up garage near a railway siding. Then she'd met Ben, who'd been on one of his retreats, times when he went off and photographed nothing but landscapes. Fenland, waterland, brown tarns in gorse-covered hills, snow light, water light – all with the same brooding darkness in them. They were supposed to be peaceful, these photographs, a break from the subjects he spent most of his life pursuing, but they weren't. You always knew, looking at these empty fields, these miles of white sand with marram grass waving in the wind, that somewhere, close at hand, but outside the frame, a murder had been committed.

Get on with it, she told herself. There must be something she could do. The solution to all the doubts was to get her hands on the wire, the pliers, above all the plaster, that first blessed gloop of white goo. She realized she was moving her hands, the way a starving bird will sometimes make pecking motions with its beak or snap the air at imaginary flies.

'Bugger it,' she said aloud, thinking she might as well swear while she still could.

A discreet cough. Turning to look behind her – she couldn't move her head without swivelling her whole body – she saw that Peter had come in and was standing by the door, a tall, thin, dark figure starkly elongated against the white wall. She'd given him the combination of the lock so he wouldn't be left waiting outside if she were late back from one of her physiotherapy sessions, but it meant he was always surprising her. She never heard him come in.

He came further into the room, chafing his hands together. His nose was red with cold.

'Have a cup of coffee,' she said. 'Get warm.'

They stood over the wood stove together, and she had a second cup, and he stared around him. He was obviously fascinated by the plaster figures that lined the walls. No, don't look, she wanted to say, they're not finished. They were part of a sequence she'd started after 9/11, not based on Ben's photographs, or anybody else's for that matter, because nobody had been there to photograph what chiefly compelled her imagination: the young men at the controls who'd seized aeroplanes full of people and flown them into the sides of buildings. There they were, lean, predatory, equally ready to kill or die. She thought they might be rather good in the end. They certainly frightened her.

Peter started on the wire, cutting and shaping under her direction. She went back to her drawings, rolled them out and pinned the curling edges down with chisels and mallets. Because her hands were not touching the material, she felt doubtful about ideas that had once seemed persuasive. She knew she was being uncharacteristically tentative. The grave cloths were a problem. All her instincts had been for a nude figure – there's no logical reason why the Risen Christ should go on wearing the dress of a first-century Palestinian Jew for the rest of eternity, and even less reason for him to have got stuck in the robes of a medieval English king, and yet she knew that a naked Christ would cause uproar. A lively faith in the Incarnation often goes with a marked disinclination to have the anatomical consequences staring one in the face. She'd compromised by having him tearing off grave cloths vigorously, but not so vigorously as to uncover those parts that would occasion letters to *The Times* if they were to be revealed. She was becoming middle aged. Once she might have fought for the purity of her original conception. These days she just didn't think cocks were worth the bother.

If only she had been able to do the work herself,

she'd have known immediately which ideas worked and which didn't. She felt frustrated, and was trying desperately hard not to show it, because, in all fairness, Peter couldn't have been any more tactful. He had such a talent for blending into the background that once or twice she'd actually managed to forget he was there.

Twelve weeks to go, and here she was still cutting wire. She fought the panic down and reached for the next bale.

Eight days later she had a complete figure. She wasn't sure about the torso, and she knew she was going to have to rethink the head, but the legs were all right. Everything depended on the legs. Once, in a television interview, dazzled by the lights, her face weighed down by more make-up than she'd ever worn in her life – she felt like a geisha – she'd heard herself say, 'You see, the thing is, you've got to make sure it doesn't fall over.'

She'd buried her head in her hands and groaned aloud when she watched the video. Profound, or what? Oh, well, yes, thank you, Ms Frobisher, that's really got the direction of twentieth-century sculpture sorted out. But yes, she thought, looking up at the chicken-wire figure, actually that *is* the thing. It mustn't fall over.

This was stable enough, though the proportions were all wrong. Cautiously, she craned her head back, trying, despite the pain in her neck, to decide what changes needed to be made. 'There's a spotlight over there. Would you mind putting it on?'

She walked round the floodlit figure. The head was

the problem. People would be looking up – well, obviously – from the foot of the plinth, and that meant the head had to be considerably larger than was anatomically accurate. She reckoned about a third larger. But the plinth itself stood on a small hill to the right of the path that led to the west door, and it was from this vantage point that the majority of people would see it – still looking upwards, but at a greater distance and from a much less acute angle. The problem was simple: the distortion that worked from the foot of the plinth might well look grotesque from the path. Simple to formulate. By no means simple to solve.

'It's a wonderful site, isn't it?' the dean had enthused, white hair blowing in the wind, when he took her outside to see it. Meaning, she supposed, that it was prominent. It was that all right. She'd stared at him in complete astonishment. *Wonderful?* she'd wanted to say. *It's a bloody nightmare.* It wasn't just the technical problems of the position, it was the fact that the statue was going to stand next to one of the most beautiful buildings in Europe. A wonderful site if you didn't mind making a total prat of yourself.

'Peter, would you mind standing there?'

He'd been hovering behind her, silent as always, waiting for her to tell him what to do next. He went and stood where she indicated, beside the figure.

Self-conscious but determined, she lay down on the floor at his feet and looked up at him.

'No, don't look at me. Look straight ahead.'

When he looked down, his eyes almost vanished.

Even staring straight ahead they were difficult to see.

'Can you take your specs off?'

He did as she asked, reaching behind him to put them on the table. His eyes still made no impact, and yet they were larger than most. The eyes on the Christ were going to have to be enormous, and she'd under-estimated how big the head had to be. She looked from Peter's head to the ball of wire on top of the figure, memorizing the changes that would have to be made before she could start on the plaster. She felt Peter tense up under her gaze.

'It's all right, don't worry,' she said, laughing a little with embarrassment as she tried to stand up. 'It's not turning into a portrait.'

He didn't help her to her feet, though she struggled on her knees for several seconds because her back had gone into spasm. He never touched her. When he handed tools up to her, his fingertips never brushed hers. Once or twice she'd seen him reach out a hand as if to steady her on the scaffolding, but he never actually did. He was elaborately formal, impersonal.

'Ouch,' she said, pressing one hand into the small of her back, laughing.

'Are you all right?'

'Fine. I just needed to get the size of the head right.'

'Does it need to come off?'

'Yeah, but it's a bit late now. We'll start on it tomorrow.'

She was smiling as she took off her gloves and put the pliers down. But trying not to sound disconsolate was one of the burdens of the situation. Her moods, the ebb and flow of hope and conviction, were supposed to be private. Her work, what she chose to show, became public at the moment when somebody pulled off the sheet and not one second before.

After Peter had gone, she walked round the figure again, comparing its shape with the figure in her head, mentally altering the proportions, itching to get up there, to feel the wire, but even looking up for any length of time produced pain. She had to admit defeat.

As she turned to go, she noticed that Peter had left his specs behind on the table, and she picked them up. Greasy fingerprints all over them. Impossible to keep glasses clean in a studio. She went over to the sink, dampened a sheet of kitchen paper and worked at the lenses till they were clean, holding them up against the light to check she'd removed every mark. She hoped he was all right to drive without them. Experimentally, she put them on, looking round the studio at the complex patterns of light and shade cast by the figure on the plinth.

Suddenly, she realized what she was *not* experiencing: the wave of nausea you feel when you put on somebody else's spectacles. And she could still see perfectly well, although somebody else's prescription lenses ought to have blurred the scene. Thinking she must be mistaken, she took them off and put them on again, but no, there was no doubt. The 'lenses' were clear glass.

Lots of people wear clear specs, she told herself. She put them to one side and started clearing up. But then she thought: who wears them? Rising young executives wanting to look older and more authoritative. But not gardeners. In any outdoor job glasses are a nuisance. Oh, well, not my business, she told herself firmly, and got back to work.

When she'd finished, she wrapped the specs in kitchen paper and put them by the sink, then, dragging herself reluctantly away from the warm fug of the studio, let herself out into the icy winter air.

Seven

Stephen woke before dawn. Nothing like this darkness in the city, ever. Deep black, like some of those nights in Africa. He located his body purely by the sense of touch: skin on sheets. His hands and feet were far-flung colonies. He daren't switch the light on, because in this state he found light more frightening than darkness. All the while the details of the dream went on invading his waking mind. Being buried alive. No source of light in this dream – only the smell, gasping breaths, other people's blood soaking him to the skin, the knowledge that if he moved or cried or stirred, the people up there, the people he never saw, were waiting with knives and guns and machetes to finish the job.

Exerting every scrap of willpower, he turned over, and stared into the darkness until beyond the swirls of orange and purple he managed to distinguish shapes: a chair, a wardrobe, the door to the landing. When he was sure he knew the way, he got out of bed – there was no point lying there, he would never get back to sleep, he was too afraid the dream would return – and naked, sweating, a pink, peeled prawn of a man – that's how he saw himself – he edged his way downstairs, feet overlapping the sixteenth-century treads at every step. He entered the stone-flagged kitchen, where he drew back the curtains and put the kettle on for coffee.

He drank it sitting by the window, the hot fluid delineating his oesophagus, another part of his living body reclaimed from the dark. He watched the stars turn pale, saw the empty road curving towards the sleeping farmhouse, and the frost-bound fields, the fires waking in the white grass as the light strengthened. All the time he was debriefing himself, sorting out the dream. He knew if he didn't take time to do this, it could stain and corrupt the whole day.

Before starting work, he jogged to the top of the hill. Not a breath of air, not a blade of grass or a twig stirred. On the crest he leant against a tree, watching darkness drain down the slopes of the hills as if somebody at the bottom of the valley had pulled the plug on night. Details emerged as the light grew: knobbly black buds of ash, brittle brown oak leaves still clinging to the tree, the veins on the backs of his hands. And then the sun erupted, shredding clouds, pouring streams of light down the valley, turning the moon, that lingered in blue translucent space, into a crazed eggshell.

All around him were the baby fists of new ferns, though there was a rawness in the air that threatened more snow. He began searching for the owl's nest. It had been hooting again last night, on and on with hardly a pause, as if it thought it was a nightingale. One tree half covered in ivy looked more promising than the rest. He scuffled through the mulch of dead leaves until he found what he was looking for, picked up three or four fibrous brown pellets and put them in his pocket.

Back in the cottage, he took them out and rolled them between thumb and forefinger. He'd picked them up automatically, as he would have done as a boy, but now he thought that Adam might like them. He'd take them up this afternoon, as soon as he saw Justine's car parked outside the house.

Relations between the farmhouse and the cottage had quickly settled into a routine. Stephen hardly saw Robert and Beth except at weekends, but observed their comings and goings almost as if they were strangers.

Both were busy, and Beth added to the strains of a full-time job by doing a lot of community work. She was a regular churchgoer. That rather surprised Stephen, because Robert was a militant atheist: 'There is no God, and Sharkey is his prophet' – that was Robert's creed. So unless Beth's brand of Christianity was remarkably accommodating, they must find plenty to disagree about.

Robert worked incredibly long hours. Sometimes, in particularly bad weather, he stayed overnight in the city rather than risk snow drifts blocking the moor road.

Or so Beth said, expressionlessly, her eyes dead.

'Where does he stay?' Stephen asked.

'Oh, there's always somebody who'll give him a bed.'

Initially, he'd been afraid Adam would ignore the unspoken rule of no weekday contact and take it into his head to visit his uncle in the cottage. He was such a still, strange, isolated little boy. In Robert's place he might not have thought it wise to bury Adam in the depths of the country, miles away from other children of his own age. Out of school he seemed to see nobody except his parents and Justine, whose little red Metro spluttered up the lane every day at four o'clock, bringing him home from school. Stephen wanted to say to Robert, 'But our childhood wasn't like this.' They'd run wild, at least until the first shades of the exam prison house started to close in. Contrasted with their childhood, Adam's seemed both overprivileged and depleted. Stephen would encounter him sometimes, trotting along, searching for roadkill or following tracks in the snow, but always, except for Justine, alone.

When Stephen spoke to him, Adam would duck his head, avoid eye contact, mumble something and then, as soon as possible, drift away.

His evident disinclination to have anything to do with his uncle made Stephen perversely more interested in him. So that afternoon, shortly after Justine's car with Adam in the back had coughed and wheezed its way up the hill, he took the owl pellets round to the house, and spread them out on a sheet of kitchen paper on the table.

'What do you think they are?'

Adam wrinkled his nose. 'Poo?'

No kid who regularly brought home roadkill had any right to be fastidious. 'Wrong end. They come out of the beak.'

'Owl pellets?'

'Yeah.'

'Cool.'

'Have you got any tweezers?' Stephen asked Justine,

who was standing by the cooker, frying sausages for Adam's tea. She didn't look as if she had. Like everything else about her, her eyebrows were flourishing and entirely natural.

'Got a meat skewer.'

She rattled about in the cutlery drawer and produced one.

'That'll do.'

He showed Adam how to tease out the small bones, skulls, feathers, fur and other indigestible parts of the owl's nightly diet. Adam was totally absorbed. Stephen met Justine's eye over the sleek, bowed head. She smiled and said, 'You can come again. This is the quietest he's been for weeks.'

Before long a neat row of skulls was lined up on the table.

'Now you can wash them,' Stephen said, starting to clear away the debris.

Adam ran off to the downstairs bathroom with his treasures in his cupped hands.

Stephen dusted off his hands and was about to go – he hadn't intended to do more than deliver the pellets and retreat to the cottage – when Justine said, 'Do you fancy a cup of tea?'

He fancied something a bit stronger than tea, but he could scarcely ask Beth's au pair to raid the drinks cupboard. 'Yeah, good idea.' He was tired, he realized, sitting back in the chair, and he'd hardly spoken to anybody all week. 'You nearly finished for the day?' he asked, as she filled the kettle at the sink.

'Just about.' She stifled a yawn. 'Beth's always late back on Thursdays. There's some sort of meeting after work, and it just seems to run on.'

How on earth had this bright girl ended up doing this? Over tea – Adam busy with his skulls at the other end of the table, snuffling through his mouth as kids do when they're interested – she talked about her life, the job, how it was this or being a barmaid and Dad had thought this would be easier. There was no mention of her mother.

'What does your mother think?'

'God knows. Buggered off years ago.'

'I'm sorry.'

A shrug. 'No need, it was a long time ago. It was a great scandal at the time, you know? Vicar's wife runs off. Not supposed to happen.' She smiled. 'You didn't know I was a vicar's daughter, did you?'

'No.' He wondered if she was a virgin. 'Do you have to do anything?'

'Do anything?' She was amused. 'Like what?'

'I don't know. Good works.'

'No. Well, I don't, anyway. No, I just keep lots of spiteful old cows supplied with gossip.' She took a sip of her tea. 'I inherited that role from my mother.'

'You could go off somewhere.'

Her face darkened. 'It's difficult.'

Deserted, possessive dad? 'You're going to stay here all year?'

'No, well, don't tell Beth, will you, because it'll freak her out, but I think I might talk Dad into letting me go on one of those crash secretarial courses. And then I could get a proper job. You can't get a job with just A-levels. Nobody wants to know.'

'Sounds like a good idea. Where would you do it?'

'London.'

'Ah.'

He thought of Justine and her milkmaid cheeks in some office in Kensington tapping away on a keyboard thinking real life had started at last. Though he was the wrong one to criticize anybody for thinking real life was somewhere else – he'd devoted his whole working life to that particular delusion.

'What's this?' Adam asked, holding up a skull with two long, orange-coloured teeth in the front.

'A mouse,' Stephen said.

'How do you know it isn't a shrew?'

He didn't, of course.

'You've got plenty of books,' Justine said. 'Why don't you look it up?'

Stephen stood up to go. She came to the door with him, looking, he thought, prettier than she had the other night. He did find her attractive, though by now he was so frustrated he would have found almost *any* young woman attractive – and his definition of 'young' was becoming more generous by the day. But this one was too young, and much too close to home. If things went wrong – and how with a twenty-year difference in age could they not go wrong? – it could become very messy. And they wouldn't be able to avoid seeing each other.

Thinking like this implied he stood a chance, whereas in fact she probably thought of him as even more decrepit than her father. At best as a nice, kind, avuncular figure helping to amuse Adam.

Not a pleasant thought.

He set off down the frosty path, raising his hand to wave to her as he reached the gate, feeling the withdrawal of warmth and light as a minor but real abandonment.

Eight

The phone was ringing as he opened the front door of the cottage, and he ran into the living room to pick it up. As soon as he heard Nerys's voice, he caught the brown fug of his breath rising from a suddenly bilious stomach. Nerys sounded controlled and strident, spoiling for a row. She'd had an offer for the house, she said, and she thought they ought to accept it. The papers were full of a slowing down in the housing market, well, they'd been talking about that off and on for months, hadn't they, but this time people did seem to think it was actually going to happen, so –

By 'people' he suspected she meant Roger. Roger-the-lodger, the sod. 'How much?'

'One and a half million. The estate agent says they've got the money. What do you think?'

'Grab it.'

'That's what I thought. Well,' she said breathlessly, 'I'll go ahead, then, shall I?'

'Yes. And thanks, Nerys. I know you've had all the work.'

'That's all right.' She managed to sound gracious and aggrieved at the same time. 'Are you well?'

'Yes, fine. And you?'

'Fine.'

Somehow in a plethora of 'fines' they managed to get off the phone. It must be over, he thought, replacing the receiver, if they'd reverted to being polite.

He'd hardly put the receiver down, when the phone rang again. He jumped to answer it, superstitiously afraid it might be Nerys ringing to say the sale had fallen through, though if so it must've been the shortest negotiation in history – but it was Beth, sounding resentful, as she always did when asking a favour. She gave generously – she was always dashing about doing some good work or other, letting this, that or the other cause eat into her scanty free time – but she'd never learnt to ask or receive gracefully, so it was a slightly petulant-sounding Beth who explained that Justine's car wouldn't start, and she couldn't stay over because it was her father's birthday, and they were going out for supper, so could he possibly run her home? Beth would have done it herself, of course, but Adam was in the bath and couldn't be left. Stephen cut her short, saying it was no bother at all and he'd be up to the house in a couple of minutes.

Fortunately, he hadn't started drinking. One of his health ploys was to put it off till later and later in the evening.

Justine was waiting at the gate, Beth just visible at the crack in the front door. 'Goodnight,' they called to each other. 'Have a nice evening,' Beth added.

Stephen waved, but didn't get out of the car.

As Justine settled into the passenger seat and pulled the seat belt across, he said, 'I don't know where you live.'

'Hetton-on-the-Moor.'

'No wiser.'

'It's the other side of the forest. Don't worry, I'll direct you.'

'Is it far?' He was wondering about the petrol.

'Six miles.'

Not far, then, though distances were deceptive here. The country lanes wound round so much that estimated travelling times were apt to be too optimistic. And then there was the forest, with its single road, its mile after mile of impenetrable trees.

'Is it anywhere near Woodland House?'

'Kate Frobisher's place? Yes, she lives a couple of miles outside the village.'

'One of your father's parishioners.'

'Yeah, but not the God-bothering kind.'

A short pause, as the car bumped off the grass verge, its headlights illuminating hedgerows laced with frost.

'Why, do you know her?'

'I've met her once or twice. I knew Ben well. I did quite a few assignments with him.'

'Bosnia.'

'Yes, that's right.' He was surprised she knew. It must be history to her.

'I read the book. Left here.'

He took the corner, his headlights revealing the dark mass of the forest straight ahead. 'That was the last book we did together.'

She mumbled something about it being very tragic. He agreed that it was. After that they drove for a while in silence, and the soft sound of the tyres over slushy snow seemed to seal him off from normal life. There hadn't been time for the news about the house to sink in, but he was beginning to realize he was free. Single. He didn't know whether he felt elated or frightened, but elation was closer. He felt he was setting off for a day out, instead of just driving Beth's au pair home.

'You scored a real bull's eye with those owl pellets.'

'Yes, he liked them, didn't he? And you don't have to boil them to get the skulls.'

'That's right.' She laughed. 'We're going to label them tomorrow so that'll keep him busy. And then we're going to do a proper survey: how many mice? How many shrews? What's the percentage of each animal in the owl's diet . . . ? I don't suppose you could show me the tree, could you? Because we're going to need a lot more pellets.'

'Of course, come over any time. It sounds like an awful lot of work.'

'I don't mind. I'll miss him, if I do go on this course.'

'I wouldn't've thought he was all that easy to take care of. He's –' He pulled himself up, sharply.

'Weird. Yes, I know, but I don't think there's all that much wrong with him. Beth was frantic when they diagnosed Asperger's.'

He mustn't let her see that he hadn't known. 'I've never really understood what that is.'

'It's basically a sort of difficulty in seeing other people as people. Like if you were looking at this' – she pointed to the trees his headlights were revealing – 'there wouldn't be any essential difference between me and the trees. So you can't change your perspective and see the situation from another person's point of view, because you can't grasp the fact that they have their own internal life, and they might be thinking something different from you.'

'So they're objects?'

'Yes.'

Stephen thought for a moment, trying to relate this to his knowledge of Adam. He didn't know him well enough. 'I don't know how much good these labels do. I was supposed to go and see a psychiatrist – the newspaper I worked for wanted somebody to have a look at me.'

'What was wrong?'

'I was starting to howl at every full moon.'

'No, really what was wrong?'

'Nightmares. The usual. If you want the label – post-traumatic stress disorder. I don't know. I decided in the end it just wasn't for me. After all, nobody forced me to go to those places. Some of them I actually begged to go to – it was my idea. And if you bring it on yourself, like that, I don't think you've got any right to complain. You've certainly no right to expect sympathy.'

'You sound as if you think you don't deserve help.'

'I don't think it's possible. I think you have to do it yourself. Especially if you got yourself into the mess in the first place.' This was the wrong conversation to be having with her – too intimate, too intense – but he didn't know how to get out of it. 'There was a guy once – a Holocaust survivor – who said something about seeing the sun rise in Auschwitz and it was black. But you see he didn't *choose* that experience. He got lumbered with it. Whereas people like me who go round the world poking their noses into other people's wars – we do choose it.'

'A black sun?'

'Yes. We risk the possibility. And if you end up with nightmares, too bad. They're part of the baggage. And you certainly shouldn't go running to a therapist, and say, "Poor little me."'

They drove for a while in silence.

'I shouldn't say anything,' she said at last, 'because I don't know enough about it, but I do think you've got therapy completely wrong. I don't think it's about feeling sorry for yourself, or even the therapist feeling sorry for you. I think it's supposed to be a lot tougher than that.'

He was surprised by her vehemence and let the subject drop. After a few minutes he asked, 'So what are you going to do after university?'

'Don't know really. Something with children.'

'Teaching?'

'No, I thought of being a paediatrician. Or a child psychiatrist, but it's years ahead. I don't really know.'

'Oh, so you're reading Medicine?'

'Yes.' She was stifling a yawn as she spoke. 'Right here and then just follow the road.'

'You sound tired.'

'It's the warmth. I'll be all right.'

The next time he looked she was asleep, hanging from her seat belt like a toddler, her full lips pouting slightly on every exhaled breath. He smiled to himself and tried to drive smoothly, taking his time on the bends, braking well in advance.

The next bend was sharper. He reached out to steady her and felt her body heat on the palm of his hand, like a burn that lingered for many minutes after he touched her. She slipped sideways until her knee rested against his thigh. He was intensely aware of her warmth. He didn't want the drive to end. For as long as she went on sleeping, she was potentially his. As soon as she woke up, he'd be back with the implacable reality: that she was his sister-in-law's au pair and more than twenty years younger than him.

On the next stretch of straight road he risked looking down at her. Her face was in shadow. He could see only her hands, which were loosely knotted in her lap. There was a dusting of gold hairs on her wrists, each hair distinct in the faint glow of light from the dashboard. He thought how smooth and firm her skin looked, how pleasant it would be to touch, then dragged his gaze back to the road.

Too late. The road was momentarily streaked with red. He thought he heard a thud, but it was lost immediately in the squeal of brakes. The car began to skid, but he righted it, though not before he'd glimpsed the slope between the trees, leading down to the stream in the valley far below. He brought the car to a jarring halt.

Justine was awake, staring. 'What was it?'

'I don't know.'

'Did we hit it?'

'I don't know. Stay here.' She started undoing her seat belt. 'No, stay here.'

He got out of the car, his stomach churning. Burnt rubber mixed with the smells of new bracken and moist earth. He inspected the ground round his wheels, his fingertips flinching in anticipation of what they might find. No sound now, except for the occasional slither and plop as an overburdened branch let fall its weight of snow. Whatever it was must be dead – that was all right, he could cope with death. What he dreaded was injury – the need to put whatever it was out of its misery. His fingers dabbled in wetness, but when he brought them close to the headlights they were merely smeared with mud. He stood up, scanning the ground, peering under the wheels, looking up and down the road.

'Can you see anything?'

'No, I think it must be further back. We must have gone right over it.'

'I expect it was a rabbit. There's lots of them about at the moment.'

He'd seen them too, baby rabbits newly out of the burrow bumping along the grass verges without fear, or caught in the middle of the road, quivering bags of blood with the headlights in their eyes. But he didn't think this was a rabbit. He remembered that streak of red.

'There's a torch in the glove compartment. Can you find it?'

He heard her hand poking about in the recesses, and then she got out into the road to hand it to him. They walked back up the lane together. The forest stretched out in all directions, full of furtive rustlings that froze as they passed, noses twitched at the air, unseen eyes followed them. A few flakes of snow, fat, splothery, loose flakes that wouldn't lie, drifted down into the wavering circle of torchlight.

'Do you know, I'm beginning to think we might have missed it?'

Stephen kept his voice casual, but inside he wanted to sing. He didn't want this drive to end in death.

He followed Justine with the torch as she climbed up the right bank and stood brightly illuminated against the dark wood. As she turned to face him, he lowered the torch to avoid dazzling her. 'What do you think it was?' she asked.

'I thought it might be a fox.'

'Could be. I heard one barking last night. They'll have started mating. It woke me up.'

He wanted to get back home, to draw the curtains against the darkness with its indistinguishable screams of lust and pain. 'There's no sign of it. I think we'd better leave it.'

'I'll just have a look in here. There's a little path, can you see?'

Before Stephen could say anything, she'd ducked

under the barbed-wire fence and disappeared into the darkness of the wood.

He stood in the lane, while all around him the snow fell faster, spiralling down into the light of the head-lights, though when they reached the wet road the flakes disappeared. Blinded at first, he slowly became accustomed to the dark. He didn't want to go too far away from the car, which wasn't parked particularly safely because the grass verge wasn't wide enough. He waited, walked up and down, stamped his feet. The full moon clung to the crest of a pine tree high above his head. Once or twice he called her name, but the sound echoed eerily up and down the green tunnel of the lane, stirring the darkness with its echoes. In the end it seemed simpler, safer even, to wait in silence. He didn't want to attract attention to himself. The thick darkness of nights in Africa came back to him, pressure building behind the thin membrane of everyday life like matter in a boil. 'Justine,' he called again.

When she didn't answer, he climbed up the bank to look for her. Here on the edge of the wood there were clumps of cow parsley almost as tall as he was. Dry, brown stalks that creaked a little as he brushed them aside. He waited on this side of the fence, in darkness because the torch battery seemed to be dying. At last a rattling of feet through dead leaves told him she was returning. He switched the torch back on and his heart turned over, for there, walking along the path between the trees, was a white-faced creature with glowing eyes.

As she came closer, he saw she looked nervous. Perhaps it was his silence, perhaps the deadness of the woods beyond. She was breathing quickly.

'Nothing?' he asked.

'No, nothing.'

Their whispering restored normality of a sort. He turned and began scrambling down the slope towards the car, his feet catching in the ferns. Then he heard her gasp. He looked round to see her doubled up, halfway through the barbed-wire fence, her jacket caught on one of the barbs.

'I'm sorry,' he said. 'I should've . . .'

He went back and in silence began working to free her. It took a long time because he didn't want to tear the cloth, and by the end he was breathing rapidly and his fingers had become clumsy. He caught his hand on one of the barbs, and was glad of the stinging because it made him think of something other than her nearness. She was grinning, embarrassed by the situation, as aware of him as he was of her. Finally he straightened up and asked, 'Are you all right? Did you hurt yourself?'

She lifted the weight of hair, and there, on the side of her neck, slanting down into the sweater, was a long red line, beaded with drops of blood that in this light looked black.

'That looks nasty.'

He was hardly aware of the words. He could only stare and stare at the red tear in the white skin. He wanted to put his hand over it. He wanted to touch it with his fingertips. It was as if his mind had been torn, a rent made in the fabric of his daily self and through this rent, slowly, all previous inhibitions and restraint dissolved into the night air. He reached out for her and kissed her. After the first shock, she started to kiss him back. He was dazed by the speed of it. His hands came up to hold her head. Her hair felt so alive, as if his exploring fingers might strike sparks, and down there at the roots were the marvellously interlocking bones of her skull. His mind went numb. There was no past, no future, only their two bodies pressing against each other in the darkness at the edge of the wood.

They stepped back at last, looking into each other's faces. Not the intimate lovers' gaze of both eyes into one pupil, but the scanning of people who are still strangers.

'Well,' he said, trying to sound casual, and not succeeding. He hadn't enough breath left to support the tone of voice he wanted.

She stared up at him, doubtful, as wary now as he was himself.

He swallowed. 'I'm sorry,' he said, 'that wasn't meant to happen.' What a ludicrous thing to say. He'd blurted it out without thinking, and immediately asked himself, why the hell not? Consenting adults, both single. She'd returned the kiss. The silence became a problem. He tried again. 'Come on,' he said. 'Let's get you home.'

She turned and strode off down the bank, looking neither to right nor left. He followed her more slowly, flashing the torch well ahead of him so it would light her way.

He'd almost reached the car when he saw it: a red mess of spiky fur and splintered bone. As he got into the car and started the engine, he was grateful she hadn't seen it. Against all reason, that thought still had power to console.

Nine

There was silence in the car. They stared straight ahead as, more slowly and carefully now, he drove along, his headlights probing the darkness between the trees. He didn't know what to say. He couldn't apologize again, and anyway she hadn't objected. It was just that he'd precipitated a situation he didn't want and was trying, clumsily, to claw his way back. He could hardly repeat that he hadn't meant it, and so he said nothing, trying to convey by silence that the incident had been trivial, but silence didn't seem able to carry that message. With every minute the kiss seemed to acquire greater importance. They were both taking quick shallow breaths, as if afraid the other would hear deeper breathing and misinterpret it. His chest felt tight. He was aware of her thighs, slightly apart, of the way the seat belt separated her breasts.

'This must be where Adam found the badger,' he said.

'Just back there. Beth doesn't like him coming this way on his own.'

'It's a long way.'

'I know I wouldn't want him coming here if he was my kid. If animals can't see the cars coming, how can he?'

Gradually, the trees thinned and they left the forest behind. Searching for something to talk about, he asked if any of her friends were taking a gap year, and had she ever thought of doing that herself? Yes, but she'd decided against it. Apparently medical schools weren't keen on the idea. 'They think you go off the boil,' she said. 'And they're probably right.' Her voice, which had been husky and constrained, became clearer and more confident as she spoke. She was having an unintended year off and she'd certainly gone off the boil. Brains turned to mush.

'You've been ill, remember.'

'Yeah, but I'm all right now.'

'What you need is a few new experiences.'

'Yes.' She sounded amused.

A slight tension returned when he stopped the car on the road outside the vicarage, a tall, narrow, Georgian house with gables set back from the village green behind a copse of trees. He walked round to open the door for her.

Standing together in the sudden cold, they looked at each other directly for the first time. The moonlight caught the whites of her eyes. Something stirred in him, something nameless and irrational and a lot less healthy than lust. He smelled the stairwell in Sarajevo, and dragged cold air into his lungs. Her mouth was slightly open.

'Yes, well,' he said, taking a step back.

'See you.'

She raised her hand, and walked rapidly away up the path. The front door released a sliver of golden light on to the trampled snow, and then she was gone.

Ten

Stephen woke next morning to find the excitement of the previous evening vanished and replaced by depression. He'd made a fool of himself. The worst of it was he was still attracted to her, but there was nothing he could do about it. She could come or not as she chose. He certainly wasn't going to pursue her.

The sense of new possibilities beginning to open up had disappeared. At nine, long after he should have started work, he was still slumped in an armchair, brooding over the failure of his marriage.

11 September 2001. Not a date anybody was likely to forget and many people had far worse personal reasons for remembering it than he had. On that day, having any kind of personal crisis seemed selfish, and yet of course they happened. People fell in love, or out of love, or down flights of badly lit stairs, got jobs, lost jobs, had heart attacks and babies, stared at the shadow on an X-ray, or the second blue line on a pregnancy-testing kit.

When he closed his eyes, Stephen's brain filled with images of shocked people covered in plaster dust. Grey dust blocking his nostrils, caking his eyelids. Gritty on the floor of the hotel lobby, trampled up the stairs and along the corridor to his room, where the television screen domesticated the roar and tumult, the dust, the debris, the cries, the thud of bodies hitting the ground, reduced all this to silent images, played and replayed, and played again in a vain attempt to make the day's events credible: the visual equivalent of what you heard repetitively on the street: *Christ, Holy shit, Oh my God.*

Sometime after midnight, too fuddled with tiredness and drink to remember the time difference, he phoned Nerys. The phone rang perhaps twenty times. Running his tongue round his mouth, he found pieces of grit lodged between his teeth, though he'd just finished brushing them. He sat on the bed, watching the second plane strike, and hoped his voice would sound normal. She came on the phone yawning. 'Nerys, it's me.' When there was no reply, he went on, 'I was just wondering how you are.'

'Stephen, I tried to ring. I couldn't get through.'

'No, the lines were jammed.'

Silence. He imagined her breasts in the moonlight, not as firm as they'd once been, but beautiful still. So many years of late-night calls from hotel bedrooms, and somehow in the process she'd detached herself. He didn't blame her. He closed his eyes and for a moment almost drifted off himself, but then the remembered thud of a body hitting the ground jolted him awake. To shut the sound out, he focused on her breasts and was rewarded by a stir of lust. Sometimes when you're so saturated in death that you can't soak up any more, only sex helps.

'Were you anywhere near?'

'Yes. I got quite close, then we were told to get back.' He was afraid she might be drifting off to sleep. 'Nerys? I've been thinking.'

'Yes?'

Something in her voice, patient, school-mistressy, exasperated, deflated him. He was trying to remember how it had been when they were first married, how one night while he was painting a door in their first home she'd come up and put her arms around him from behind, rubbing his cock against the palm of her hand while her breath exploded between his shoulder blades in sharp hot bursts. 'I can't wait till bedtime,' she'd said. 'Come to bed now.' And how once in grey, early-morning light, randy, waiting impatiently for her to wake, he'd slipped inside her, guilty, forcing himself not to move, but then miraculously she'd arched her back and giggled and let him in more deeply, and he'd realized she was only pretending to be asleep. They'd been so passionate then, insatiable. He'd wake up in the mornings, feeling the imprints of her hands all over his body, already hard and wanting her, even before he was fully conscious. 'Perhaps we could go back to Suffolk sometime?' Their first weekend together had been spent in Suffolk, on the coast at Shingle Street.

'Did you ring me up to say that?'

'I was just thinking.' What he'd meant was not, 'Can we go back to Suffolk?' but 'Can we go back?'

'I expect it's changed,' she said. 'Shingle Street. It'll have been ruined by now.'

A sound in the background.

'Are you in bed?'

'Of course I'm in bed.'

'I thought I heard somebody.'

'Well, you didn't.'

He had to believe her. But then he thought, There's the man who does the garden, the man who does odd jobs around the house, the man who does repair work on the car, the man who helps her with the VAT – 'I'm thinking of packing this in.'

'What?'

'This.'

'Oh.' She sounded disconcerted, though she'd been on at him to get a desk job in London for years. 'You say that, but you don't really mean it.'

'Actually I think I do mean it – this time.'

'How much have you had to drink?'

'A few.'

'Say it again when you're sober and I'll believe you.'

If this went on, they were going to quarrel. 'OK. Anyway, I'm sorry I woke you up.'

And then, just as he was about to put the phone down, he heard a man's voice, drowsy, bad-tempered, too fuddled with sleep to be cautious, say, 'Who the fuck is it?'

Nerys said quickly, 'I just switched on the World Service, darling. I think it might help me get back to sleep. Bye!'

The phone went dead. Stephen lay back against the pillows, thinking, Christ. Oh my God. And then, almost simultaneously, he thought, *Yes*. He'd known for a long time that something was going on. Nerys hadn't been the same for, oh . . . months, years probably, only it had suited him to look the other way. His mind groped in darkness. One phone call, and everything changed. But then he thought, Nothing's changed. They'd probably been sleeping together every night he'd been away. For years perhaps. The only thing that had changed was his awareness of the situation.

Resigned to a sleepless night, he got up, put on a scratchy, over-washed towelling robe and took himself and a bottle of whisky along the corridor to Ben's room. Thick carpets, twice-breathed air. Only the puddle of grey footprints outside Ben's door seemed real. He knocked, bracing himself for disappointment.

'Come in.'

Ben was still dressed, watching television in the darkness, a bluish light from the screen reflected on to his face. He pressed Mute as Stephen came into the room, and turned on the lamp beside his chair. His eyes were bloodshot, his hair damp. Like Stephen, he'd showered off most of the dust. His cameras were on a table by the window. 'I can't stop watching it.'

'No, nor me. Ridiculous, isn't it? When it's out there.' He sat down. 'Are you going back out?'

'Yes, in a few minutes. I just had to get the dust off.'

Stephen offered the whisky. Ben fetched glasses from the bathroom and held them as Stephen poured. They clinked silently, then turned again to face the screen.

Ben said, 'Do *you* think the world just changed?'

'I think America will.'

'I think things have changed. I mean real change. That was designed to be a photo-opportunity, and what have I done? I've spent the whole bloody day photographing it. Along with everybody else. Because we can't escape from the need for a visual record. The appetite for spectacle. And they've used that against us, just as they've used our own technology against us.'

'So what are you saying? We shouldn't cover it?'

'I don't know what I'm saying. But I know something happened here – and it isn't just that the Americans found out that they're vulnerable too.'

Stephen took a gulp of whisky. 'I just rang Nerys.'

'Oh, good. I haven't managed to get Kate.'

'She was in bed with another man.'

A pause. At last he looked away from the screen. 'Oh, my God, Stephen, I am sorry.'

'It's nothing. You compare it with what's happened to a lot of people today . . . Going to work this morning . . .'

'Have another drink.'

He didn't want another drink. What he wanted was to be outside his own skin, but there was no way of arranging that. He pressed his fingers deep into his flesh, round the jaw, under the cheekbones, into the sockets of his eyes, reminding himself of how it all fitted together. 'No, I won't, thanks. I'm going to take a couple of sleeping pills and blot it all out.'

Getting up to go, he saw the cameras on the table. 'Did you get any good shots?'

Couldn't remember what the answer had been, but

knew it now anyway. Yes, he got some very good shots. He always did, right to the end, right up to the last shot that killed him. He missed Ben. More than he missed Nerys. Now that was a shock, though perhaps it shouldn't have been. He'd shared more with Ben.

It snowed hard all day. By evening the ground was completely covered. After a bad start, Stephen worked till four o'clock and only then allowed himself to think about Justine. He felt she would come, though he almost managed to hope that she wouldn't, but when, unnaturally alert, he heard the crunch of her feet, he had got to the door and opened it before she knocked.

'Adam couldn't come,' she said, stamping her boots on the mat. 'He's got a temperature.'

Perhaps it was true. 'Wouldn't you rather wait till he's better?'

She stared at him. 'No, if he's going to be off school, I need something to keep him busy.'

'Then we might as well go straight away. There's no point in getting warm just to get cold again.' He put on his coat. 'How's the car?'

'Fixed. Beth got the AA out. Well, it's almost as big a disaster for her as it is for me. If I can't get to work, she can't go to work.'

He opened the back door. There, improbably large and veined, was the full moon, a cratered desolation hanging in space. The snow was unmarked except for the imprint of birds' feet around the bird table. It levelled everything: even the garden pond was level with the lawn, its fringe of dead reeds casting blue shadows on the snow.

'I'll go first, shall I?'

Cautiously, he felt his way down the path, each step scuffing up a fringe of snow. Once he turned and looked back. Snow-light was reflected palely up into her face. She was looking down, choosing where to put her feet. The hawthorn hedge that divided the garden from the path was thick with snow. Brushing against it in his struggle to open the gate, he dislodged dollops of snow that landed on his head and shoulders. His breath was everywhere.

Side by side now, they set off across the field. It would have helped to talk, but he couldn't think of anything to say, and anyway needed his breath for the climb. He didn't want to be too obviously gasping for breath. The moon filled the sky, casting their shadows long and black against the snow. Once they were in the copse, he stopped and listened, but, apart from the creaking of the branches, there was no sound. 'Up there,' he said.

They found the tree, and groped about in the snow between its roots to find the pellets. She stuffed about a dozen into her pocket. 'That'll do.'

It was harder going down. Once she tripped and he put a hand out to steady her, but she moved away again as soon as she recovered her balance. They came out from between the trees and stopped for a moment, gazing down over the white fields. Suddenly she caught his arm. 'Look,' she said.

A barn owl, perhaps even the owl that owned this nest, was hunting, quartering the frozen fields, relentless in its precision. Nothing that lived and moved could hope to escape its beak and feathered claws. He pictured it eating, the obscene delicacy of the raised claw feeding a recalcitrant tail into its beak, huge golden eyes slowly blinking. Backwards and forwards, up and down. It was an illusion, probably, that he could feel the ripple of disturbed air across his face. At last it detected movement and stooped to the kill, scattering snow, huge wings flapping and beating the air as it struggled to lift off, something small and warm wriggling in its claws.

'Isn't it odd?' Justine said. 'You always feel lucky when you see something like that, and yet it's bloody horrible, really.'

As they started to walk down the hill, he said, 'Would you like a drink before you go? You must be frozen.'

'In the cottage?'

'Yes. Or we can go out. Whatever.'

She considered, the roundness of her cheek in the pale light making her seem momentarily no older than Adam. 'In would be fine,' she said, and smiled.

She surprised him. He'd been prepared for anything, even virginity. Instead there was a swift, almost soundless orgasm, followed by sharp fingernails clutching his buttocks and urging him on. And it took him a long time. The last thing he'd expected, after several weeks of celibacy, was to be left standing on the starting blocks with his running shorts around his ankles. Evidently she felt extra help was required, because at the last moment she shoved her forefinger hard into his anus. When he was at last able to speak, he said, 'Bloody hell, woman.'

She looked up at him like an affronted kitten. 'Some people like that.'

People? She was the vicar's daughter, for Christ's sake. They lay, side by side, watching snowflakes fumble at the pane. The room was full of moonlight reflected off the snow. She'd asked him not to turn the lamps on, and at the time he'd thought he understood her shyness. Now he wasn't so sure. After a while, he started to laugh, deep convulsive laughs that banged the headboard against the wall.

'What?' she asked. 'What?'

'That was wonderful.'

Snow had been falling steadily for the last hour, muffling every sound other than that of their own breathing. He saw how the moonlight caught the whites of her eyes. Anchoring himself in the present, he concentrated on the briny smell of her on his fingertips, closing his eyes.

Abruptly, in a single powerful movement, she launched herself off the bed, pulled on her T-shirt and raced downstairs.

Following her, a few minutes later, feeling sticky, drained, spindle-shanked and middle aged, he found her in the kitchen, frying bacon and eggs.

'I'm famished,' she said. 'Aren't you?'

Eleven

During the first few weeks of their working together Peter seemed simply bored. He turned up on time, fetched, carried, lifted, mixed plaster, held buckets, cut cloth and, when not required, retreated to the corner of the room, between the plaster figures, so that often Kate would forget he was there, and then be startled when something moved on the periphery of her vision.

That changed when the figure began to take shape. She was familiar with this process: the sense, growing stronger by the hour, as she built up, carved, cut back, built up, carved again, of another presence in the room. The decisive moment came when it – he – acquired a face. With some amusement she noticed how Peter's posture changed. Before, he'd stood easily with his back to the armature. Now he opened his shoulders when he was talking to her, as people do who feel the need to include another person in the group.

He noticed her observing this, and said, with a little self-conscious laugh, 'I keep feeling I ought to speak to him. It seems rude to ignore him.'

He'd become fascinated by the process, or by the figure perhaps, by what it represented. Either way he was no longer the impersonal, passive assistant. Now, every day, he brought his brain as well as his muscles to the task, and that didn't make it easy to maintain the clarity of her own conception. She was always aware of his mind pushing against hers, in the silence.

It's in the nature of plaster that you have to work fast. It forces decisiveness on you, and yet there were many times now when she had to wait to be helped. Between the decision and the action, there was this hiatus, while she waited for him to mix the plaster, or hand the chisel up to her. Once, worn out and in great pain, she had to let him apply the plaster, and that was a small death. She watched his hands stroke it on, and told herself it didn't matter who applied the plaster as long as she, and she alone, did the carving.

Only it did matter. Her grasp on the figure had become tentative – 'fluid', if you wanted to sound positive about the situation, but then 'fluid' wasn't the way she worked. Normally she had the conception clear in her head from the beginning, so that the process of carving seemed almost like the uncovering of a figure already there, waiting to be released. Peter had destroyed that. Sometimes she looked down from the scaffold and saw him standing below, and his fingers would begin to twitch and she knew he was imagining the chisel in his own hands.

Her attitude to him changed. Previously she'd said almost nothing to him, apart from a brief greeting in the morning, a comment on the weather – once they'd started work, not even that. And, whether because his own inclination accorded with hers, or because he was adept at picking up what other people wanted, he had been resolutely impersonal.

But now those twitching hands made her curious. Had he, she asked, any artistic ambitions himself? No, he said, not art, he was no use at that. He wanted to be a writer. Even this admission, which was hardly intimate, had to be dragged out of him. He made her feel she was being intrusive, though the question was natural enough in the circumstances, and scarcely intimate. 'So that's why you do gardening? To support the writing?'

'Yes. I could teach, but –'

'No,' she agreed. 'The trouble with teaching is you're using the same part of your mind. It's creative if you're doing it properly. Worst possible job for an artist. Or a writer I suppose.'

'And not just that. It's so circular. I did an MA in creative writing and most of the people on the course were going to teach it.' That rare charming smile again. 'Anyway, I enjoy gardening. I like doing things with my hands.'

Kate found that conversation reassuring. It was a situation she could easily identify with: doing odd jobs, scratching a living, because the one thing you wanted to do couldn't be made to pay. It put him into a context she could understand. She'd done jobs like that as a student – waitressing, bar work, hotel work, anything – and for a number of years afterwards. She felt she knew him better. But then it was back to the long hours of silence, looking up from the work now and then to see his hands making those odd, involuntary movements. Once she came into the studio and found him holding the mallet and the chisel in his hands, feeling the weight of them. He put them down as soon as he saw her.

She had no conceivable reason to object.

Winter was teasing this year. No sooner did a day of glancing sunlight suggest that spring might be on the way than another frost set in. Once again the moorhen skittered across a frozen pond, and a pale sun scarcely summoned up the strength to disperse the mists, even at midday.

On one such day she asked Peter to take her to the timber yard to stock up on logs and incidentally to buy a bag of wood chippings for the sculpture. She wanted a rougher texture, and wood chippings mixed in with the plaster might just do it. She was aiming for an almost scabby surface, not unlike the trunks of some trees.

It was the first time she'd been out in Peter's van. It was on its last legs, a miracle it stayed on the road – but there was something nice about it nevertheless. Peter loved it. You could tell by the way he held the steering wheel. She accepted his help in hauling the seat belt across.

Travelling as a passenger, she felt her disability most keenly. She hadn't got back behind the wheel again yet, and that made her totally dependent on other people. She was even beginning to wonder whether her reluctance to drive was not, now, more a matter of nerves than of physical incapacity. She ought to make the effort. It was quite simple really: if she didn't drive, she couldn't live where she lived. Perhaps she could ask Peter to sit with her in her own car for fifteen minutes afterwards while she drove round the back roads. She looked at his profile, keen and concentrated as he checked his rear-view mirror, and thought, No, I'll ask Angela. She wanted to keep her relationship with Peter focused on work.

At the sawmill she climbed down and greeted Fred and his son Craig with pleasure. While Peter and Craig collected the logs, she chatted to Fred, who was saying, as everybody did, that foot-and-mouth had put a stopper on his business. You heard the same story in various voices and accents everywhere you went. The path that ran past the timber yard was a public right of way through the forest, and that was still closed off. Originally they'd tied their blasted yellow tape right across the entrance so nobody could get in or out of the yard at all, and it had taken three visits to the council offices and God knows how many phone calls to get them to come and shift it so Fred could carry on with his business.

'Isn't it picking up at all?' she asked.

No, he couldn't see it. It was a body blow, he said. His skin was sagging on his bones, and she saw that the red veins in his cheeks no longer looked like the natural high colour of an outdoor life but something much less healthy: hectic, purplish, mottled, the precursor of a stroke perhaps. Craig, standing behind him, suddenly looked less like a gangly teenager, more like a young man, stronger than his father, resilient. And so the generations pass, she thought, as they went off to pile logs into the back of the van, but would Craig keep the business on? Would there be a business to keep? Oh, but surely, she thought, looking at the forest that hung over the clearing like a green wave about to break, surely anything based on timber would survive? Some of the farms might not restock, shops and restaurants might go bust – in fact they had, they did, you saw it all around you – but the forest would survive.

It was growing colder, the puddles iced over. Her eyes watered with the cold. I will ask him if I can drive back, she thought, feeling Fred's depression as something she had to counter by taking the next move on her own path to recovery. It was only a mile or so along the forest road, and it would do her good to drive past that place in particular. It would lay the ghost of that night.

She was looking at the back of the van as she thought these things, the three men standing a little to one side, talking, in clouds of breath now that the setting sun was beginning to slip behind the trees. Fred's red tartan jacket matched the raw red of his cheeks and nose. She looked at the number plate on the van, the mud splashes, and suddenly she was back on the forest road, at night, tailing a white van. She'd forgotten that till now. Or had it been another occasion? Her mind reached back into its own darkness. No, definitely that night.

Peter's van. How could she tell? There'd been no reason to focus on number plates then – and there must be dozens of white vans around in this area alone. Virtually every small business for miles around seemed to have a white van. And yet she felt it was Peter's van she'd passed that night. He hadn't mentioned seeing the accident.

Because he hadn't seen it.

But if it was his van, he must have seen it. There was no turning after the crossroads. So he must have been the first person on the scene. If it was his van. The man who came and stood beside the car could have been Peter, but he hadn't phoned the police. Another person turned up and did that. She could hear a voice saying, '. . . and an ambulance.' Not Peter's voice.

Because he hadn't been there. He didn't ring the police because he wasn't there. He didn't mention it because he wasn't there. She was getting herself into some kind of paranoid spiral over nothing.

He was coming towards her. She framed her face muscles into a smile. 'I've been thinking,' she said. 'Would you mind if I drove back?'

'No, of course not. The gears are stiff, mind.'

'I think I can manage.'

He held the door open for her, always so polite, so helpful. She climbed into the driver's seat and leant out of the window to say goodbye to Fred.

Peter was standing by the passenger door, also saying goodbye. She turned and saw his apparently headless figure in the jacket, the only jacket he seemed to possess. Her heart bulged into her throat.

She couldn't say anything. This might well be based on nothing more than the delusion of a semi-conscious woman, a woman who forty-eight hours later had been unable to give her own name and address to the nice young woman doctor. Who hadn't realized she was in hospital. Who couldn't remember the crash. No, she couldn't mention it.

He opened the door and slid in. 'What's the matter?' he asked sharply.

She remembered the incident with the glasses. Next morning she'd handed them back without comment, but somehow he knew she'd tried them on. They went straight into his pocket and never reappeared.

'Nothing.' She forced a small, hard laugh. 'I'm just a bit nervous, I suppose.'

'No, well, don't be. I'll keep an eye out.'

He was turning round, looking over his shoulder, doing the checking for her, as he spoke.

She took a deep breath and turned the key.

Twelve

Despite his closeness to Ben, Stephen had met Kate Frobisher only twice, the last time in an art gallery where some of Ben's photographs were being shown. Stephen had walked round the exhibition, finding some of the images very hard to take in this setting. You needed to be alone with them to achieve an honest reaction. He'd left as soon as possible after congratulating Ben.

Despite the map, he struggled to find Woodland House, which was set back from the lane behind a thick shrubbery that virtually hid it from sight. It was, as Beth said, isolated.

The spray of gravel under his wheels was as good as a burglar alarm. Kate emerged at once, arms crossed under her bosom, bending down to peer into the car with a shy, friendly smile. She was still wearing a surgical collar, though it must have been weeks since the accident. He looked for obvious marks of grief and found none, except for two broad white streaks in the dark hair that she'd bundled off her face anyhow. They hadn't been there before, or perhaps they had, and she'd just stopped bothering to hide them. He wound down the window and she offered her hand and then immediately withdrew it, apologizing, laughing, wiping wet clay or plaster off on the already streaked side of her smock.

He got out of the car and, after a moment's hesitation, they kissed, briefly, on each cheek. It felt foreign here, belonged in the overcrowded art gallery with trays of cheap white wine. Here in the country they didn't know each other well enough to kiss. Answering polite inquiries about the difficulty of finding the house, he followed her over the threshold and into a stone-flagged corridor.

One ladder-backed chair, a small uncurtained window, an earthenware jug with three gigantic heads of hogweed casting an intricate pattern of shadows across the white walls. A cool, even chilly interior, but then she threw open a door and ushered him into a room full of deep reds and blues, pools of golden light from the lamps falling over books and paintings. Pale yellow sunlight flooding through the large windows made the fire burn dim.

'Would you like a drink? Gin, wine . . . ?'

'White wine, please.'

While she poured, he turned to one side and there, on top of a carved oak chest, was a portrait bust of Ben – obviously her work – and powerful, he thought. Suddenly there were three people in the room, and this third presence produced a charge that was too strong, too complex, for the length of their own acquaintance-ship. Stranded between small talk and the conversation they didn't know each other well enough to have, they smiled and nodded, but found it difficult to think of anything to say. She had a streak of white plaster on her chin that was beginning to dry and flake. He was aware of wanting to brush it away with his thumb. His hand actually began to move towards her, but then he stopped, horrified by the inappropriate intimacy of the gesture.

'That's amazing,' he said, pointing to the bust.

'I'm glad you like it. I did it last summer.'

So easy and light the reference, but as she spoke the firelight leapt over the bronze face and for a moment the features seemed to move.

Lunch served at the kitchen table was simple but good. Chicken casserole, hot, crusty bread, followed by cheese and fruit.

He remembered Robert saying how much she loved the house so he asked her about that, and she became animated at once. Her face flushed – but she had been too pale before – as she told him about how she and Ben had found it, the state it was in, filthy, the old farmer who owned it had no children and so, as he sank into senility, the place had become not merely dilapidated but squalid. They'd walked round it with a torch on their first visit, dismayed by the dark rooms – the windows had been almost overgrown with ivy – but then, drifting out into the yard with an increasingly disconsolate estate agent in tow, they'd seen the outbuildings and immediately, in spite of all the work that would be needed to put it right, they'd known this was the place. Had to be. 'Can you imagine what it would cost in London to get a place with two studios? Two million?'

'More than that.' It wouldn't come cheap even here

in the North, where you could get a country house with a deer park for the price of a three-bedroomed flat in Notting Hill. 'Aren't you nervous here by yourself?'

She shrugged. 'People come for the weekends. Obviously, it's quieter at this time of year.'

She genuinely didn't seem to mind the isolation. He guessed her loneliness was the deeper kind that comes from the absence of one person, and she really didn't care whether other people were around or not.

'I've got an assistant,' she said, after a slight pause. 'He comes in every day except Sunday.'

'Yes, Robert said you'd had an accident.'

'I crashed the car – just down there, on that bend – and it's left me with neck and back problems. So I just had to bite the bullet and take somebody on.'

'You don't like the idea?'

'Hate it. I like to be able to walk up and down and shout and swear when it doesn't go right.'

She was smiling, but he guessed she meant it.

'But he's all right. It seems to be working.'

She looked strained. If this had been an interview, he'd have been on to it at once, probing what was obviously an area of doubt. But it wasn't. He was visiting a friend's widow. And he was beginning to like her a lot. He liked her lack of pretension, the brisk, workmanlike approach.

He didn't mention the reason he'd come till they were back in the living room and she was serving coffee. Then he said, 'Have you had time to think about the photographs?'

'There's nothing to think about. I know Ben would have wanted you to have them. And that's good enough for me.' She handed him a cup of coffee and sat down with her own. 'He often talked about you.'

'I miss him.'

A pause. 'I've got some of his Afghanistan stuff over in the studio. The last things he took.' Her voice stayed steady, but her eyes were bright. He looked away, giving her time to recover herself, but there was something she had to say first. 'And I want to thank you for sending this back.' She touched the amulet round her neck. 'It was you, wasn't it?'

'Yes.'

'You found him?'

'Yes. It was instantaneous. He couldn't possibly have suffered anything. I doubt if he knew.'

She nodded. 'I hoped it was like that. They said it was, but you don't always get the truth, do you?'

'No, it was.'

'I'm glad.' A deep breath, 'So what's the book about?'

'Ways of representing war. It's not what they want me to do, they want me to write anecdotes. You know: Amusing Mass Murderers I Have Met.'

'But this is the one you need to write?'

'Yeah. I can even tell you what started it. Jules Naudet, the guy who was following a rookie fireman round New York on 9/11 and just found himself filming the attack on the towers? Well, something he said haunted me. At one point he turned his camera off – he wouldn't film people burning – and he said, "Nobody should have to see this." And of course immediately I thought of Goya.'

'"One cannot look at this"?'

'Yes – but then "I saw it." "This is the truth." It's that argument he's having with himself, all the time, between the ethical problems of showing the atrocities and yet the need to say, "Look, this is what's happening" . . . and I thought, My God, we're still facing exactly the same problem. There's always this tension between wanting to show the truth, and yet being sceptical about what the effects of showing it are going to be.'

'Yeah, I know exactly what you mean. I had this conversation with Ben . . . oh, hundreds of times.' The sadness returned. 'You should be doing this book with Ben, really.'

'If I use his photographs, I will be. In a sense. And I'll talk about things that happened, you know, making the ethical decision when you've only got a second to make it. You see, the thing Ben and Goya have got in common is that they went on doing it. Whatever the doubts, it didn't stop them.'

'Rightly.'

'Yes, I think so.'

A short silence. He was aware of the flicker of firelight across Ben's features.

'Would you like to see where he worked?'

'I'd love to.'

He finished his coffee and stood up. They walked across the yard, the brief thaw already giving way to night and frost. The ruts were harder now, crusted on top. His feet bit into them, then held. A low building faced them across the yard. Kate got out her keys, fumbled with the lock and stood aside. He thought she was just letting him go first, but no, she stayed outside. Was she being tactful and giving him a few minutes to himself? Or had she not been in since Ben died?

He stepped over the threshold, thinking that perhaps the last person to breathe the air in this room had been Ben. The carpet held flakes of his skin, hairs from his head must lie on the cushions of the sofa over there. The forensic science of grief. We shed ourselves all the time, he thought, shed and renew and shed again until that final shedding of our selves.

Dust everywhere, and a cobweb in the corner of the window. The last rays of the setting sun caught the glass and turned the death trap into a thing of beauty.

'The light switch is on your right.'

He flicked on the switch, hating the glare of light that dissipated the shadowy presence he'd sensed in the room. But he pulled himself together and went across to the table. Computer, scanner, a printer – far more advanced than anything he ever needed to use – but along the wall facing the desk there were box files neatly labelled: date and place. The archive of a working life.

What was missing was the one box he hadn't come back to label: Afghanistan, 2002.

He heard a man's voice behind him speaking to Kate. Then she called from the door: 'I'm just going across to the studio. I won't be a minute.'

He pulled out the file on Bosnia and looked through

some of the prints, recognizing places and people. A chandelier in a devastated ballroom; an old Serbian woman surrounded by icons, scraps of food on the table in front of her; a queue of women and children waiting their turn at the tap; an old Muslim woman, tottering down the street with a milk bottle full of water, the only container she was strong enough to carry; and then, without warning, there she was: the girl in the stairwell.

He gaped at the print, unable to understand why it was there. Obviously Ben had gone back the next morning, early, before the police arrived, to get this photograph. He'd restored her skirt to its original position, up round her waist. It was shocking. Stephen was shocked on her behalf to see her exposed like this, though, ethically, Ben had done nothing wrong. He hadn't staged the photograph. He'd simply restored the corpse to its original state. And yet it was difficult not to feel that the girl, spreadeagled like that, had been violated twice.

Quickly, he replaced the photographs and went out into the yard.

The long shadows cast by the house and trees were creating an advance guard of deep frost. Chickens, stepping out cautiously on their cracked yellow feet, were pecking about on the frozen ground, where wisps of straw shone like gold. The cock looked up at him with a bright amber eye.

Kate came across the yard, smiling. 'Would you like to see the ones I had framed? Have you got time?'

Her studio was a taller building on the third side of the farmyard. A narrow door led into a small lobby used to store raw materials: bags of plaster, bales of hessian, yellowing piles of old newspapers. Through another door into a vast barn, one wall made entirely of glass. Outside darkness was falling – only the crests of the hills still caught a glint of light.

The studio was heated by a wood-burning stove whose flames flickered all over the dim interior. Kate switched on the lights. In the centre, partly obscured by scaffolding, was a huge, crudely carved male figure.

'That's it,' Kate said sighing, hands pressed hard into the small of her back, like a peasant woman who's been doing hard physical work all day. He'd noticed her hands over lunch. They were certainly not glamorous. Thick veins, rough skin, splitting nails – you'd expect to see hands like hers on a building site.

Clustered in the corner was a group of white plaster figures, striding out. Extraordinary figures: frightened and frightening.

Kate, meanwhile, had walked over to the far corner where there was a screen displaying some of Ben's photographs. He joined her there and glanced across them. As she'd said, these were mainly from the last trip to Afghanistan. One showed a group of boys on the border between Afghanistan and Pakistan, ragged, thin, peering out at the camera from behind a fence, and flashing mirrors into the sun to blind the photographer. A flash of light had whited out the face of the boy holding the glass, so in a narrow technical sense the picture was a failure. Further along, a man's face, distorted with anger, one hand half covering the lens. Another was of an execution. A man on his knees staring up at the men who are preparing to kill him. But Ben had included his own shadow in the shot, reaching out across the dusty road. The shadow says I'm here. I'm holding a camera and that fact will determine what happens next. In the next shot the man lies dead in the road, and the shadow of the photographer, the shadow of a man with a deformed head, has moved closer.

This wasn't the first execution recorded on film, nor even the first to be staged specially for the camera, but normally the photographer's presence and its impact on events is not acknowledged. Here Ben had exploded the convention.

'I'd like to use those,' Stephen said. He was thinking that Ben might almost have taken them for the book.

'They were sent back after . . .'

Right at the bottom left-hand corner he saw another photograph, this time of Soviet tanks, disused, rotting, corroded with rust. This mass of military debris filled most of the frame, so that from the viewer's angle they seemed to be a huge wave about to break. Behind them was a small white sun, no bigger than a golf ball, veiled in mist. No people. Hardware left behind after the Russian invasion of Afghanistan: the last war. But the composition was so powerful it transcended the limits of a particular time and place, and became a *Dies Irae*. A vision of the world as it would be after the last human being had left, forgetting to turn out the light.

'That's a great photograph,' he said, knowing he would have to find a way to use it.

'Yes.' She was struggling with tears again, not looking at it. He wondered if she knew it had been taken seconds before Ben died.

All this time he'd been aware of the plaster figures on the edge of his vision, and when he turned round he felt compelled to count them again. No, still seven. They hadn't been breeding while his back was turned. He remembered reading that Arctic explorers sometimes suffer from the delusion that there is one more person present on the trek than can actually be counted. He couldn't see any reason why that would apply here, unless the overwhelming whiteness of the room was a factor.

Everything was white, even the floor. During the day the northern light would bounce off every surface, leaving the room, as far as possible, shadowless. Perhaps that was enough to create a mild form of sensory deprivation. He wondered if Kate was aware of it, whether she too suffered from a compulsion to count the figures.

'Would it be all right if I came over sometime and looked through the prints?'

She nodded at once. 'Good idea.'

She sounded cheerful, as if the prospect of somebody working in Ben's room revitalized her. This had been so much a place where two people lived, worked, talked, squabbled, drank, cooked, made love. And yet

Ben had been away for six weeks at a time. She must be used to being alone.

The place was making him uneasy. He went to the window and looked down at the pond, where the last light of evening clung to the water. The overhead lights were reflected in the glass, making him feel vulnerable to the outside world, to the dark hillside. He turned and saw a man standing in the doorway. He was wearing a dark coat and had come in so quietly that he might have been there for a while before Stephen noticed him.

Kate followed the direction of his gaze. 'Oh, come in, Peter. This is Stephen Sharkey. A friend of Ben.'

Peter was tall, good-looking, with pale, watchful eyes. He nodded to Stephen.

'I've got the hessian, but they only had the really thin stuff. I said I'd take a roll and ask you.'

'I'll have a look.'

Stephen and Peter were left alone in the cavernous interior, surrounded by the white figures.

'So you're Kate's assistant.'

'Yes, I do the lifting. It's just a temporary job.'

'I can't imagine how it happens. I mean, how does that' – he pointed towards the huge, plaster figure – 'turn into bronze?'

Peter smiled. 'The lost-wax method. Just don't ask me what it is.'

'You're not a budding artist, then?'

'No, I just do odd jobs. Gardening, mainly.'

Kate came back. 'That's fine. I don't mind it being

thin as long as the weave's coarse enough. We could do with another two bales.'

'Do you want me to get them now?'

'If there's time.'

'No problem.'

He raised his hand to Stephen and went out. A moment later they heard the cough and sputter of an engine.

Kate smiled. 'I don't know how he keeps that thing on the road.'

She sounded preoccupied, gazing up at the big figure. Stephen took the hint and went back to the photographs, but continued to watch her out of the corner of his eye. Now that she was absorbed in her work, he felt he was seeing her clearly for the first time. Not an easy woman to get to know. The rather jolly outgoing manner disguised a formidable inner reserve. If he'd met her at the church fête, or organizing a jumble sale, or whatever women like her – he meant women with that rather clipped, upper-class accent – found to do in the country, he wouldn't have attributed very much to her in the way of an inner life. Yet obviously she had, and not a comfortable one either. She'd got the chisel out now and was trying to reshape part of the upper thigh, but almost at once she stopped, grimacing with pain. 'Bugger it.'

The sound of her own voice seemed to remind her she was not alone. 'I shouldn't be doing this,' she said, with a slight, embarrassed laugh. 'I'm too tired.'

'It's time I was off anyway. I'll give you a ring, shall I, to arrange when I can come over?'

'Any time. I'm always here.'

They walked together to the door.

'What's Peter's other name?'

'Wingrave.'

'He's very striking-looking.'

'Yes.' She smiled. 'You didn't like him.'

He shook his head. 'I haven't seen enough of him.'

It was acute of her to detect the reserve he'd felt on meeting Peter, though it wasn't a matter of dislike. He hadn't asked himself whether he liked him or not – though remembering the sudden, warm smile he rather thought he had – but he sensed instability. He'd been in so many dangerous places he'd learnt to decide on the spot whom he could trust, and he wouldn't have wanted Peter watching his back.

'It'll be nice having somebody using Ben's room,' she said, as they walked out into the yard.

'You don't use it?'

'No, I just leave it locked up.' A twist of the dry lips. 'Sometimes I think he's in there, you see, working, and it's quite a soothing feeling. I'm in the studio, he's over there, and in a few minutes we're going to meet and have a drink. And as long as I think that, I can keep going.' A little self-conscious laugh. 'I know it's not healthy.'

'People survive whichever way they can. I'm quite sure a lot of the things I do aren't healthy.' She looked so sad standing there that once again he had the urge to reach out and touch her. Instead he said, 'I don't know if Ben mentioned it, but my marriage broke up.'

'He did. I'm sorry.'

He nodded, and they walked to the car. This time they shook hands, which he found rather touching, a sign that they were groping their way into their own relationship, one that didn't depend entirely on knowing Ben.

'See you,' he said, slipping into the driving seat.

He saw her in his mirror, waving, and then she turned and walked back into the house.

Thirteen

Stephen spent the second week of February at The Hague, covering the Milosevic trial at the war-crimes tribunal.

Whole days dragged past while he stared at Milosevic through the bullet-proof glass that divided the ex-dictator from the public gallery. There was a flaw in the glass, and, as Stephen moved his head from side to side, the pudgy, truculent features rippled and re-formed like a reflection on water.

Milosevic also appeared on a small wall-mounted screen to Stephen's right, much of the time in brutal close-up. You could see the small patch of shaving rash he'd developed on the left side of his chin. Screen, reality, screen, reality, Stephen switched between the two, the screen image always more informative and in one sense more accurate, since it lacked the distortion of that flaw in the glass.

At intervals the drone of speeches and translations was interrupted as a photograph was displayed on the screens, or a short video recording played. A young, brown-haired, vigorous Milosevic, surrounded by security guards, made an impassioned speech. The grey-haired old man in the dock stared at his younger self and smiled a little ruefully, and for a moment a murmur of fellow feeling ran along the public benches. Every-body had done that. Everybody had been confronted unexpectedly by a younger version of themselves and had thought, My God, where did it all go?

But then the screens filled with other images and there were no more smiles.

'This,' said the prosecuting counsel, 'is a corpse exhumed from a mass grave in Kosovo.'

The decomposing head of a young man appeared on the screen, blindfolded, his mouth open in what was difficult not to identify as a scream. It might well have been a scream. Some of the men had been castrated before they died. Blindfolded, not because he might identify his tormentors – they were going to kill him anyway – but because it's easier to torture a man whose eyes you can't see.

'And this,' said Milosevic the next day, embarking with some enthusiasm on a gruesome game of Snap, 'is the severed head of a Serbian child lying on a pavement in Belgrade.'

You had to take the child's nationality on trust, though it might equally well have been the head of a Bosnian child lying in the market place in Sarajevo. It wouldn't be the first time the dead had been made to work overtime, appearing as victims in the propaganda of both sides.

The child's eyes stared up from the pavement. People shuffled their papers, coughed, turned pens round and round in their fingers, ashamed of their inability to go on feeling. Then the child vanished and was replaced by carbonized corpses in a railway carriage, baked faces set in lipless grins, leaning towards the windows as if waving goodbye to friends and family on the platform.

None of this had been visible at the time. Not even to the pilots who dropped the bombs, still less to the audience watching Pentagon briefings on television in their living rooms. On the screen set up in the briefing room, and on the television screens, puffs of brown smoke appeared underneath the cross-hairs of the precision sights. Doubly screened from reality, the audience watched, yawned, scratched and finally switched channels. Who could blame them? War had gone back to being sepia tinted. Sanitized. Nothing as vulgar as blood was ever allowed to appear.

And all the while, under the little spurts of brown dust, this. A child torn to pieces. Human bodies baked like dog turds in the sun.

In the bar that evening, Stephen glanced up from his newspaper and saw his old friend Ian Brodie, wearing his trademark black trench, come in through the swing doors – a silhouette as unmistakable as a stealth bomber's. Stephen jumped up, greeted him, offered him a drink, and got two pints from the bar while Ian took off his coat.

They managed to find a small, relatively quiet table in the corner. On the sofa directly opposite a Serbian politician was being interviewed on camera. From the next table, where a young man was editing another interview, came the chipmunk chattering of voices on fast-rewind. Stephen looked round, wondering if he missed all this. How much he missed it.

Ian sat down, his bullet head covered with hair so thin it looked like gosling down, bringing a smell of clean air in on his clothes. They spent the next hour swopping gossip: who was here and for how long. Pity the poor sods who'd landed this as a long-term assignment, Ian said, because it was going to run and run. 'Slobo'll die of old age or a stroke,' he said, 'before we get a verdict.'

They all called him Slobo – it sounded affectionate but wasn't.

'At least they've nailed the sod,' Stephen said.

'Victors' justice.'

'Is it?'

A gleeful cackle. 'Well, he sure as hell wouldn't be here if he'd won.'

'Yeah, OK. Yeah, I know. But it still matters that he's here. *Raison d'état?* No, sorry, mate, you're a crook.' Stephen leant forward. 'I love it.'

The bar was filling up. Stephen could put a name to everybody in the room. One or two had that curiously rubbery look of people seen mainly on television. Others were old friends. It was a travelling village.

'You know I've resigned?'

'Yeah. Finishing a book? How's it going?'

'Slowly. It's taking a bit longer than I thought it would.'

'They always do. But you'll come back?'

'I don't know.'

Ian raised a yellow-palmed hand – somewhere on the long road from Glasgow to Wapping he'd picked up the old soldier's habit of smoking with a fag concealed in his fist – to attract the barman's attention. 'Why's that?'

'I've had enough.'

'Couldn't you just take a year off?'

'No, I think it's decision time. I'm forty this year. I don't want to spend the rest of my life trotting off to other people's wars till I'm only fit for the knackers' yard.'

Ian bent to lick the head off his pint with a grey and felted tongue. 'Like me, you mean?'

Stephen said awkwardly, 'You know I don't.'

They left it there. Ian began reminiscing about the time they'd spent in Sarajevo during the siege. Stephen ordered another round of drinks. They laughed a lot, drank a lot and ended up talking about Ben.

'I saw him,' Stephen said, 'in London the day before he left. I was going out a week later. He had a bad feeling about it. Almost a premonition. I've gone over that conversation so many times – I wish I'd said, "Look, if it doesn't feel right, don't go. Let somebody else go." Because if you've been in the game as long as he had you do develop an instinct.'

'Definitely.'

'You know that little amulet thing he used to wear? He kept fiddling with it. The catch was loose and he wasn't going to have time to get it mended. And that really bothered him.'

Ian nodded. 'It wouldn't have made any difference if you had said something. He'd have gone anyway.'

'Yes, I know. But I still wish I'd said it.'

Around midnight, still to all outward appearances sober, Ian glided to the door, keeping his head very still, like a bride who fears her tiara may not make it down the aisle.

They stood together on the wet pavement. Stephen put a hand on Ian's shoulder. 'Well, good night.'

'You stay in touch now.'

'Next time I'm in London – I'll give you a ring.'

Ian set off to his hotel. After a few yards, he turned and, walking backwards, called, 'You couldn't have saved him. He'd have gone whatever you said.'

Stephen raised his hand. ''Night, Ian.'

He walked slowly upstairs to the first floor, struggled to turn the key in the lock and then flopped down on the bed. He closed his eyes and saw the photograph of the young man exhumed from a mass grave in Kosovo. He'd been there when that was taken, pressing a handkerchief over his nose. Summer. Dusty trees. Chequered light and shade. They followed the smell up the valley, plagued by flies that zigzagged above the narrow path between the trees. Drunk on sweat and the smell of decay, one kept settling on his upper lip. Flies settled on the blindfolded man too, but he didn't try to brush them away. Stephen watched a fly zoom into the gaping hole of his mouth.

You couldn't have saved him.

Jerking awake, he realized the bedside lamp was still

on, thought about getting up, undressing, pouring a glass of water, but couldn't in the end be bothered to do any of those things.

Instead, he groped for the switch and turned off the light.

Over breakfast he read the article he'd written the day before. At the last moment Ted had rung to say they'd got a terrific photograph of Milosevic entering the tribunal, so could the story start with that? Reluctantly, he'd rewritten the first paragraph – with difficulty, since, like most people, he hadn't seen Milosevic come in.

The photo – it had pride of place at the head of the page – showed the chief prosecutor, Carla del Ponte, laughing in triumph as the ex-dictator, a shadowy figure with bowed shoulders, was escorted to his seat.

Ted was right, it was a terrific photograph. A dramatic moment. Unfortunately, it had never happened. He'd been watching Carla del Ponte, her helmet of blonde hair gleaming under the lights, sharing a joke with the other prosecuting attorneys, wholly absorbed in that conversation. Not only had she not laughed in triumph at Milosevic's downfall – she hadn't even noticed him.

So much for photography as the guarantor of reality. It pissed him off. He kept telling himself it didn't matter, but all the time he knew it did. Image before words every single time. And yet the images never explain anything and often, even unintentionally, mislead.

*

That afternoon, he played truant from the tribunal and went to the Mauritshuis, where he spent a long time in front of Vermeer's *Girl with a Pearl Earring*.

Enormous eyes, blackness all around her, a dazzle of pain and tears. She reminded him a little of Justine, and the time he spent with her did more than anything else to rinse his mind clean.

Fourteen

Back home, rattling his key in the lock – the front door was hard to open because the wood swelled in damp weather – he braced himself to face the dark and chilly cottage, no fire, no food in the fridge, and the manuscript, lying in wait for him on the table, which even after this short break seemed about as appetizing as a bowl of cold porridge.

Instead he opened the living-room door and saw a fire blazing in the grate and smelled food cooking. The whole room had been tidied up and cleaned. All he had to do was sit down by the fire, pour a glass of whisky, and wait for Justine to get back from the farmhouse.

And upstairs – he knew without going to look – there would be clean sheets and pillowcases and a vase with flowers on the table by the bed.

That first time had set the pattern for all their subsequent encounters. If it made sense to speak of practical orgasms, then that is what Justine had, and always they were followed by this sudden sharpening of her appetite. Sex never made Justine fancy grilled fish and steamed spinach, seasoned with lemon juice and freshly grated nutmeg. Oh, no, Justine's taste was death-on-a-plate fry-ups, washed down by plenty of booze.

'If you're going to be a doctor, you'll have to change the way you eat,' he said sourly from the kitchen door. 'And drink less.'

She looked up, flashing her sudden broad smile. 'Ah, but I'm going to be a medical student first.'

He found the sex extraordinary, like nothing he'd ever experienced. *Foreplay?* he wanted to croak as Justine got her leg over for the second time that night. Or, *What happened to romance?* OK, he found the idea of quick, impersonal sex as exciting as the next man, but he didn't want it in his own bedroom night after night with somebody he knew. Something had happened to Justine to make her both sexually uninhibited – there was nothing they didn't do – and emotionally withdrawn. She still wouldn't let him switch on the lamp, or even light a candle, so on cloudy nights they made love in pitch darkness. It began after a while to have an almost mythical quality, this prohibition against seeing her face, and it was her *face* that she was hiding. She joined him in the shower afterwards with no trace of embarrassment.

Sometimes, as on the first night, she spoke airily about 'people'. People liked this, people didn't like that, though he guessed, from various clues she let slip, that she'd had only one previous lover. Increasingly he was aware of this unknown man as an invisible third in their love-making, a secret sharer, his presence falling like a shadow on her skin.

Once or twice she talked about it, the affair she'd had last summer after A-levels, how shocked she'd been when the young man dumped her. No warning. She'd thought everything was all right, and then one evening he'd said, 'I don't think this is working.' Her eyes filled with tears as she said it, and she rubbed her wet cheek on his shoulder. 'Why do you think he thought that?' Stephen asked. 'I don't know. I don't think he ever meant it to be permanent. It was just for the summer.'

She gave no further details, but she returned to the subject again and again, and always, whenever she mentioned it, her eyes filled with tears.

There's an old saying that a man is only as old as the woman he feels, but Justine made him feel ancient. He wanted to say, 'Look, this time next year you'll be in love with somebody else. You won't be able to remember what you saw in him.' And when you're my age, he thought sadly, you won't even remember who he was. He didn't say any of that. Instead he watched her face, blind and groping through pain, and thought that all this so-called wisdom was useless, because it couldn't be conveyed without sounding patronizing. And perhaps he was being patronizing. No, patronizing wasn't the right word, he cared too much about her for that. Paternal, that was more like it.

They went to bed and made love, and for once he saw her, or part of her, the shadows of clouds dissolving and re-forming over her breasts. He groaned and clutched her hips, grinding her pelvis into his, throwing his head back and baring his teeth as he came.

Nope, paternal wasn't the right word either.

★

After ten days of intensely hard work, bending over the computer until his eyes burned, Stephen began to find the cottage unbearably claustrophobic. The fact was that Justine had insinuated herself into his living space. Not his work space, but almost everywhere else. She rearranged objects, tidied up, washed up, vacuumed the carpets. He never protested, except once when he found her ironing his shirts and told her roughly to stop being a doormat.

'I'm sorry,' she said, flushing. 'Dad's pretty helpless, and –'

'I'm not.'

It might have been better if they'd gone out more, but she didn't want to go out. If he suggested a meal in a restaurant, or a drink, she always referred to some parishioner of her father's who was sure to be there. 'So what?' he felt like saying. She was single; he was, if not single, at least separated from his wife. It was nobody else's business.

When he finally stopped work in the evening, they watched television, like an old married couple. It was strange watching news bulletins, or programmes like *Panorama* that in the past he'd often contributed to, but he soon found that Justine disliked them anyway.

'Why won't you watch the news?' he asked. It staggered him, this indifference to what was going on in the world.

She shrugged. 'I don't see the point. There's nothing I can do about it. If it's something like a famine, OK, you can contribute, but with a lot of this there's nothing anybody can do except gawp and say, "Ooh, isn't it awful?" when really they don't give a damn. It's all pumped-up emotion, it's just false, like when those families come on TV because somebody's gone missing, or thousands of people send flowers to people they don't know. It's just *wanking*.'

That last word was the give-away. 'But you can't have a democracy if people don't know what's going on.'

'You can read the papers. It's the voyeurism of *looking* at it, that's what's wrong. Do you know, some people never watch the news, on principle?'

'I don't know how *people* tell the difference between principle and just being too fucking self-centred to care.'

The long hours alone with Justine, in bed and out of it, had the unexpected effect of waking him up sexually. Like Cleopatra, but rather earlier in life, she made hungry where most she satisfied. Now, as he walked through the streets of Newcastle on his way back from the university library to his car, he noticed every woman he passed. The sensation was almost painful, like blood flowing back into a numbed limb.

The sky was a deep turquoise, and the starlings were beginning to gather, huge folds and swathes of them coiling, spiralling, circling, and everywhere their clicks and chatterings, as insistent as cicadas. Beneath this frenzy, another frenzy of people rushing home from work, shopping; young people setting off for a night out; girls, half naked, standing in shop doorways; young men in short sleeves, muscular arms wreathed in blue, green, red and purple, dragons and serpents coiled round veined biceps. He passed a gaggle of girls, the pink felt penises on top of their heads bobbing about in the wind that blew up from the Quayside. Perhaps he gaped too obviously, for one of them turned round and stuck two fingers in the air.

He walked through all this, muffled up against the weather, sensible, middle aged and cautious, but also, as the blue light deepened and the girls became lovelier, racked with lust. He stopped at the foot of Grey's Monument, craning to look up, while thousands of starlings broke in waves above his head and a few stars pricked through the darkening sky.

Standing here like this, in his dark mac among the half-naked boys and girls, he looked, he suspected, not merely middle aged but furtive. The man in the park peering up the skirts of little girls on the swings. He needed a drink, and that was a problem because he had the car with him. And yet he didn't want to go tamely back home with a bottle as he had on previous nights. Not bloody likely. He looked around for a wine bar – he could have one drink, for God's sake, there was no harm in that, and even one at the moment felt like a life-saver, softening his mood, dissolving the hard edges of memory so that he could flow into the lives around him.

And then he saw Peter Wingrave, standing in the doorway of Waterstone's, obviously waiting for somebody, a girl, probably. Or perhaps not. He watched Peter watching the crowds and saw an echo of his own loneliness, his own desperation. It was enough. Peter glanced up as soon as he realized he was being directly approached, with a face prepared for strangers, cautious, polite, ready to take evasive action, balanced on the balls of his feet. Excessively cautious, surely. Stephen could well believe it might get rough a bit later in the evening, but not now.

'Hi,' Stephen said.

A flash of recognition, succeeded almost immediately by a dull flush. Now why? Because he's on the pick-up, on the prowl, or perhaps not even that. Perhaps just ashamed of being alone. He was very attractive-looking underneath the nerdy specs and the designer stubble, but you couldn't see him fitting in easily with his contemporaries, though he knew nothing about him, really. He had no grounds for thinking that. Peter might be the linchpin of a thriving social network, for all he knew. Good looks, intelligence, charm . . . And something else, something that undermined them all.

'Mr Sharkey.'

'Stephen.' Despite Peter's confident use of the name, he seemed uncertain. 'We met at Kate's studio.'

'Yes.' He was glancing from side to side, as if looking for a way out of the encounter. But when Stephen suggested a drink, his gaze immediately focused on Stephen's face and after only a second's hesitation he said, 'Yes.'

They went to a wine bar a few hundred yards down the street. It was crowded, but not with the kind of young people who were walking past outside. This was job-related drinking, people disguising from each other the fact that they had nothing else to do and nowhere else to go, clinging to this extended version of the working day because outside it they didn't exist.

Or because they love their jobs, he reminded himself, remembering how much he'd loved his.

A man with a roll of pink fat overlapping his collar was speaking urgently into a mobile phone, a finger blocking out the din from his other ear. They had to push their way past him to get to the bar. Stephen was sweating, though outside he'd been cold in spite of the coat. Peter asked for a whisky. Stephen bought him a double, himself a single, and stood pinned against the bar, wondering why he was doing this. Glancing at Peter, Stephen saw him looking round, searching the faces round the bar, and, as he leant closer to speak to him, he caught a whiff of sweat, fresh, but not the normal scent of a healthy body reacting to heat. He'd always meant to ask somebody – Robert might know – why fear sweat smells different from ordinary sweat. It certainly did. An intimate acquaintance with his own armpits in various sticky situations had taught him that. And yet these people were, what? Accountants? Lawyers? Not the kind of people to tear strangers in their midst limb from limb. But at least he now knew why Peter interested him – had done from the moment he walked into the studio. Something was wrong, something didn't fit, and Stephen's nose for a story was twitching.

It was hard to get a conversation going. Partly the

noise, partly his own state of mind. When he'd been working as hard as he had recently a kind of verbal dislocation set in, in which it was hardly possible to string another sentence together, and names of even very common everyday objects escaped him. He'd hear himself say 'thingy' or 'whatsit'. It had irritated the hell out of Nerys, but then so had everything else he did, in the end.

'Have you been working for Kate long?'

'No, just a few weeks. It's useful because gardening dries up in the winter months.'

'Oh, yes, I remember. You're a gardener.'

'I've done a lot of gardening.'

'But it's not what you want to do?'

'No, I want to be a writer.'

Oh, God. No wonder he'd been so keen on coming for a drink. He was on the lookout for contacts, agents, publishers. Stephen was already working out a cast-iron excuse for why he couldn't read whatever it was Peter'd written.

It's a haiku.

I really am pressed for time at the moment . . .

'Have you had anything published?' An unkind question, perhaps, but then he wasn't trying to be kind.

'A couple of stories in *New Writing*. I did an MA in creative writing.' He winced fastidiously, forestalling Stephen's reaction. 'And the Writer in Residence sent them off to the editors and . . .' He shrugged. 'They accepted them.'

'You don't sound very pleased.'

'To be honest, I wish I'd had the guts to say no.'

The bar had suddenly become less crowded as a group of people left together. Stephen waved Peter across to a table. It was a relief not to have to shout and, tucked away in a corner like this, Peter seemed to relax. 'Why's that?' he asked, as they settled at a table. 'I thought it was quite prestigious. A showcase.'

'Yes, but unless you're Damien Hirst, you don't want to put a dead sheep in it.'

Stephen took this to be mock modesty, and it made him impatient. 'C'mon, they can't be that bad.'

'You know that poem, I can't remember the words, something about using the snaffle and the curb, but where's the bloody horse?' He looked charming, modest, vulnerable. Self-mocking. 'They're a bit like that. Equine deficiency syndrome?'

'Do you think there's a cure?'

'Oh, no, I shouldn't think so.' His voice had gone flat, as if he'd stumbled into talking more seriously than he'd intended. 'Terminal.'

'I'd like to read them.' As if to explain this unusual desire to himself, Stephen went on, 'Too much control. It's an unusual fault in a young writer.'

'Yes, I suppose it is. If you give me your address, I'll let you have them. If you really mean it?'

'Of course I do,' Stephen said, already regretting it. 'How are you finding the job with Kate?'

'Fascinating.'

'Have you found out how it turns into bronze?'

'More or less. I'm still not sure I understand it.

Nothing you actually touch appears in the finished product, I know that much.'

'Does she talk about what she's doing?'

'Not really – sometimes when we're having coffee she'll say something, but mainly it's just, "Where's the chisel?" "I need more plaster."' He was smiling, but his eyes were alert. Perhaps he'd detected more interest from Stephen than he could account for. 'You knew her husband?'

'Yes, we were in Bosnia together. And various other places. Round and about.'

'Rwanda?'

'For a while.'

'Afghanistan?'

'Briefly.'

'I've seen some of his photographs.'

He didn't say any of the things people normally say, and Stephen was grateful for that. It was the last thing he wanted to talk about. 'Have you tried your hand at a novel yet?'

'Ye-es, but I don't know . . . I'm quite attracted to writing screenplays.'

'More money?'

'Less publicity. You can be quite successful and still not be well known.'

'That's an advantage?'

'For me it is.'

'You'd be quite good at it, though. Publicity.'

Peter shrugged.

'You don't like the idea?'

'It's a perversion. It should be the work.'

'Isn't that a bit ivory tower? They've got to sell the stuff somehow. It's the marketing people who matter these days. USPs.'

Peter looked puzzled.

'Unique Selling Points. What's your Unique Selling Point, Peter?'

'I'm not sure I've got one.' He reached into his pocket for a packet of cigarettes. 'I suppose this is all right?' he asked, looking round.

'I think so. There's somebody smoking over there.'

He coughed as he inhaled.

'Have you ever been in the army?'

'No. Why do you ask?'

'I just wondered. I've got a theory you can tell if somebody's lived in an institution.'

'And you think I have?'

Stephen shrugged. 'I think it's probably true of me. Boarding school, in my case.'

'Yeah, well, snap.'

'Which one?'

'You wouldn't have heard of it.'

He was tightening up. Why the fear of publicity? He had youth, good-looks, charm. Given a modicum of talent, or preferably a great big chunk of talent, he was there.

'Anyway,' Stephen said, 'I look forward to reading the stories.'

'Do you have an agent?'

'Yes, but I don't think he'd handle short stories.'

'I've got half a novel.'

This was becoming a predictable conversation. 'I think with a first novel you more or less have to finish it.' He decided to change the subject. 'Do you like Kate's work?'

'Yes.' He looked up, the cold grey eyes thoughtful. 'I like the way she uses the male nude. She gets a lot of flak. Some people think she ought to sculpt women more, but the fact is she couldn't explore the ideas she wants to explore using the female body. I mean, look at the way painters display martyrdom. You almost never see a woman saint being martyred, because it just wouldn't have the same . . . A naked man being tortured is a martyr. A naked woman being tortured is a sadist's wet dream.'

Stephen thought for a moment. 'Suppose you're gay?'

'Ye-es?'

'A tortured male nude might be a bit of a turn-on.'

'Only if you were a sadist as well.'

'Be a real challenge, though, if you were a Christian, wouldn't it? Crucifixions, beheadings, floggings, breaking on the wheel, burning at the stake, roasting on spits –'

Peter said sharply, 'I don't know how many Christian sadists there are.'

'Oh, I reckon they make it into double figures.' He drained his glass. 'I wonder what Kate would say?'

'Nothing. She doesn't find abstractions helpful.' He got up to go to the bar. 'Will you have another?'

Watching him talk to the barman, Stephen wondered

how old he was. There were lines round his mouth and eyes, he couldn't be much under thirty, even allowing for the weathering effect of an outdoor life. And if, at times, he seemed unformed, Stephen suspected it was less a matter of immaturity than of some basic confusion in the ground plan. He was like a cold bright star circling in chaos.

Stephen glanced round the room. A young girl with dark hair and enormous eyes was talking animatedly into a phone, her face veiled in cigarette smoke. Why is that movement so erotic? he thought, staring at the inside of her wrist. She looked up, caught him watching her and glanced quickly away. He turned back to catch a slight smile on Peter's lips. Hey, Stephen thought, I'm the one with the teenage girlfriend. And then immediately he felt ashamed of thinking of Justine like that, as a high score in a competitive game. This evening was nonsense. He'd somehow got out of step with himself.

He finished his drink quickly after that. As he stood up to go, he remembered he hadn't given Peter his address, and felt in his pockets for paper and pen.

'It's all right, I've got some somewhere.' Peter was groping about inside his crammed rucksack. Books, tissues, bread rolls, milk, photocopies of newspaper articles, a pair of white socks were piled on to the bench between them. 'Here we are.'

He handed over a notebook and pen, and Stephen printed his address, slowly and carefully, in block capitals, because he wanted time to check something out. Some of the photocopies – perhaps all of them – were about Kate. There was no mistaking the white wings of her hair.

'Right,' he said, handing the pen back. 'I look forward to reading them.'

For once this was not entirely insincere. The stories might be dreadful, but Peter was interesting.

Outside, in the street, Stephen felt the tingle of sweat evaporating from his face. It had been raining. All along the greasy pavement reflections of street lamps blurred into supernovae.

They said goodnight and set off in opposite directions. After a while, Stephen looked back to see Peter moving rapidly along, threading his way between groups of young people out on the town, a dark bead on a brightly coloured string.

There was no reason why Peter shouldn't have copies of articles about Kate. By his own admission he'd become fascinated by her work, and it was natural for him to want to know more, now that he was so intimately involved.

All the same, Stephen couldn't help wondering if Kate knew the extent of his interest.

Fifteen

Kate had arranged to meet Stephen at the Bowes Museum. She wanted him to see the Goya.

Always she approached it slowly. From the moment she entered the gallery she was aware of it immediately, like a beam of infra-red light on her skin, but she refused to look in its direction, wandering off instead into the sixteenth-century room, trailing round countless crucifixions and depositions and pietàs. Wonderful things here, not least the El Greco, but on balance it was a dark place, she thought, full of unmastered cruelty.

She came out of it hungry for the Goya. It was so small, not much larger than a sheet of typing paper, all the colours subdued. The interior of a prison, seven men in shackles, every tone, every line expressing despair. She stood back. Knelt down. Stared. And because she'd only recently been talking to Stephen, she wondered whether any photograph, however great, could prompt the same complexity of response as this painting. Photographs shock, terrify, arouse compassion, anger, even drive people to take action, but does the photograph of an atrocity ever inspire hope? This did. These men have no hope, no past, no future, and yet, seeing this scene through Goya's steady and compassionate eye, it was impossible to feel anything as simple or as trivial as despair.

She felt almost disloyal to Ben, thinking this. She got up, fleetingly aware that six weeks ago she couldn't have made that movement without pain, and belatedly realized the man standing with his back to her, looking at the Canalettos, was Stephen. He looked, she thought, rather like his surname: lean, grey, elegant and danger-ous. Hearing her approach, he turned and smiled. 'I didn't want to disturb you,' he said.

'Have you seen it?'

'Yes, amazing.'

'Do you want to go on looking round?'

'No, I think I've done enough for one day. I even went to look at the two-headed calf because I thought Goya would have gone to see it.'

'He would, wouldn't he.'

They smiled as if enjoying the quirks of a mutual friend. She said, 'That used to be part of a really quite sinister exhibition. There was a whole wall of mur-derers' death masks – done by the hangman, I suppose. All very pseudo-scientific – the facial features of degeneration and all that.'

'What did they look like?'

'Anybody else.'

Downstairs, on the steps, looking out over the formal gardens, she said, 'I suppose that's how he survived.' She squinted up into a pale sun that was rapidly being obscured by trails of black cloud. 'Otherwise . . .'

Yes, Stephen thought, otherwise . . . Deafness. The war. 'Mind you, when you look at the "black" paintings you wonder if he *did* survive.'

'Have you noticed how noisy his paintings are? You normally don't think of paintings as making any sound, but they absolutely roar at you.'

'Yes. I think his deafness must've been the sort where you have horrible meaningless noises all the time. But then, of course, he was very good at diverting himself.' They were walking down the steps to their cars now. 'Therapists are quite scathing about "taking your mind off it", but there's no doubt it works. At least for some people. It worked for him.' Circuses, freaks, markets, fiestas. An odd collection of fragments to shore against his ruin.

'And Leocadia,' he said, unaware that he was completing a train of thought she hadn't shared.

'A mixed blessing, some people thought.'

'They stayed together.'

'Perhaps she had no other option.' She glanced at him and smiled. 'Forty-two years younger than him.'

'I know.' He was thinking with a challenge like that in the bed there wouldn't be much time to brood. The wind was blowing hard across the formal gardens. He had to turn his head sideways to speak at all. 'Where shall we go for lunch? Is there anywhere close?'

'The Fox and Hounds. I'll show you.'

Over the meal they talked about Goya, the dating of the painting, which the museum gave as 1794, though

all the books he'd read – and the museum's own cata-
logue for that matter – suggested 1810–12 as more likely.
'I feel that's right,' he said. 'I think he'd been through
the war when he painted that. One of the rape scenes
has a similar background.'

'Isn't it amazing, the way he shows rape? You still
can't do that now.'

'They're not generally keen on an audience.'

As he spoke he had a flashback to the stairwell in
Sarajevo. One of the worst he'd had for quite a while.
It's not true, he thought, that images lose their power
with repetition, or not automatically true anyway. That
memory, which was now subtly different because Ben's
photograph had been grafted on to it, never failed to
shock.

'How did Ben cope?'

'Buried himself in the country. He didn't see people,
when he came home. He just went to ground.'

'I used to do that. Trouble is, Nerys didn't want
to go to ground with me. Understandably,' he added
quickly. 'She had her own life.'

Kate was looking down into her glass, ruby-red lights
reflected up into her face.

'Did Ben ever go to a therapist?'

'No.' She hesitated. 'Did you?'

'Yes, quite recently.' He smiled. 'Everybody seemed
to think it was a good idea.'

'What did you think?'

He shrugged. 'He was good. Only I suppose in the
end I think Goya's a better guide.'

'He lost his wife, didn't he? Goya. Just after the war.'
She shook her head. 'Poor woman.'

'Why poor?'

She looked surprised. 'Six dead children. Miscarriages galore. Read his letters. She's forever in bed, bleeding.'

'You identify with her?'

'Sympathize. There's nothing to identify *with*. We don't know anything about her, except the obstetric history, and we only know that because she married Goya. He didn't paint her. Or did he? – I can't remember. If he did, it was only once.'

Stephen was smiling. 'You think he should have done?'

'It would have been *nice!*'

'Why don't you sculpt women?'

'Wrong body. It's not the right vehicle for the ideas I want to explore.'

'That's what Peter said.'

'Peter?'

'I bumped into him the other night. He's going to send me some of his stories. Did you know he wants to write?'

'Yes, he mentioned it. I haven't read anything.'

A short silence. 'He's very interested in your work. I noticed he had photocopies of articles about you in his rucksack.'

'Yeah, well, I know he's . . .'

Her voice trailed away. When it became clear she wasn't going to say any more, he asked, 'How's it going? Or shouldn't I ask?'

'Pretty well, actually. I've got a good bit of the carving done. I'm not sure about the head, though.' She looked abstracted, unconsciously rubbing a morsel of bread between thumb and forefinger until it turned into a small grey bead. 'But you can overwork things.' She realized what she was doing and put the bread down.

'And Peter? Is that working?'

'Seems to be.'

He waited.

'Well, no, not really.'

'What's wrong?'

'Difficult to put your finger on it. And it could just be me being paranoid. Things keep changing position.' She glanced at him. 'I know my studio looks as if a bomb's dropped, but actually I do know where everything is, and I keep coming in and things have been moved.'

'What sort of things?'

'Chisels, mallets, scrapers.'

'Nothing's missing?'

'No, and they haven't been moved far. A few inches.'

'You're sure?'

'Positive. He's got a key, he knows the combination on the burglar alarm – he has to, because he sometimes delivers stuff outside working hours.'

'Why would he do that?'

'I don't know.'

'He doesn't touch the figure?'

'Not the Christ. Some of the others have moved. The group in the corner. They shift about a bit.'

'You haven't confronted him with it?'

'No. It's mad. Nothing's missing. Nothing's been damaged. And I suppose I keep thinking if I don't say anything it'll go away.' She looked directly at him. 'It could be me. I'm sure I don't need to spell it out. I have been in better states.'

'I don't think it's you.'

She smiled, then laughed. 'Good.'

'You think he's getting a bit obsessed?'

'A bit. He's really got into it –'

'No, I meant with you.'

She considered for a moment. 'No, I don't think so. I'm old enough to be his mother.'

'As Jocasta said.'

'Oh, c'mon.'

She was laughing now, slightly flushed. How long since she'd thought of herself as an attractive woman? But he knew the answer to that. To the day. Almost to the hour.

'Anyway, he's got a girlfriend. Justine Braithewaite. The vicar's daughter.'

He managed not to show surprise. He didn't for a moment believe anything was still going on, but he remembered how reluctant Justine was to go out to any of the local pubs or restaurants. She'd always said she didn't want to bump into any of her father's nosy parishioners. But perhaps there was another explanation. He wasn't jealous, but he was surprised, and a bit hurt, that he hadn't been told.

A few minutes later he paid the bill and followed

Kate into the car park. 'You're right about that place. It's very good.'

As they left the shelter of the building, a gust of wind caught them. She staggered, and he put out a hand to steady her.

'March coming in like a lion,' she said, pushing the hair away from her face.

Battling across the car park, they had to turn their heads sideways to escape the wind that threatened to snatch the breath from their mouths.

She almost shouted, 'Are you going back to Goya?'

'Yes, I think I'd better. Can we arrange a time for me to come across and look at prints?'

'I've got to go to the hospital tomorrow. They're going to give me an anaesthetic to try to free up the shoulder. How about Tuesday?'

'Fine. See you then.'

It was impossible to talk. He saw her into her car and waved as she turned off into the road.

Sixteen

Next morning the book from Peter arrived, with a short note giving his address and telephone number. Normally Stephen would have put it aside to read later, but by now his curiosity had been awakened. This was Justine's boyfriend – ex-boyfriend. Why on earth hadn't she mentioned his name?

Peter's story 'Inside the Wire' was longer than the other pieces in the issue, though the potted biography at the end of the book gave less information than other contributors had thought necessary. His MA was mentioned, but almost nothing else.

Andrea White teaches Art inside a high-security prison. When people expressed surprise that her entire working life was spent locked up with some of the country's most dangerous men, and asked if she did not feel nervous, she replied that she often felt safer inside the prison than she did waiting at the bus stop after dark to start the long journey home.

Andrea lives in a one-bedroom flat, in an area that was supposed to rise but hadn't risen yet. A year before, she'd split up with her boyfriend. Two years before that, she'd had an abortion after her boyfriend decided he was too young to be saddled with a family. Now, despite his fear of being a child bridegroom, he's married and his wife is pregnant. Andrea passes her sometimes trundling her trolley round Sainsbury's.

Once safely home, Andrea puts on soup for supper – home-made – warming it through, gently, as you should, while cutting the bread – home-made, warm from the oven. She knows all about the deep demoralization of the microwave, does Andrea, and she wants none of it – she's fighting back. But it's a precarious little life she leads – trying and failing to get over the boyfriend, getting drunk at a party and having a one-night stand, but lacking the emotional toughness not to feel bad about it afterwards. Next morning, getting up and staring at herself in the mirror, she notices that the creases at the corners of her eyes look deeper when she's tired, and then she drags herself off to work.

She's a good teacher, though she rarely encounters any actual talent. The prisoners generally go in for disturbingly sentimental portraits of children, chocolate-box flowers, gooey pictures of Christ – Peter was very good on the links between sentimentality and brutality. But one prisoner, James Carne, is doing something different. He returns again and again to a single image: a figure of indeterminate sex, the face hidden by bandages or tape, enclosed in a double helix of barbed wire. It's a bit like the Amnesty International candle. 'Did you,' she asks James, 'have the Amnesty International candle in mind when you drew it?' 'No,' says James. 'But you were thinking of imprisonment and the impossibility of escape?' 'Oh, yes.'

Andrea's starved of meaning, so she attaches meaning to this. After a while she begins to suggest that perhaps he should do something else. 'When I'm outside,' he says. 'Shut up in here I can't think about anything else.'

She goes out of the prison gate, feels the wind and rain on her face, sees the barbed wire outside the high perimeter walls, hears the snapping of scraps of cloth and paper caught on the barbs. Of course he can't do anything else. It was stupid and insensitive of her to think that he could.

James is a tall, rather good-looking man, muscles toned from long hours spent in the gym, obsessively working out. Andrea's feelings for him, though, have nothing to do with physical attraction – or so she tells herself, hurrying through the weekend's shopping so she'll have time to go to the hairdresser.

James notices the new haircut, as he notices the shorter skirts, the brighter lipstick, the way the lipstick bleeds ever so slightly into the lines around her mouth. He watches her tug the skirt down over her knees when she catches him looking at her. He's a man who notices things.

Without actually saying so, he implies that he's inno-cent of the crimes for which he was sentenced, and she believes him. How could a murderer, a drugs dealer, an armed robber or a rapist – Andrea prefers to remain vague about the details of precisely what it is that James didn't do – paint pictures as sensitive, as beautiful, as this? The figures glow inside their cages of barbed wire.

And then he comes out. He waits for her at the bus

stop where so often in the past she has felt afraid, with the floodlit rain-streaked walls of the prison towering over her.

There was no suspense. The ending had never been in doubt, and yet Stephen couldn't stop reading. There's a horrible fascination in watching an innocent human being become complicit in their own destruction. The violence, like everything else, was beautifully controlled, neither shirked nor lingered over. Barbed wire figured prominently, as did masking tape.

Andrea died a terrible death because she projected her own values on to an image created by somebody else for his own purposes. Stephen felt enormous compassion for her, but then he wondered whether he was not projecting his own values into the story, doing, in fact, exactly what Andrea had done with the paintings. You bring everything you are, everything you've ever experienced, to that encounter with the sculpture, the painting, the words on the page. But behind the smoke the sibyl crouches, murmuring too low for you to catch the words, 'Ah, but I don't mean what you mean.'

There was great insight into the small rituals of middle-aged female loneliness – remarkable in a young man. Insight, yes. But compassion? Stephen looked back at the description of James noticing the shorter skirt, the brown spots on the back of Andrea's hand, the leaking of lipstick into the lines around her mouth. Peter was inhabiting James's mind with disconcerting ease.

The second story, 'The Odd Job Man', was about a

widow who employs a man to do the small jobs around the house that she'd always relied on her husband to do in the past. There are a great many odd jobs to be done – it seems no sooner has Reggie (a rare false note) mended one thing than another breaks down. Eventually Reggie declares his passion, and she refuses him, saying she's not over her husband's death. The next morning, setting off for work, she finds her husband's decomposed body on the doorstep with a note, saying, 'What's he got that I haven't got?'

Christ. Stephen put the book down. That was one story he wouldn't be reading twice. Again the emphasis on female helplessness, the detailed observation that always implied empathy, and yet, somehow, mysteriously failed to deliver it. The stories kept slipping into sympathy with the predatory behaviour they attempted to analyse. There was no moral centre. That was Stephen's final verdict, and it was this ambiguity in the narrator's attitude to predator and prey, rather than the actual events, that made the stories so unsettling.

He read them over breakfast. They recurred throughout the morning in that second life of fiction that generally confirms the first impression, though in this case his estimate of the skill involved went up. It was the setting that gave the writing such authority. The smells on the landings, semen, socks and stew; the sour smell of chicken shit from the man trusted to work on the farm; the smell of dried urine from the cells of inveterate bedwetters; the grey cruds of chewing gum stuck to the undersides of the top bunk; the iron taste of the mist that hangs over the prison, the only tangible evidence that there is a world outside.

Of course, it's amazing what research could do to suggest that first-hand experience was being used. Saul Bellow wrote *Henderson the Rain King* without setting foot in Africa.

But that was Saul Bellow.

He left the book lying on the coffee table in front of the fire, where that evening Justine found it. She said nothing, but curled up on the sofa to read, a fuzz of golden hair visible under the T-shirt, which was the only garment she wore. He watched her brow furrow in that elusive expression of pain that was, he realized suddenly, the thing he found most erotic about her. She was so strong, so full of energy and hope. What did it say about him that it was her capacity to feel pain that aroused him?

She closed the book with a snap. 'Thank God I did Science.'

'They're good, don't you think?'

He assumed she'd been reading Peter's stories, and she didn't contradict him. 'They're horrible.'

She was quiet for a while. At last he went across to her and held out his arms as one does to a sulky child, and she came into them and cried. Rubbing her shoulders, he tried not to get excited by the smell of their earlier love-making and to focus simply on consoling her, but she pushed him away. 'How long have you known about me and Peter?'

'Kate mentioned it.'

'Kate Frobisher?'

'Yes.'

'How the hell does she know?'

'I don't know. Perhaps she saw you together.'

She was wiping her eyes fiercely, her chest too tight to support her voice. 'Typical. You can't do anything in this sodding place without being spied on.'

'I'm sure she wasn't spying. Did your father know?'

'Of course he did.'

'Did he approve?'

'Why shouldn't he?'

'I don't know. You tell me.'

She tried to stare him out and failed. 'Actually, Dad was a bit of a hypocrite about it. You know, he belongs to this Fresh Start initiative that tries to help people who've just been released from prison? That's how he met Peter. Years ago, this is, and then he showed up again last summer and asked if he could stay for a few weeks. And as long as he was just doing the garden, it was fine, great, we were all doing this great Christian thing, but then I started going out with him – and that was a bit different.'

'So he was actually *living* with you?'

'Yeah, for a few weeks.'

'And you fell in love with him.'

'He made the running, not me.'

'You'd be still a child the first time you met?'

'Yeah. Which is what you think I still am. I don't know what that makes *you*.'

'Of course I don't think you're a child. C'mon, don't take it out on me, I'm only trying to help.'

'Sorry.' She smiled, wiping her nose on the back of her hand. He got up and found her some tissues.

'What was he in for?'

'I don't know. Except it wasn't sex offences, because Dad said he couldn't take those, not with me in the house.'

'He didn't tell you?'

'Peter or Dad?'

'Peter.'

'No.'

'Didn't that surprise you?'

'No, and it wouldn't surprise you either if you knew Peter.'

'I don't see how you can have a relationship with somebody and not tell them something like that.'

'Don't you?' Her mouth was pursed as if she'd been sucking lemons. 'He didn't. He didn't talk about the past much and when he did . . . I learnt to avoid the subject.'

'Why?'

'Because there was never any depth. It was always one-layer thin. You could poke your finger through it – and I didn't want to because I didn't want to know what was on the other side. But I did think one day . . .' She was struggling for composure. 'When we went out – that night, the night we finished – I thought it was going to happen, I thought he was going to tell me, because he obviously had something on his mind.

Instead of that, he cut my head off.' An attempt at a laugh. 'Chalk it up to experience, I suppose.'

'Was he cruel?'

'I don't know.' She was staring into the darkness beyond the ring of firelight. 'I don't know if cruel's the right word.'

'They're cruel stories.'

'Yes, but he isn't James. He certainly isn't Reggie.'

'He created them.'

She shrugged.

'Did he hurt you?'

'Of course he did.'

'I mean physically.'

'You mean was he violent? Oh, for God's sake, do you think I'd put up with that?'

'Some women do.'

'Not me.'

He could sense that in her. 'So how?'

'I don't know. It was . . . like everything was turned against you. Sometimes I'd open my eyes when we were making love and he'd be just staring at me and . . . It felt like being an insect on the end of a pin . . .' Unexpectedly, she chuckled. 'You know, not coming, but going. But I was in love with him. None of it mattered. And I thought it was going really well, and then . . . *chop.*'

'Do you think your father had talked to him?'

'No, I don't think so. If he went in for that kind of heavy-handed father stuff, he'd be talking to *you.* No, I think Peter always intended it to be just for the summer.

Because I was going to university, I think he thought it was limited, off I'd go, and that'd be that. Only I got ill, and suddenly there was no obvious end-point. I think he was afraid of saying too much.' A pause. 'He did love me.'

'Are you sure?'

Again that baffled, groping look. 'No.'

'Would you have wanted it to go on?'

'Yes.'

'In spite of not knowing what he'd done?'

She shook her head. 'Whatever it is, he's served his sentence. You can't hold things against somebody for ever.'

That depended on what they'd done, he thought. 'You must have some idea.'

'No.'

'Drugs?'

'He hates them.'

She was starting to defend him, the last thing Stephen wanted. 'It sounds as if you're well rid of him anyway.'

'That's exactly what Dad said.'

He was glad to know Christian charity hadn't entirely stifled common sense. 'Yeah, well, we're the same generation.'

He looked at her again in her ridiculous baggy T-shirt and thought, I've got to stop patronizing her. All along he'd assumed she was suffering from nothing more than the pangs of disappointed calf love, as painful as a toddler's temper tantrum and as difficult for an adult to take seriously. He'd never allowed for the possibility that she might have encountered, early in life, a man who would have been bad news for any woman at any age. Or man, perhaps, remembering certain nuances in his conversation with Peter.

Coldness, manipulation, a passion to control, an abnormality of mind that makes generosity in giving count against the giver . . .

He patted her ankle, then impulsively bent and buried his face in the golden hair between her legs, groping, flicking, sucking, nuzzling while his hands pressed her thighs gently apart. For a second her pelvis arched, like a flower in a dark corner angling to find the light, and her stomach muscles tensed and quivered.

But then, almost immediately, she was laughing and pulling away from him, pushing his head to one side as she wriggled free.

'I've got to go home.'

He looked at his watch. 'It's not time.'

'Beth says there's a tree down on the forest road. I'll have to go all the way round.'

She was looking down at him almost as if she were sorry for him.

'Will I see you tomorrow?'

'Yes.'

More love-making in the dark. 'Do you still love him?'

The pupils of her eyes were so large the blue eyes looked black. 'I'm not sure I know what love is.'

'The truth is you were too good for the little sod.'

She smiled and shrugged. 'I'd better get dressed.'

'You're probably too good for me.'

She wrapped her arms around him and kissed him. 'Oh, you're not so bad.' A subterranean explosion of laughter shook her breasts. 'You'll do.'

For now, he thought, as he watched her dress.

Seventeen

Kate got back from the hospital on Monday afternoon, amazed at the improvement to her shoulder, but still drowsy from the anaesthetic. After making a few phone calls to tell people she was home, she stood at the window, pulling Ben's amulet up and down the chain. It was some comfort, but no substitute for his arm around her shoulders.

She resisted the idea of going to sleep, and set off for a walk instead. She needed to clear her head, but also she wanted to enjoy the improvement in her mobility. She walked along, bending her head from side to side, circling her right arm. If anybody had seen her she'd have been locked up, but there was nobody to see. The weather was keeping everybody else indoors.

It had been blowing a gale all day. Even in the hospital she'd been aware of it, great blasts hurling rain against the window, though inside her cubicle there was only the heat of the radiator and mingled smells of antiseptic and rubber. Never mind, she was free of all that now. No more hospitals. No more surgical collar, and for the next two days at least – no Peter. She'd given him Monday and Tuesday off – paid, of course – partly because she hadn't known how she'd feel after the operation, but also because she needed to spend some time alone with the Christ, to try to recapture her original conception.

Above the forest the clouds massed together, a huge black anvil obscured by veils of drifting grey. The trees heaved and thrashed, and then suddenly went quiet, only the topmost branches tweaking, like the tip of a cat's tail while it's watching a bird. And then the rain came, great slanting silver rods, disappearing into the black earth.

The deer would still be dry, she thought. She imagined them, moist nostrils quivering as the storm passed over their heads. Other animals were less lucky. In the fields cows huddled around their feeding trough in muddy trenches they'd dug for themselves; horses tilted a hind hoof and stood, blank with misery, water matting the coarse hair on their flanks; rabbits raced for cover, the wind making pale grey stars in their fur.

She ran the last few steps to the front door, struggling to keep her balance, and let herself into a house whose fading warmth told her at once that the fire was either dead or dying. She managed to rescue it, and sat down by the fire with a stiff whisky to warm her through. Outside in the yard dead leaves were blown about like specks on an ageing retina. The hens, affronted by the constant ruffling of their feathers, had retired to the barn, where they clucked peevishly on their brooding perches.

After a while, feeling fully restored by the walk, she got out her drawing pad and looked back to her original sketches for the Christ commission. They worried her because they had an energy that she knew the finished, or nearly finished, figure lacked. She spent a couple of hours working out what had gone wrong, increasingly convinced that something had and knowing there was very little time left to put it right. In the end she put the work aside in despair and went to the window, resisting the urge to go across to the studio and try out new ideas. It would be mad to work now. She was in no state to take decisions.

The sky had darkened. Trees strained and groaned in the yellow light. A flock of birds flew over, rooks, probably, flapping big, black, ungainly wings, but after that there was nothing. Feeling suddenly exhausted, as much by doubts about her work as by the anaesthetic, she switched off the lights and went early to bed.

She felt she would sleep at once, and did, only to wake again, half dreaming, thinking how the wind in the trees sounded like the sea. It was like being back in the lighthouse she and Ben had rented once, where one stormy day she'd forced the window open to find a seagull level with her face, its rapacious golden eyes glinting as it rode the wind. And that night she'd run her hands along Ben's spine, feeling the knobs of his vertebrae as secret and mysterious as fossils.

'Hey,' he'd said, turning to face her. 'I'm not clay.'

You are now, she thought. Oh, my love. At such moments, stranded between sleep and waking, the pain tore into her, as fierce as it had been the day she took the call. Sleep, she told herself, turning over and curling up. The only cure for this was sleep.

But the long fall from waking into sleep ended with a thump. She was sitting up in darkness, dry-mouthed, staring, knowing that some particular sound had dragged her back into consciousness. Not the spatter of rain on the glass, or the whistling of the wind – these were natural sounds and easily screened out. No, some specific, *wrong* sound – a sound that shouldn't have been there at all – had woken her. She stared into the darkness, tense, waiting for it to be repeated.

Nothing. She settled back against the pillows, telling herself she couldn't have heard anything unusual against the clamour of the storm, and that a noise in a dream can seem to come from the outside world if you wake suddenly. But she couldn't get back to sleep. At last, she got out of bed, reached for her dressing-gown and looked out into the yard, through the buffeting of the wind that seemed, in some extraordinary way, to have become visible, bending the trees sideways, beating the bushes till they showed the white undersides of their leaves as if in fear. Light came and went in fitful gleams on the choppy surface of the puddles, and for one insane moment the eye of the moon stared up at her from the yard.

Anything could've woken her, she thought. A dustbin lid clattering against a wall, a door banging, but then she saw it, a glow of light from inside the studio where no light should have been. A moving light, a torch or a small lamp. She saw the reflection on the hillside rather than the light itself, a tinge of purple on the heaving grass.

Police. She picked up the phone, unable at first to understand why there was silence rather than a steady purr, then realized the lines must be down. Checking, she switched on the bedside lamp. Dead. She went downstairs, trying lights on the staircase and landings, then found the torch she kept in a drawer of the hall table. Through into the living room, swinging the beam around her, she brought the light to a stop on Ben's portrait. Oh, my dear, she thought, and touched his face.

If there'd been burglars in the house, she'd have locked the bedroom door and let them have the lot. But this was her work. She wouldn't let that be stolen or destroyed.

In the kitchen she pulled on wellies, her bare feet jamming against the rubber, cold toes wiggling in space – too much space – she must've put on Ben's boots, not her own. No time to change, she was out in the yard, switching the torch off as she left the house. She felt that carrying a light would make her conspicuous, though she switched it on again as she ventured out into the yard, briefly creating a wobbling sphere of light with slanting, silver lines of rain sweeping across it, then switched it off again, paused for a moment to get her eyes accustomed to the dark, and set off to the studio door. She opened it quietly, and stood in the lobby among the familiar daily smells, aware of somebody on the other side of that door. Deep breaths. Blood clamouring in her head and neck, destroying her ability to think. She put her eye to the crack in the door, wanting to know who and what she had to confront.

She couldn't see anybody. The shadow of the huge Christ lay across the floor and climbed the wall, and a second smaller shadow flickered around it, like a grey flame. She pressed closer to the door, wondering if she dare push it open, trying to remember if it creaked, and then she heard the last sound she expected to hear – though it was the sound that filled the studio almost every day of her working life – the tapping of a mallet on a chisel. She pushed the door further open.

Peter Wingrave stood there, a torch propped up on one of the benches behind him, his shadow huge against the wall of the studio, but this was Peter as she'd never seen him before. Her mind grappled with the wrongness of the image, and then she realized he was wearing her clothes, even to the fur hat with earflaps that she sometimes wore when the studio was really cold. He looked ridiculous – and terrifying. Deranged. His bare arms protruded from the plaster-daubed fisherman's smock. She was a tall woman, but on him the sleeves were barely past his elbow, and his legs stuck out of her tracksuit bottoms, bare legs, white and hairy in the torchlight, more clearly visible than the rest of him. Only her moon boots had defeated him. He was bare-foot, his strong prehensile toes gripping and relaxing as his feet moved across the mess of white plaster dust, towards the figure, pause, strike, away. Decision, action, contemplation: the constant comparison of the shape in the mind with the shape that was emerging from the plaster. The shadow of the figure thrown on to the wall in front of him, one shadow threading in and out of the other, like a weaver's bobbin.

He looked mad. He looked totally, utterly deranged, and he was destroying her Christ.

But then, a second later, something that had been tugging at the edges of her mind became clear. There was something wrong about the sound. She strained to listen. The scuff of his feet moving across the floor, a snap as a larger piece of plaster broke under his weight, then again the tap of mallet on chisel. There was no impact, no jar and squeak of the chisel biting into the plaster. He was miming. Pretending to be her. In his own mind, perhaps, he had become her.

The first rush of relief at knowing the figure wasn't being damaged gave way immediately to a deeper fear. If he had been destroying her work, she must and would have confronted him, but this was so different from anything she'd expected to see that she stepped back into the darkness and stood there, thinking. He was stealing her power in an almost ritualistic way. She couldn't confront him, because she couldn't begin to understand what she was dealing with – she couldn't foresee what his reaction would be.

Slowly, being careful to make no noise, she backed out of the lobby and ran across the yard into the house, where she locked and bolted the door behind her.

She began searching for her bag, but when she found her mobile she couldn't get a signal. And in any case, she thought, putting it down, what could she say? There's a man in my studio. Did he break in? No, I gave him the key. Is he doing any damage? No. Is he threatening you? No. Are you frightened? Yes. Terrified. Are you a neurotic, stupid bitch? Yes – probably.

They wouldn't say that. All the same she didn't particularly want to have the conversation. She put the mobile down and sat at the kitchen table, in darkness, torn between the desire to go back over there and ask him what the hell he thought he was doing, and her fear that what he was doing made so little sense, even on his own terms, perhaps, that he wouldn't be able to answer, and that the question might therefore topple him over into some state she couldn't predict and wouldn't be able to deal with. No, better left.

He was wearing her clothes.

She felt a spasm of revulsion, not from him but from herself, as if he had indeed succeeded in stealing her identity. It was easy to believe that what she'd seen in the studio, through the crack in the door, was a deranged double, a creature that in its insanity and incompetence revealed the truth about her.

Half an hour later, perhaps a little less, she heard the studio door close, footsteps walking along the side of the house and then the noise of his van driving away.

Eighteen

The storm blew itself out over the next few hours. Kate made no attempt to sleep again, but sat at the kitchen table, tense and watchful, eyes prickling with tiredness, mouth and stomach sour with too much caffeine.

After a while, as the light coming through the window panes strengthened, she crept out of the house into the opening eye of day, and in that watery yellow light made her way across the yard, which was strewn with twigs and small branches torn off the trees, to the studio.

The huge figure towered over her. It had changed, and yet there were no fresh chips of plaster on the floor, and no chisel marks she couldn't remember making herself. If it looked different, it must be because her way of seeing it had changed. The belly was scored in three, no, four different places. She put her hands into the cracks. Chest and neck gouged – it looked like a skin disease, bubonic plague, a savagely plucked bird. Pockmarks everywhere. Slowly, she raised her eyes and looked at the head. Cheekbones like cliffs, a thin, dour mouth, lines graven deep on either side, bruised, cut, swollen. Beaten up. Somebody with a talent for such things had given him a right going over. This was the Jesus of history. And we know what happens in history:

the strong take what they can, the weak endure what they must, and the dead emphatically do not rise.

She'd made this, not Peter, and yet it seemed to her, remembering last night, that everything she found most disturbing in this figure corresponded with his mimed movements.

Putting the problem aside as too complex to solve now, she looked round the studio, thinking he might have left things behind, and sure enough, there was his jacket on the bench. Putting scruples aside, she felt inside the pockets and found loose change, three five-pound notes and a credit card. She'd have to find a way of returning these: she didn't want him coming here to collect them. Perhaps she could drop them off at the vicarage. He could pick them up there.

She went out, locked the door and changed the combination on the alarm. It took her a long time to remember what she had to do to achieve this, and while she was doing it the rain started again, though only a few scattered drops, just enough to freshen her burning face.

Back in the house, she forced herself to wash, dress, comb her hair, though her efforts only seemed to make the shadows under her eyes more apparent. She looked dreadful, ancient. Felt it too. And yet the improvement in her shoulder was even more remarkable this morning. They'd told her that if it worked at all, the effects would be dramatic, but she hadn't dared hope for anything as good as this.

The lights came on at ten o'clock. Various pieces of

electronic equipment clicked and whirred, the freezer light glowed red but quickly turned to green. A hum in the distance resolved itself into the sound of a car's engine. Peter? She immediately wished she'd phoned Angela and asked her to come round, but it was too late now. The car stopped by the side of the house, and with relief she saw Stephen Sharkey walk past the kitchen window.

He was making for the studio, taking it for granted that at this time of the morning she'd be there.

'Hello,' she said, opening the kitchen door.

'Hello. Rough night?'

She must look even worse than she thought. 'Yes, it was a bit.' She stood to one side. 'Come in.'

He stepped over the threshold. 'Did your lights go off?'

'Yes, they came back on half an hour ago. And yours?'

'The same. I expect we're on the same bit of the grid. Did you manage to sleep through it?'

'Not really.'

'Do you know,' he said, taking off his coat, 'I saw an owl sitting on the fence back there, in broad daylight. I think I could have walked up to it.'

'Perhaps it's lost its tree, poor thing. There'll be a good few of them down.'

She was remembering he'd arranged to come this morning to look through Ben's prints. It had completely slipped her mind. 'Would you like some coffee before you start?'

She put the kettle on, but had peppermint tea herself.

Her mind buzzed and fizzed with caffeine, but not in any way that produced useful thought. Stephen watched her sip the greenish-brown liquid. She looked shaken, he thought.

'Don't you like thunder?'

'No, it wasn't that. I was woken up by I think it was a dustbin lid blowing around – but then I saw a light in the studio. So I went across . . .'

She told it, or attempted to tell it, as an amusing incident, unaware of the expression of fear and distress that had spread across her face and deepened as she spoke.

'Anyway, there he was with my clothes on.'

'Your clothes?'

'Yes, you know, work clothes. He wasn't prancing about in high heels and a bra.' A spasm of irritation born of exhaustion. She controlled herself. 'He was pretending to carve the plaster.'

'Pretending?'

'Oh, yes, he didn't touch it.'

'Imitating you.'

Imitating domesticated it, she thought. It had been a lot more than that.

'What did you do?'

'Nothing very heroic, I'm afraid. I just came back here and locked the door.'

'Did you phone the police?'

She shook her head. 'The lines were down.'

'Have you tried this morning?'

'No, I don't see the point.'

'Was there any damage?'

Good question. 'No, not really.' She couldn't explain that the damage was to her belief in herself and in the project. There was nothing the police could do about that.

Stephen was silent for a moment, holding the steaming mug in his clasped hands. 'Did you know he'd been in prison? Did Alec tell you?'

'No. How do you know?'

'Justine told me. It's about five years ago, so he's been out for a while.'

'I don't suppose he did anything dreadful. Possession of a Category A drug?'

'I think it was a bit more than that.'

'Doesn't Justine know?'

'No, he never told her.'

'Alec would know.'

'Oh, yes, he'd know.'

'I can't believe he didn't mention it.'

'No, well, I agree. I think you had the right to know what you were taking on.'

'Yes.' She was starting to feel angry. A simpler and much more enjoyable response than the mixture of disgust and self-doubt she'd experienced till now.

After Stephen finished his coffee, she took him off to Ben's studio, tapped in the combination and unlocked the door. 'Look,' she said, 'why don't I write this down for you? Then you can come and go as you want.' He gave her his notebook and a pen, and she leant against the wall to write the numbers down. 'I hope you have a good morning,' she said, handing the pad back to him.

She went back into the house, but a few minutes later she came out, got in her car and drove away.

Parking outside the churchyard gate, Kate realized she could see the headstone of Ben's grave, backed by bleached blond grass. She'd wanted him to be there, on the edge of the cemetery, with the rolling moors shrugging their bare shoulders behind him, rather than close to the village with its dense, secretive life, its rivalries, feuds and gossip.

As she walked up the path to the front door of the vicarage, she saw pale gashes in the trees that had been damaged overnight. Twigs and small branches were scattered over the lawn as they were over her yard, but, more worrying for Alec, there were broken slates mixed in as well.

She rang the bell twice, resigning herself to a long wait and possible disappointment, but after a few minutes she heard footsteps – too light to be Alec's – and turned to the door, expecting to see Justine.

But it was Angela who stood there. They stared at each other. The buttons on Angela's blouse had been done up in the wrong order, obviously fastened in a hurry. Kate blushed, Angela didn't. Trying to keep her eyes off the button, Kate asked, 'Is Alec in?'

'Yes,' said Angela, not moving aside.

Somewhere in the depths of the house Kate heard the slapping of bare feet on lino. 'Could I have a word with him, please?'

She had never spoken to Angela in that chilly, formal

way before, but it had an effect. Angela stood aside and let her in. Kate followed her along the corridor and down a flight of steps to the basement kitchen. A dreadfully old-fashioned place. The gas cooker had clawed feet. Kate sat at the table. Angela filled a whistling kettle at a tap that juddered with the effort of producing water, and put it on the cooker to boil.

The window looked out over the churchyard. It said a lot for the kitchen that one appreciated the comparative cheerfulness of the view. Kate said, 'I'm not surprised Victoria ran away.'

Angela shrugged. 'She'd only herself to blame. The bishop offered them a modern house, but she wouldn't have it because it was on a housing estate. She was quite county, you know, Victoria.'

'Was she? I never really got to know her.' A pause. 'Where's Justine?'

'With Stephen, I suppose.'

'With Stephen?'

'Oh, yes. That's been going on quite a while.'

Alec had come in on slippered feet and was standing just inside the door. 'Hello, Kate. What can I do for you?'

She didn't want to say anything in front of Angela, but it was difficult to make that clear without appearing to snub her. She looked so pink and pleased with herself, presiding over the teapot in this desolate kitchen with its smells of congealed fat and mice. Poor Justine.

'I'd like to talk about Peter, but there's no hurry. Have your tea, first.'

Alec beamed as he accepted a cup. He looked so happy, so nice, so rubicund and smiling, so engagingly and endearingly well fucked above his clerical collar, that it was difficult to go on being angry.

But Kate made the effort, and, sensing her mood, Alec suggested they should take their tea into his study.

Kate followed him down the corridor, wondering what the smell was. Some powerful floor cleaner that failed to live up to its promise and simply pushed the grime around from place to place. Though perhaps there was no grime. Perhaps it was just that the lino had reached a stage of wear when all the colours run into each other and become shades of grey. It reminded her of high teas with her great-aunts when she was a little girl. That graveyard smell of boiled beetroot leaking red on to wilted lettuce leaves.

Alec's study was overshadowed by trees. He closed the door behind them and stood at an angle to the window, facing her. 'I dream about them sometimes. The trees. I dream the branches come in at the window.'

Kate realized, with some surprise, that in over five years of so-called friendship this was the most intimate thing she'd ever heard him say. 'You should cut them down.'

'Oh, I couldn't do that.'

'They're too close, Alec. Anything that's been blocking the light for 200 years needs to come down.'

He sat down with a creak and protest of ancient wood. 'What's wrong?'

'Something rather strange happened last night.'

In telling the story again, she rediscovered her anger. She was flushed by the time she finished. 'It's thrown me completely. I was really frightened.'

Alec steepled his fingers, as if she had posed some abstract question in moral theology. 'I wonder what made him do that? He does have problems with boundaries between people.'

Kate was getting angrier by the minute. She could have accepted any amount of Christian preaching – he was paid to do it, after all – but this was just psychobabble. And he hadn't acknowledged the salient fact, which was that *she* was the injured party.

'You mean, he can't tell where he stops and other people start?'

'He's not dangerous.'

'Alec, that *is* dangerous.'

'I can see it must've been a terrible shock.'

She felt like giving him a few shocks of her own. 'Why didn't you tell me he'd been to prison?'

'It didn't seem relevant. He hasn't been in trouble with the law for more than five years.'

'I was the person to decide if it was relevant. It's quite simple, Alec. If you want him in your house getting off with your daughter, that's your business. But I have the right to decide who I want to trust. You should've warned me.'

'Well,' he said at last, after a long dragging pause. 'It's difficult.'

'What did he do?'

'Do?'

'What did he do to get sent to prison?'

'I can't tell you.'

'Can't or won't?'

'It wasn't a sexual offence. I always specified I couldn't take sex offenders because of Justine.'

Her eyes narrowed. 'What, then? Murder?'

She expected, hoped, that he'd laugh and accuse her of being melodramatic. Instead, he sighed. 'I really can't talk about this.'

And that was that. She could tell he wouldn't budge.

'I was alone with him, hour after hour, day after day, and you can't say, "Well, so what? Nothing happened," because last night something did happen.'

'Did he threaten you?'

She was silent. 'Alec, do you know what it is to be really frightened?' She wasn't explaining this well, because she didn't understand it herself.

'Are you going to tell the police?'

She stared at him. His glasses flashed in a glint of light that struggled through the leaves. 'Why? Why is it so important for me not to tell them?'

'It could be very serious for him.' He started to speak, stopped and started again. 'He hasn't really *done* anything, has he?'

'You mean he's on parole?'

Alec looked down at his hands.

'No, I won't tell them.' She looked at the carrier bag at her feet. 'I've brought all his stuff. I haven't got his address – I always paid in cash. And this' – she held up the envelope on top – 'is payment to the end of the month.'

'What's he done, Kate? Except get a bit obsessed?'

'Mucked up the contents of my head. But I quite agree that's not a crime. You see, I'm not being spiteful. I'm trying to understand, but I *don't* understand, and I don't think you do either. And it does seem to me that while you were dishing out the Christian charity, you might have spared a bit of it for me.'

'Perhaps he's in love with you, Kate. Have you thought of that?'

She shook her head vigorously, involving her shoulders, back and arms, like somebody trying to shake off an unpleasant insect. 'No, I don't think that's it, at all.'

She was almost in tears. Alec reached out his hand, but she moved out of range. 'Don't bother getting up, Alec. I can see myself out.'

Nineteen

Stephen listened in silence to Kate's account of her meeting with Alec. When she'd finished, he said, 'You won't weaken and take him back, will you?'

'Good God, no.'

She looked so tired and lonely he wanted to hug her, but they weren't on hugging terms, so he touched her gently on the arm and wished her luck.

When he told Justine about Peter's midnight visit to the studio, she shrugged her shoulders and went back to chopping peppers.

'Was that your impression? That he's got problems dealing with boundaries between people?'

She thought for a moment. 'It's not the way he sees it. He thinks he's got exceptional powers of empathy. And he hasn't, of course. What he does is dump his own emotions on to the other person and then he empathizes with himself.' She shrugged again, this time violently. 'It's a mess.' She scooped up the chopped peppers and threw them into the pan.

He thought the conversation was over, but a second later she surprised him by laughing. 'You know what his ambition is, apart from being a writer? To be a therapist. He thinks he'd be better at it than most of the ones he's known.'

'How many has he known?'

'Oh, a few.'

'He's addicted to therapy?'

'He's addicted to giving therapists hell.'

'Justine,' he said, coming up behind her and putting his arms around her. 'Do you know what he did?'

'No. What does it matter anyway?'

'You don't think Kate had the right to know what she was dealing with?'

She turned to face him. 'I don't see the point of hounding people.'

'No,' he said, taking the plates from under the grill. 'Neither do I. But I've got to do something about those stories. I've either got to send them back, or . . . I don't know. Respond, anyway.'

Justine had promised Beth she'd take Adam to the fair, and persuaded Stephen to go with them. He'd agreed with reluctance, but found himself looking forward to it by the end of the week. He'd been working so hard cooped up in the cottage that he was starting to go stir-crazy.

They could hear the music while they were still half a mile away. Behind Stephen, as he braked and turned, the Sainsbury's carrier bags, with their sober reminders of the routines of adult life, rocked and swayed, and one of them spilt its contents on to the floor.

'Just leave it, Adam,' Justine said, turning round. 'We'll sort it out when we get back.'

The moor was not far from the centre of town, but

so big that on dark nights you could feel lost crossing it. Music thumped from loudspeakers stationed at every corner of the fairground. They seemed to wade through noise, lean into it. Young girls, faces blank in the yellow, green and purple lights, shouted and screamed, while gangs of youths stared after them, their bristly scalps slick with sweat. In the male guffawing, which both acknowledged and discounted the girls' presence, there was a yelp of pain. The clammy night, the syrupy music oozing like sweat from every pore, the smell of beer on belched breath as another group of youths walked past, combined to produce a sexual tension that hung over everything as palpable as heat.

Stephen was beginning to enjoy himself. Even the muddy ground, the sparse, trampled grass, purple under the revolving lights, tugged up memories from way back.

'We've got to go on something,' Justine shouted.

'Yes,' he shouted back, looking around for some innocuous ride, one that didn't involve being pinned to the walls of a spinning globe by centrifugal force while your cheeks were dragged back to your ears. He pointed at the Ferris wheel, not because it looked safe – it didn't, it looked like a great spinning Catherine wheel that might at any moment be torn off its base and go hurtling and fizzing all over the sky – but because it was familiar from his childhood. 'What about that?'

'OK,' she shouted, through a mango-yellow mouth.

Stephen had no head for heights. His stomach knotted as the bar clanged shut across their legs. Adam insinuated a small, sticky hand into his and he smiled reassuringly, and hoped he wasn't going to be sick. Portrait of the intrepid war correspondent at play, he thought. They were whirled aloft, jerkily at first, then more smoothly as the carriages filled up. Finally, the wheel began to spin.

He risked one look down. By the ticket booth was a group of people, disappointed this time, waiting for the next ride. Their faces, upturned to watch the spinning lights, looked like small pale flowers on long stalks. He shut his eyes as the chair swung beneath him, braced his already rigid arms and felt a rush of warmer air as they neared the ground.

The third time round he felt Justine's hand on his sleeve and turned to look at her. Her mouth was wide open but no sound came out, or none that he could hear above the blare of music. At first he thought she was screaming, then realized she was laughing. He tried to speak, but the words were torn out of his mouth by the wind. They swooped down, down towards the flashing lights, and a strand of Justine's hair came loose and whipped across her mouth. Adam, squashed in between them, shrieked, but seemed to be enjoying it. He was warm all along Stephen's side, like a puppy, and had the grey wool, gym shoes and custard smell of little boys everywhere. Incredibly, Stephen was starting to enjoy the ride. He actually looked forward to that moment when he would see the whole fairground spread out between his feet, Adam's fingers clutching his arm, Justine's involuntary cry, and then the gasping headlong descent.

When he got out he seemed to have rubber thigh bones, and wobbled about, not immediately sure where the ground was. 'Would you like a beer?' he shouted.

'I'll get it. I think Adam needs the loo.'

'Do you, Adam?'

'Yes.'

He looked a bit white. Stephen put a hand on his shoulder and steered him off to the Portaloos at the other end of the field. 'Did you feel sick?'

'A bit.'

'So did I.'

He waited outside, but Adam seemed to take an enormously long time. He was worried until he remembered something Justine had said about Adam's toilet rituals – one of them involved lining the bowl and seat with paper before he could bring himself to perform.

Stephen didn't mind waiting. He was thinking about Goya, about his love of visiting circuses, fiestas, fairs, freak shows, street markets, acrobatic displays, lunatic asylums, bear fights, public executions, any spectacle strong enough to still the shouting of the demons in his ears. Portrait of a man who'd come through. Looking round, it was clear why Goya's self-medication had worked. Stephen felt dazed by the colours and shapes around him, by the way his bombarded senses began to assume each other's functions, so that colour became noise and noise colour. All these mouths shouting, laughing, screaming, eating, drinking; mouths everywhere. You saw the mouths first, as you saw the mouths first in Goya's paintings, combining to produce that roar that even in the Prado, off season, early in the morning, almost deafens you. But he didn't want to think about Goya now. He was looking forward to the beer, hoping it would be cold, picturing the sweat of condensation on the can.

When Adam came out, they looked round for Justine, but at first they couldn't see her. He felt a tweak of anxiety as he stared along the queue, willing her to be in it. Passing faces now looked merely grotesque; he was aware of the dark open spaces outside the fairground, of the stars, pale in the lights, wheeling and turning in the chaos of space.

Then he saw her standing under one of the huge lamps that lit the entrance to the car park. Moths attracted to the light fluttered all around her, so that she stood in a haze of white wings. Adam ran up to her, she handed Stephen a can of beer, and they walked through the car park, talking about where they should go.

They set off down the road to a pizza bar, Adam trotting along between them and discussing Ferris wheels in his usual professorial manner. God knows what they made of him at school. Justine said he had tummy ache on Monday mornings, which suggested something was wrong. He'd be bullied, of course, had to be, and he'd be defenceless against it, unable to do anything except go on being his unacceptable self.

Most of the outdoor tables were taken, but they found one close to the entrance, and sat looking out over the river with its floodlit bridges. Small candles flickered on every table, casting a warm glow over the circles of faces, finding answering points of light in raised glasses.

Glancing round, Stephen noticed Peter Wingrave was sitting at a table in the far corner, with a man and a woman, both older than him, the woman heavily pregnant. He was facing away from the entrance and hadn't noticed them come in. Deciding not to mention it to Justine, Stephen drummed his fingers on the cloth, while Adam read the entire menu through carefully three or four times before deciding to have what he always had – vegetarian lasagne.

'Who's driving?' Stephen asked.

'All right,' Justine said. 'But I want a drink when we get back.'

He got up to get the drinks and coincided at the bar with Peter. Stephen was content to wait at the back of the crowd, giving Peter the opportunity of approaching him if he wanted or avoiding him if he didn't. It was a bit awkward that he hadn't yet responded to the stories. The rest – his antics in Kate's studio, even his previous relationship with Justine – was not, strictly speaking, Stephen's business.

'Hi,' Peter said, coming straight up to him.

Peter looked well, Stephen thought, even slightly tanned, and then wondered why he was surprised. He'd expected somebody more obviously unbalanced. 'How are you?'

'Fine. Apart from the usual aches and pains.' He smiled that fleeting and extremely charming smile. Not overused. In fact, rather carefully rationed. Stephen felt cynical and yet aware that cynicism was perhaps a shallow response to the capacities he sensed in Peter. 'I'm gardening again. The first few weeks are always a bit tough.'

'Oh. So you're not working for Kate now?'

'No, she's virtually finished. And she's a lot better – that manipulation under anaesthetic thing really worked. Apparently the improvement was dramatic. She said it might be. I can't wait to see it.'

This was all said smoothly, and perhaps he believed it. Perhaps Kate, not wanting the relationship to end unpleasantly, had given her improved mobility as the sole reason for ending the arrangement. 'You must have plenty of gardening in this weather?'

'God, yes. The phone never stops ringing.'

'Good.'

A pause. They looked around them.

'I liked the stories.' Liked was definitely not the right word, but then a crowded bar on a warm spring evening isn't the place for precision. 'I thought what I might do is photocopy them and send them to my agent with your address and then he can get in touch with you directly if he wants to pursue it.'

'I could do the photocopying.'

'It's no problem. I'd rather they went off with a covering letter. I don't want them ending up in the slush heap.'

'It's very kind of you.'

Stephen shrugged. He hadn't missed the flicker of

speculation in Peter's eyes. 'But I don't think he's going to be interested in short stories. Though I suppose short stories do work as a first book, sometimes. McEwan.' They were almost at the front of the queue. 'Was McEwan an influence, by the way?'

'He was a bit. Though you soon slough off influences that aren't right for you.'

It was a surprisingly confident speech for a young man. Stephen had a picture of a snakeskin, faded and paper thin, left behind on the sand, as the new gleaming skin emerged into the light. How many sloughed-off skins had there been so far? 'Did you know those men? James. Reggie.'

A wary laugh. 'Ye-es, in the sense that I've known people like them. But you can't take a character straight from life.'

'So what do you do? How do you turn a real person into a fictional character?

'Add bits of yourself.'

'Really? I'm tempted to ask, "Which bits?"'

'We all have a dark side.' A banal little remark intended to end the conversation. Peter was looking out of the window at the corner of the courtyard where Justine and Adam were sitting. 'Isn't that Justine Braithewaite?'

'Yes. The kid's my nephew. She looks after him.'

They looked at each other, Peter visibly registering that he didn't know Stephen well enough to ask the question he wanted to ask. The pain in his eyes and the smile on his lips were an uncomfortable combination to witness. Stephen looked away. He'd loved her – whatever else was fake, that, at least, was real.

A second later Stephen was able to say, 'I think it's your turn.' And then he moved deliberately further along the bar so that they wouldn't need to speak again.

But when, an hour later, Justine said, 'I think we ought to be going. Adam's got school tomorrow,' Peter immediately swung round to look in their direction, almost as if he'd heard what she said, though that was quite impossible. As Stephen counted out a tip, then followed her into the street, she turned and looked back, scanning the crowded tables. Peter was standing up under one of the tall lights, hair gleaming, face in shadow, watching her go.

Twenty

A man gets off a train, looks at the sky and the surrounding fields, then shoulders his kitbag and sets off from the station, trudging up half-known roads, unloading hell behind him, step by step.

It's part of English mythology, that image of the soldier returning, but it depends for its power on the existence of an unchanging countryside. Perhaps it had never been true, had only ever been a sentimental urban fantasy, or perhaps something deeper – some memory of the great forest. Sherwood. Arden. Certainly Stephen had returned to find a countryside in crisis. Boarded-up shops and cafés, empty fields, strips of yellow tape that nobody had bothered to remove even after the paths reopened, just as nobody had bothered to remove the disinfectant mats that now lay at the entrance to every tourist attraction, bleached and baking in the sun.

The weather continued fine, amazingly warm for the time of year. Every morning he looked up at the trees and thought that today – with only a few more hours of sun – the green-gold haze on the branches would burst into leaf, but evening came and the trees were unchanged. He lived in the hollow of a green wave, knowing it couldn't last, that it must end soon. These weeks seemed to have the shaped quality of the past.

One evening he was standing in the garden looking into the copse, when he heard a cough behind him. Robert.

'I came through. I did ring the bell, but I couldn't make you hear.'

Typical of Robert to emphasize that he hadn't overstepped the bounds of propriety, but also typical that he didn't assume he could enter the cottage whenever he chose merely because he owned it. Sometimes Stephen made an effort to see his brother as a stranger might, to discard the past faces that lay under the skin of this middle-aged face. The good little boy, breathing through his nose as he pushed a crayon across the page; the priggish adolescent – he had been priggish, surely? – this couldn't be all sibling rivalry – the brash medical student who talked about diseased bowels till he made you want to puke. Shy at his wedding, proud at Adam's christening and no doubt, in countless consultations, day after day, kind, sensitive, tenacious, efficient. A proper life. That was the way Stephen thought about Robert – a man who lived a proper life. By implication, a life unlike his own, and yet he didn't regret his choice of career.

They stood together by the hedge, with this life-long competition behind them, and talked about the weather.

'The lawn needs mowing,' Robert said.

'Big garden.'

'Yeah, too big.'

'Beth likes gardening. She always seems to be potting on or pricking out or something.'

'Yes, but it's too much for her. You need somebody going at it full time.'

They drifted back into the cottage, where Stephen, after a glance at his watch, offered Robert a whisky. He expected Robert to refuse – he was almost ostentatiously abstemious – but this time he nodded, and sat down heavily on the sofa.

Stephen poured himself his usual generous double, then paused. 'You're not driving again this evening?'

'No. I'm in now for the night.' He sounded like somebody returning to an open prison. Stephen revised his estimate of what might be acceptable and handed him a glass so strong he choked on the first gulp.

'My God, Stephen.'

'You sound as if you need it.'

Robert sighed noisily, puffing out his cheeks, making a joke of unhappiness. 'Is it that obvious?'

Stephen sat in the chair opposite. 'Not to somebody who hasn't known you all your life.'

'Oh, I'm all right,' Robert said. 'I must say, Stephen, you look a hundred per cent better than you did when you arrived.'

'I feel it. I jogged three miles yesterday.'

'Good.'

'*And* it was up hill all the way. Do you know from the top of that hill you can see three burnt areas? Where the pyres were. I'd no idea they were as close as that.'

'It started two miles down the road. We got the first blast. They closed the roads – sent in the army. You could smell the carcasses for miles. I used to smell them on my skin at work.'

'Yes, the smell does linger a bit.'

Robert took another gulp of whisky. 'I say "we" but of course it isn't "we". We're not part of it. Country life, I mean. We just float on the surface like scum.'

'Scum?'

A short laugh. 'You know what I mean. Buy up the houses. Commute into work. We don't give anything back. I suppose Beth does a bit, more than me, anyway.' He shook his head, drank again. 'She's a pillar of the community, in fact.'

It's difficult to deal with anger when the topic under discussion isn't what's causing the anger. That was Stephen's impression of Robert this evening, that he was above all else a very angry man, though the anger was continually suppressed. A kind of ongoing genial rage. No doubt working in the NHS gave plenty of cause for irritation, but he suspected the roots of Robert's malaise lay closer to home.

'Bad day at work?' Stephen asked reluctantly. He didn't really want to talk about it.

'No, not particularly. In fact, we got the grant. Do you remember I told you, the one I was applying for?'

'Good. Well done. How much?'

'Three million.'

'My God, Robert.'

'It's not going into my pocket.' He hesitated. 'Beth finds it very difficult.'

'Oh? Why?'

'Because part of the research involves the use of human embryos. And she has ethical objections. I suppose I shouldn't have told her . . . But then if you can't talk about the big moments, what kind of marriage is it?'

'Pretty typical, I should think. A lot of married people live separate lives. They reach some kind of *modus vivendi*, and . . .' He shrugged. 'Don't ask me. I didn't manage it.'

'All I know is I'm bloody well pig sick of it. I'm fed up with getting into bed every night with somebody who thinks I'm Josef Mengele.'

'I can see you might get tired of that.'

'It's not funny, Stephen. She thinks I kill babies.'

'And it's not a minor flaw, is it? Not something you can overlook.' He smiled. 'There must be one or two women around who *don't* think you're Josef Mengele.'

'Yes.'

Said flatly. Evidently no confidences were to be offered on that subject. 'How bad is it?'

'I don't know. There's Adam . . .'

'Oh. That bad.'

'And there's the house. I can't leave her stuck in there. She's scared stiff when I'm away.'

'You do go away quite a bit.'

'I have to. It's part of the job.'

A pause. 'So what are you saying, Robert?'

'That I've got to make a go of it.'

'Would moving into town help?'

'She loves the garden.'

Stephen had become aware of strains in his brother's marriage, though when he first arrived he'd assumed it to be entirely happy. It seemed to him now there'd been a lot of masochism involved in his first impressions. He'd almost wanted Robert's life to be in every way more successful than his own. It was a kind of wallowing in his own failure. But he was surprised to find Robert was thinking of moving out. 'Are Beth's objections religious?'

'Yes. And they seem to be growing on her. It happens to some women at the menopause. I can't respect it. I wish I could.'

'Then you have to shut up and leave it alone. Can't Alec Braithewaite talk to her? Isn't he –'

'He agrees with her.'

'Ah, not entirely a menopausal symptom, then?'

'No, I know. I'm being arrogant. Anyway, thanks for the drink. Thanks for listening.'

He tossed back the last of the whisky, almost like a foreign correspondent. Stephen was proud of him.

'Do *you* have any views about it?'

'What? Research on human embryos?' Stephen shrugged. 'I've seen too many kids blown to bits to worry about that.' He took Robert's glass. 'How's Adam?'

'Running Justine ragged, poor girl.'

A slight constraint. Of course Robert and Beth knew. They couldn't not know, with Justine's car parked outside the cottage most evenings and occasionally all night.

'Oh, by the way, Beth wants to know if you'd like to come round for lunch on Sunday.'

Stephen nodded. 'Yeah, love to.' He showed Robert to the door and watched him stride away along the country lane, looking bizarrely out of place in his shiny black shoes and dark grey suit.

Twenty-one

Sunday dawned bright and clear. After a good morning's work – he was on the home straight now, beginning to relax – Stephen set off to the farmhouse. He knew Justine was going to be there because she'd mentioned it, but he wasn't sure if there were to be any other guests. It had crossed his mind that a family lunch, just the four of them – and Adam, too, of course – might be Beth's way of acknowledging the relationship.

A tight-lipped Justine met him at the door. She'd seemed doubtful about the invitation when she first mentioned it, but evidently something had happened to disperse the doubt. She was now unequivocally livid. 'You'd better wait in the conservatory,' she told him rather ungraciously. 'Beth'll be along in a minute.'

She was wearing an apron over her dress, and he supposed that was what had made her angry – being forced into the dual role of guest and kitchen assistant. She bustled off. Looking at that rather broad and firm backside, he thought, God help the patients who don't watch their cholesterol levels – she'll give them hell.

Adam was in the conservatory, his freshly brushed hair sticking up in spikes, and, beside him, glass in hand, was Robert, chatting to a man in black with silver hair. When he turned round, he revealed an intelligent sheep's face, the eyes at once keenly alert and innocent.

'Alec, this is my brother, Stephen,' Robert said. 'Stephen, Alec Braithewaite.'

They shook hands.

'Justine's father,' Robert added.

'Yes,' said Stephen.

'Justine's talked about you a lot,' Alec said.

Stephen took the glass Robert held out to him, noticing that without being asked Robert had poured him an extra stiff whisky. Alec was on sherry. Stephen raised his glass, looking intently into Robert's eyes, trying to relay the message, 'If you think a double whisky's going to get round me, you two-faced, treacherous, lying, conniving bastard, apology for a brother, you can think again.'

'Oh?' Stephen said.

'She admires your work. Bit of hero-worship, I think.'

The doorbell rang. Robert was about to move off when 'I'll go!' Justine called from the hall.

Feminine flutterings and flutings and cooings, though a bit one-sided – Justine seemed to be growling – and then Angela came into the room, looked at Alec, blushed, looked down and said in reply to Robert's question that she might just have a glass of white wine. But only a small one, she was driving.

'You can leave your car here,' Alec said. 'If Robert doesn't mind. I can't drink anyway. I've got Evensong.'

'Oh, dear.'

Much to Stephen's relief, Alec and Angela had eyes only for each other, and he was able to withdraw from the conversation and corner Robert. 'He's an intelligent man,' Robert said blandly. 'You'd like him.'

'Is that why he's here?'

Robert raised his eyebrows. 'He's here because he's Beth's vicar and our neighbour and we like him. Don't be so bloody paranoid. Here, have another whisky.' He looked round the room. 'We don't do this often enough. It's bad for a marriage when you get too isolated.'

'Is it?'

An awkward pause.

'Well, isn't it?'

'I think the trouble comes first. The isolation's just a symptom.'

'All I know is, it's bad for mine,' Robert said, wincing.

'You're hardly an isolated *couple*. You're never here.'

That wasn't tactful, but Stephen couldn't help himself.

'I thought I might take Beth away for a few days. Try to sort things out.'

'Oh, where are you going?'

'Paris, I thought.'

'Oh, very nice.'

'Paris in the spring.'

'Don't spend all the time arguing about stem-cell research, will you?'

'No-o, I thought we'd do the sort of things people normally do in Paris.'

'Eat croissants in bed.'

'That sort of thing. Bed, anyway.'

'"Not tonight, Josef."'

'You're a cruel bastard, Stephen.'

A wisp of cloud drifted across the sun. The shadows of the trees in the garden lay in a network all over the black-and-white tiled floor, gleaming and dancing.

'The right time of year for it, anyway,' Stephen said, feeling a stab of envy, not of Robert and Beth but of some ideal couple – himself and Nerys twenty years ago, perhaps. Not as they actually were, but as they ought to have been.

Robert turned. Stephen became aware of a very tall, red-haired youth, all angst and acne, hesitating in the doorway. The doorbell hadn't rung, so he must have been in the bathroom or somewhere else in the house. Robert waved to him and he came across, head down, taking his time.

'Mark, this is my brother, Stephen. Stephen, Mark Callender. I'm supervising Mark's Ph.D., which' – a broad smile – 'is going very well.'

Mark was so shy he needed all the boosts Robert could give him. Unless he had something dreadfully wrong with his bladder, he must have been hiding in the bathroom rather than visiting it. Watching Robert with him, turning the full force of his attention on Mark, making him feel at ease and eventually even risk a smile, Stephen saw what only a few days before he'd tried to see, and failed: Robert as he might appear to a stranger meeting him for the first time. Charismatic was the word that sprang to mind, not because he made a parade of charm and intelligence, or tried in any way to attract attention to himself, but because he didn't. His whole attention was focused outwards. At the moment, this awkward young man felt himself to be the centre of the universe, and he blossomed. With women, the technique would be devastating.

Beth appeared, presumably leaving Justine to put the finishing touches to the meal. She looked tired, and again he had the sense of somebody who was being gently and persistently erased. She and Angela were evidently close and were soon deep in conversation, leaving him to talk to Alec.

'I met a friend of yours in Newcastle the other day. Peter Wingrave.'

'Ah, Peter, yes.'

'I gather he's been in prison?'

Alec blinked rapidly. 'Did he tell you that?'

'No, I –'

'Ah. Justine.'

'No, not Justine. I guessed. It wasn't particularly difficult – he gave me two stories to read, one of which could only have been written by somebody who'd been inside.'

'I suppose he might have worked in one?'

'He might.'

'What did you think of the stories?'

'Very good. Very disturbing. And both of them – it's only just struck me – were about stalking.'

'Yes, he's interested in that. Because it's a pattern of behaviour that's been known about for centuries and has only quite recently been declared pathological. He's interested in the way psychiatry's expanded and laid claim to previously . . . neutral, or . . . anyway non-pathological areas of human behaviour.'

'There was nothing "neutral" about the behaviour in his stories. Torture. Mental and physical. Murder.'

Another sip of the sherry, another blink of the mild but far from stupid blue eyes.

'What did he do?' Stephen asked.

'I can't tell you.'

'You mean you don't know?'

'No.'

'No, you don't know, or no, you won't tell me?'

'No, I can't tell you.'

'Stalking?'

'I can't tell you.'

Stephen stayed silent, and, as he'd rather expected, Alec cracked. 'I doubt if he'd use his personal experiences in his stories.'

'Why not? People do. He certainly used the setting.'

'I just don't think he would.'

Beth was looking in their direction, aware of some exchange going on that went well beyond pre-Sunday lunch chat.

'You won't mention Peter's prison record to anybody else, will you? I mean, it could be very damaging, and' – a deep sigh caught and held – 'I do think he deserves some credit for the way he's rebuilt his life.'

'Oh, don't worry, I won't go round blabbing.'

'Good.'

'Of course, you're committed to the idea that people can change. I mean . . .' Stephen's gaze lingered almost insultingly on the dog collar. 'Professionally.'

'Can *be* changed. As an act of individual will, no, I'm not sure I do believe it. I think that's actually quite a secular belief. Therapy. Self-help books . . . It's an industry, isn't it?' A pause. 'And what about you? Do you believe people can change – or be changed?'

'I think they can learn to manage themselves better.'

'Sounds a bit bleak.'

It was strange to be forced to delineate his beliefs in this way. A taboo was being broken. 'I believe people can heal themselves.'

'Themselves?'

'Yes.'

'How?'

'How?'

'Ye-es. How?'

Stephen spread his hands. 'Create something. Almost anything. Get your body moving. Have sex.'

'Sex? Not love?'

'Love's a bonus.' He'd forgotten, as he spoke, that he was having this therapeutic sex with Alec's teenage daughter, and that in the nature of things Alec was unlikely to be pleased.

Beth appeared at his elbow and he turned to her with some relief. 'I hear you're off to Paris.'

'Yes.' She flushed and looked sideways at Robert, who was chatting to Mark and Angela. 'I just hope things'll be all right here.'

'I'm sure they will,' Stephen said. 'Justine's very competent. You're a lucky man,' he added to Alec, raising his glass.

The doorbell rang again. So that's what they'd been waiting for. Another guest.

Robert went this time, and came back into the room with Kate Frobisher, almost unrecognizable, to Stephen at any rate, in a smart dress, earrings and make-up. She looked around the room as Robert gave her a drink, and her eye lighted first on Stephen. He moved towards her and, aware of being the focus of all eyes in the room, kissed her on the cheek. When he looked round, he saw Justine standing inside the doorway watching him.

A couple of minutes later Beth announced that lunch was ready and they all trooped along to the dining room.

So that's it, Stephen thought, looking around the group. Beth and Robert, Alec and Angela, Justine and Mark, Kate and himself. The animals went in two by two, the elephant and the kangaroo. It wasn't, to be fair, easy to see what else Beth could have done, but it had made Justine very angry. He wasn't particularly thrilled about it himself. Ah, well, two hours, three at the most, and they could all go back home.

He'd have to watch what he drank, though. Three whiskies on an empty stomach had already loosened his tongue, and in retrospect he regretted the conversation with Alec.

*

Lunch was surprisingly pleasant, given that two of the guests were thinking of murdering their hostess. Beth appeared relaxed, though she listened more than she spoke. Stephen, observing her, thought that he'd never seen her properly before. He was still struck by that curiously blurred quality of her features, but he also noticed now a certain steeliness, even aggression. Robert, at the other end of the table, though he radiated energy, would be no match for her. Or at least not in this domestic setting, but then, like so many workaholic men, Robert was passive in his own home, content to leave everything to his wife, to be physically present and emotionally absent at the same time. He wouldn't leave her. It would take too much time away from his precious research.

Kate was charming, and he spoke mainly to her. She looked ten years younger, and not merely because of the make-up. Her shoulder was better. The manipulation under a general anaesthetic had worked brilliantly. Even if it hadn't been for the problems with Peter – here she lowered her voice – she'd have been able to manage on her own now.

'Did Peter get back to you?'

'Yes, he sent me a very nice letter saying how pleased he was I was better and thanking me –'

'What was he thanking you for?'

'The experience – he said it had been very important to him, and . . .' A self-deprecating smile. 'I gave him a month's wages in lieu of notice.'

'Kate.'

'We-ell . . . I thought, in the end, what's the point of having a confrontation? And when I look back, I think my own reaction was pretty odd. Mad. I must have been very low in confidence or something because I really felt that dressing-up thing was saying something about *me*. And, of course, it wasn't – it was entirely about him.'

'You think you overreacted? I don't think you did.'

'No, I think I was right to get rid of him. It'd . . . It was really peculiar. It'd turned into a kind of battle . . .' She raised her hands. 'Anyway, it's over now, and my shoulder's better, and . . . It's great, just to be able to put on a sweater and not get stuck halfway.'

Faced with the mental image of Kate pulling on a sweater, Stephen became aware of her perfume, her closeness. Sunlight gilded the lines of her throat and neck where Ben's amulet caught the light and glittered. She asked how he was getting on with the book, and he told her quite well. He was two thirds of the way through the final draft, though he might have to break off and go down to London for a few days to sort things out down there. 'The money's come through on the house. So we ought to be able to get the divorce settlement sorted out, and then . . .'

'Will you move back to London?'

'I don't know. The obvious thing to do is rent and wait for the market to collapse. And I'm happy here, for the time being. I don't know what it's going to be like when the book's finished and I'm trying to earn my living freelance. I know people say you can do it with just e-mails and faxes, but I'm not sure. I don't know to what extent you really need to be a face on the scene.'

'You won't go back full time?'

'Oh, no.'

'Congratulations. You've actually done what Ben always said he would do.' Her fingers strayed to the amulet round her neck. 'And never did.'

Stephen said quickly, 'Anyway, all that's in the future. At the moment I feel everything's on hold till the book's finished. It's ridiculous. I know I shouldn't be doing it.'

'What?'

'Sacrificing life to work.'

She laughed. 'Tell me about it.'

She seemed genuinely interested in his plans, and that meant a lot. If he only came away from his time in the north with Kate's friendship, it would have been time well spent. Meanwhile, he really ought to cut back on the drinking. Robert, who was a generous host, kept replenishing his glass, which made it difficult to keep track. He was slightly drunk, not incapacitated, but floating on a golden cloud two or three inches above the carpet. He'd reached the stage of being in love with all the women in the room: the glint of down on Angela's cheek, Justine's ferocious blue-eyed stare – she seemed to be glaring at him, he couldn't think why – Kate's hands, which she was so ashamed of. Even with make-up on, and jewellery, she did nothing to draw attention to them, no nail varnish, no rings, except her wedding ring, and he wanted to say, 'You're wrong about them. They're beautiful.' Justine's mouth was up to its usual trick of erasing lipstick. He found that incredibly erotic: the body rejecting artifice, so much sexier than any of the obvious things. He was trying to remember a time – he couldn't even recall where, let alone when – he and Ben had been at some kind of lap-dancing club. God knows why, it wasn't the kind of thing they went in for, but somehow there they were. Crowded room, smoke, drink, blue berets everywhere. Wherever two or three peace-keepers are gathered together in the UN's name, there is a lap-dancer in the midst of them – not always voluntarily either. And despite knowing that many of these women were victims, he'd had a glimpse of why some men hate women. It's demeaning to find yourself salivating like one of Pavlov's bloody dogs just because some woman you don't even fancy pushes her arse into your face. How much sexier the glimpse of a nipple under a white shirt blouse, especially when the girl doesn't even know she's showing it. Justine was now positively glaring, but when he raised his eyebrows and mouthed 'What?' she turned away and focused her whole attention on Mark, who was gazing at her like a love-sick calf.

When the time came to clear the table, Justine did it with such a startling bang and clatter he feared for the plates. Alec looked at her, reflectively, and then at Stephen. Stephen found it surprisingly difficult to meet his gaze. Are your intentions towards my daughter honourable? Somewhere, in the air above their heads, the ridiculous Victorian question hovered, and could not, despite the modern world with all its changes and complexities, be entirely discounted. No, not honourable, Stephen said, looking at the flicker of sunlight on the table cloth, but, at least, I hope, kind.

They went into the drawing room for coffee, and Stephen sat by Angela, who answered his remarks almost at random, her eyes never leaving Alec's face. There were two hectic spots on her cheeks, she had a general air of recklessness and abandon. She'd grown tired, he could tell, of being the person she was, this silly menopausal woman who kept rams as pets and arranged flowers in the church and fell obviously, humiliatingly, in love with the vicar. What an identity to cart about in the twenty-first century. She had no possible grounds for believing in her own existence. Yet here she was, and he could sense her summoning up the courage to change or ruin her life.

Alec was talking to Robert about the ethics committee they both served on. Oh, God, Stephen thought, blastocysts again. Robert was unfailingly courteous, but he was off duty. Alec, of course, was not.

After a while Stephen became aware that Justine had not joined them. He went down to the kitchen to find her beginning to wash the dishes. Beth, he knew from previous visits, never trusted this particular service to the dishwasher. Justine squirted washing-up liquid at the bowl as if she were wielding a flame-thrower. A huge foaming monster drooped and glooped over the edges of the sink, and when she turned round to face him, shaking her hands, great blobs of foam flew off into the air, one landing on his cheek where it popped stinging bubbles into his eye.

'Leave that. Come on upstairs.'

'It won't take a minute.' Tight-lipped. 'Anyway, I'm surprised you noticed I wasn't there.'

'What does that mean?'

'You know what I mean.'

He put a hand on her shoulder. 'Justine.'

'Sober up, Stephen, you're pathetic.'

'What?' He tried a cooler approach. 'What's wrong?'

'Your bloody sister-in-law, for one thing. She should concentrate on her own marriage, not go poking her nose into other people's lives. I suppose you know Robert's screwing around?'

'I think he might have a girlfriend.'

'*A* girlfrien*d*? He fucks his way round the conference circuit like a rabbit on amphetamines.'

He was shocked. 'Has he tried it on with you?'

'Oh, come on. Do you really think your brother's stupid enough to shit on his own doorstep? I don't think so. Anyway, he's never here. And neither of them' – she jerked her thumb at the window – 'pay anything like enough attention to *that.*'

Adam had slipped away from the table as soon after the pudding as he reasonably could and was now mooching about in the garden, poking a long stick into the pond.

'What's he doing?'

'Getting dead leaves out.'

'She wasn't really interfering. She just invited a few people for lunch. That's all she's done.'

'Bollocks.' Another plate banged down on to the

draining board. 'She knows exactly what she's doing. It's bad enough having Romeo and bloody Juliet up there, without you slobbering over Kate as well.'

He couldn't believe his ears. 'Slobbering?'

Another clatter of irreplaceable Georgian glass.

'Justine. Leave the dishes. Hit me.'

'Don't tempt me.'

There was a tremor in her voice that he hoped was the beginning of laughter, but he wasn't confident enough to presume on it. He was right.

At that moment they heard an embarrassed cough and turned to see Mark Callender hovering in the doorway, red-faced and awkward, with a tray of coffee cups in his hands.

'WHAT DO YOU WANT?' Justine roared.

It was blindingly obvious what he wanted, the poor sod.

'I brought these.'

Stephen pointed to the table. 'Just put them down there, will you?'

Mark retreated to the safety of the hall. 'I think Mr Braithewaite's leaving.'

'Right,' Justine said, pulling off her apron. 'I'm out of here.'

Stephen tried to take her in his arms, but she pushed him away. 'Don't burn too many boats,' he called after her.

'You're the one who's done that. The whole bloody armada.'

Twenty-two

Stephen hadn't expected Justine to come to the cottage that evening, but she did, late, tear-stained and miserable.

'Dad and Angela are getting married,' she said.

'Good,' he said, after a second's pause.

'Good?'

'It's going to make it a lot easier for you to go away. You wouldn't want to leave him on his own.'

'No-o.'

Then the wails started. He hadn't believed her capable of such uninhibited, childlike distress. 'What's wrong?' he said. 'What is it?'

'Nobody loves *me*.'

'Your father loves you.' A bit late, lamely and lacking all conviction, he added, 'I love you.'

She uncovered her face, and gave him a sharp look. She wasn't so far gone that insincerity didn't penetrate. 'You don't have to say it.' Suddenly, she stopped crying, and said briskly, 'My mother didn't love me.'

'I'm sure she did.' But he cringed as he said it, aware of the pointlessness of pronouncing on the feelings of a woman he'd never met.

'Not enough to stick around. You know, it's difficult to expect other people to treat you decently when . . .'

'No, I know.' The darkness at the uncurtained windows pressed in on them. 'And Peter can't have helped.'

'No. So OK, he was bad news, and he would've been for anybody, I don't think it was just me, but I fell for him. I can't help thinking somebody else mightn't have done, not in the same way. I clutched at it.'

'Oh, for heaven's sake, stop beating yourself up. He's attractive, he's charming, he's good-looking. If it came to a pulling contest, he'd do a helluva lot better than Mark.'

'That's true.'

'Though apparently not as well as my brother.'

'You're jealous.'

'Too bloody right I'm jealous.'

How could he have got his own brother so wrong. But he couldn't sort that out now. 'Look, getting back to Peter, in ten years' time you're going to believe you had a bloody good screw and dumped him. *You* dumped *him*. So just press fast-forward and start believing it now.'

She was lying in his arms on the bed, looking through the open curtains at the moon drifting between high towers of cloud.

'It isn't as easy as that. And in any case you don't mean it, you know you don't.' She sniffed, wiping tears away on the back of her hand. 'Dad liked you, by the way.'

'I can't think why. He must know I'm married.'

'I haven't told him.'

'He knows.'

'Well, I am nineteen –'

'More to the point, Mark liked *you*.'

'Yes, I know. He asked me to go out with him.'

'Before or after you yelled at him?'

'After.'

'Kinky sod. Will you go?'

'Do you think I should?'

'Do you want to?'

'I didn't think he was all that attractive. Perhaps as a friend . . .'

'If he's a possible friend, you should go. Mind you, I'm not sure that's what *he* wants.'

'He's just finished doing Medicine at Cambridge.'

'Well, then.'

'You're supposed to be jealous.'

'I've no right to be jealous. Have I?'

She didn't answer. After a few seconds, she rolled over and, in a tense silence, they tried to get to sleep.

He woke the following morning knowing before he opened his eyes that something was wrong. Looking into the mirror as he shaved, his expression was not that conspiratorial self-acceptance he'd found so attractive in Goya's self-portrait. Far from it. He craned his head back, guiding the razor underneath his chin, and he didn't like anything he saw.

He made coffee and then took his toast into the living room to watch the television news. Israeli tanks bombarding Jenin. An old woman in a headscarf crying in the ruins of her home. Justine, who seemed to have lost her appetite for fry-ups, peeled and ate an orange.

When the news was over, she said, 'Dad says you were asking questions about Peter before lunch. Why?'

'I wanted to hear what he'd say.'

'He says you kept asking what Peter did.'

He didn't answer.

'Whatever it was, he's been out five years and he hasn't done it again.'

'How do you know, if you don't know what it was?'

'You don't give anybody the benefit of the doubt, do you?'

'Not often.'

'The truth is, you've been digging around in violence so long you can't see anything else.'

'I see you.'

'Do you?'

Stephen sighed. This was a surprisingly married conversation to be having with a girlfriend. It had that intense acrimonious pointlessness that only comes from long years of cohabitation.

'Why do you do it?'

'What?'

She jerked her head at the girl who was talking to camera. 'That. Be a war correspondent.'

'Foreign.' The distinction mattered. He was damned if he was going to call himself after an activity he despised.

'You covered a helluva lot of wars.'

'They were there to be covered. I didn't start them.'

'You know there's a Barbara Vine book called *A Dark Adapted Eye*? That's what you've got.'

'Now you're being silly.'

'No, I'm not. People get *into* darkness, to the point where it's the light that hurts.'

'OK,' he said. 'Why did I do it? Adventure, proving myself, proving I could take it – and once that wore off, which it does, very quickly, being in the know. That sort of thing.'

She was looking at him scornfully.

'Yeah, OK. I know – pathetic. But why do you think people become doctors? Pure altruism? I don't think so.'

'Why, then?'

'Knowledge. Access to secrets. Power.'

'Not the only reasons.'

'There are plenty of good reasons for being a war correspondent. Witnessing. Giving people the raw material to make moral judgements.'

'But you said yourself, the witness turns into an audience, and then you're not witnessing any more, you're disseminating.'

He'd forgotten he'd said that. 'If you mean, "Was I damaged by it?" Yeah. I don't think it's inevitable, I can think of plenty of people who haven't been, but, yeah, I think I was. Can it be repaired? Some of it. Probably not all of it, but that's me –' He turned to face her. 'Imperfect, messed up, thoroughly unsatisfactory – and you'd better get used to it, sweetheart, because there's a couple of million more of us out there.'

She stared directly into his eyes, the skin around her own eyes swollen from last night's tears. 'You're getting tired of this, aren't you?'

'It's not that.'

'What, then?'

'I've always known it can't last. I accept that. And whenever you go, I won't try to hold you back. You will go with my blessing.' That sounded cringe-makingly pompous, but it had to be said.

She nodded. A few minutes later, still silent, she started to get dressed.

At the door, as she was leaving, she said, 'Oh, I almost forgot. Beth wants to see you.'

'What about?'

A shrug, and she was gone.

He couldn't guess what the summons to the farmhouse might be about. If it had anything to do with Justine, he was prepared to hit back. He no longer saw his brother's wife as the fragile half-erased victim of Robert's more forceful personality, but as somebody altogether more formidable. But she had no possible right to interfere. Locking the door, deciding that no, he didn't need to wear a sweater for the quick walk up the lane, he planned what he would say: something about the advisability of taking care of her own family first. Adam was getting a bloody raw deal in this situation, and, if provoked, he was prepared to come right out and say so. At some level, anyway, she must know that.

He walked to the farmhouse along the narrow path that led between high hawthorn hedges bursting into leaf, passed the pond with its rutted edges, green goose shit everywhere, and the geese themselves hissing and swaying towards him. The back door was open. In the band of sunshine that fell across the stone-flagged floor, there were three pairs of wellingtons, standing side by side, two of them green, the other, smaller pair in navy-blue and red. Once, not so long ago, he'd have felt a twinge of envy.

Beth's voice came drifting out to him. 'In here.'

She was in the conservatory. None of the windows was open, and he felt the clammy heat slick his face with sweat before he reached her. She was standing in front of a long table filling pots with compost. There were blue hyacinths blooming in a bowl beside her, spiralling up towards the light. Her fingers were covered with soil. She wiped the sweat away from her upper lip with one freckled forearm and smiled at him.

'Hello,' he said, and stood waiting. When nothing, apart from the returned greeting, was forthcoming, he said, 'What a marvellous colour.'

'Yes, isn't it? I like them so much better than the pink ones.'

He waited. She seemed to be finding this difficult.

'Robert and I were wondering if you'd do something for us?'

'Of course. Anything I can.'

'It's just that, you know we've been planning this little trip to Paris? It's not long, just the three nights, but I'm a bit worried about leaving Justine here on her own. We've had a few silent calls, and . . . well, they're always a little bit disturbing, aren't they? You always think it might be burglars checking to see if you're in . . .'

Or one of Robert's girlfriends trying to reach Robert.

'I mean, I know she's nineteen and plenty of girls that age have their own children . . .'

'Not ten-year-olds.'

'No, that's true. Anyway, we were wondering if you'd step into the breach, as it were.'

'You mean live in?' He was enjoying this.

'Yes, I think it would have to be in. There are plenty of beds.'

'And Justine would be . . . ?'

'She'd be here too. And of course she'd take care of Adam during the day, so you wouldn't have to stop work. Only we'd be happier if you were here at night.'

'Sounds all right to me. When?'

'Next weekend. We thought Friday till Monday.'

'Yes, fine. What brought this on?'

'Oh, I don't know.' She was about to say something bland about the long winter, working too hard . . . 'Things aren't good,' she seemed to surprise herself by saying.

'Between you and Robert?'

An embarrassed nod, but then immediately she began to back off. A lot of it was just tiredness, Robert working all hours, she was doing a full-time job . . . 'And this is a big place.' She gazed round her with a hopeless expression, though the house was beautifully kept.

'You're obviously happy doing what you're doing now. The garden . . .'

'Yes, but –'

'I suppose it's a big place to run on one income.'

'No, we could afford it, all right. The truth is I think if I were "just a housewife" . . .' She was sketching inverted commas in the air as she spoke, but she meant it. '. . . Robert would get bored with me. Correction. Even more bored. You know he's seeing somebody?'

Everybody, according to Justine. 'No?'

'I just wondered if he'd talked to you.'

She didn't know, she was just guessing. 'No, and I wouldn't want him to.' He hesitated, wishing he hadn't started this conversation. 'He won't leave you.'

'You mean he won't leave Adam.'

That was exactly what he'd meant, but he could see she mightn't find it encouraging. 'Marriages go through all sorts of phases, Beth. The fact is you chose each other. And that says something about you which is probably still true.'

Stephen was feeling uncomfortable. His only qualification for advising on marriage was having made a mess of his own.

'You know what I'd really like?' she said, suddenly brightening. 'A greenhouse. A big one, the kind they have in nurseries, not one of those fiddly little things. That's what I really like – plants.'

'Then go for it. You're lucky to have a passion like that – most people don't. And it'd fit in better with Adam.'

'Oh, Adam's all right.'

As if summoned, like the devil, by the mention of his

name, Adam appeared in the doorway. Stephen turned to him. 'You know what, Adam, I think it's time we went and saw Archie again.' One of the most successful days he and Justine and Adam had spent together had been at the Bird of Prey Centre. 'If we're very nice to Phil, he might let you fly him this time.'

Adam was beaming.

'Who's Archie?' asked Beth.

'An eagle owl,' Adam said. 'He's huge, isn't he, Stephen? Bigger than an eagle.'

'And he's in love with Phil, isn't he?'

Adam giggled. 'He keeps trying to mate with his glove. When can we go?'

'Next weekend, when Mum and Dad are in Paris.'

'Right,' Adam said, and marched up the stairs, not looking back.

Stephen turned and found Beth looking at him with a rather wry expression. She said, 'It's very easy, you know, being an uncle.'

'Oh, I'm sure. Uncles aren't responsible for how they turn out.'

Twenty-three

And so, that Thursday, after driving Robert and Beth to the airport, Stephen moved some of his things up to the farmhouse and started playing house with Justine. That's what it felt like – a holiday from adult life. The mere fact that the house was not his gave him an Alice-in-Wonderland feeling. He seemed to be wandering around between the chair legs while items of furniture loomed above him, mysterious with withheld significance. They made him feel insubstantial, these rooms with their carefully selected antiques, the fruits of years of settled, successful endeavour, and yet the feeling was not entirely unpleasant. Like Goldilocks in the house of the three bears, he had a sense of danger and transgression. He and Justine cooked meals for themselves and Adam, and sat down at the long table in the kitchen to eat them, and there was always this feeling of innocence and danger combined.

It was a happy time. He felt as irresponsible and carefree as Adam, or rather as Adam would have felt if he'd been a different sort of child. But even Adam seemed to feel liberated. He flew Archie, and Stephen took photographs of the moment when the eagle owl landed on his glove. Adam's face was screwed up in fear, braced to take the weight, then amazed, as the great wings settled and folded and the golden eyes turned on him, that the bird was so light.

Stephen had the photos developed in Sainsbury's, bought frames and hung them on the wall of Adam's room.

They lived an old-fashioned circa 1950s family life, playing Monopoly in the evenings, going for walks in the forest, feeding the deer, running Adam to the point of exhaustion on the sands. His ambition, he told Stephen, was to have a dog.

'Well, why not?' Stephen said.

'Because there's nobody here in the day. It'd be cruel.'

'What's cruel,' Stephen said, as he and Justine sat by the fire that evening, after Adam had gone to bed, 'is the entire situation. I mean, if Beth was desperate to be a hospital administrator, fine, but she isn't. She'd far rather be at home with the garden. That's what she really wants to do, and if she did that, Adam could have his dog.'

'Yes,' Justine said. 'But there's no status in it.'

'There is. I'd respect her for it.'

'Robert's friends wouldn't. Or anyway she thinks they wouldn't.'

'It shouldn't matter what they think.'

'But it does. She's terrified of being a stay-at-home mum, that's all.'

'So what's your solution?'

'Don't have kids.'

'It's a bit late for that – he's ten. Seriously.'

She shrugged. 'If I ever had one, I'd like to think I could stay at home and take care of it myself and not feel I was making some kind of inferior choice. It's quite old-fashioned, that idea that all your status comes from work.'

Oh, the joys of being nineteen. Everything's so easy.

'It's about sex, though, isn't it? She thinks if she's not out there, she'll lose him.'

'She's lost him anyway. Sexually.'

Stephen wanted to press her for more information – he felt she knew more than she was saying – but he didn't think he should. Her outburst in the kitchen after Sunday lunch had been driven by her own unhappiness and he knew she regretted it. He wondered how she knew, but then remembered she had a friend in the medical school where Robert taught. It might be no more than student gossip. The private lives of lecturers never lose anything in the telling. But he couldn't ask. 'Come on,' he said, standing up. 'Let's go to bed.'

Bed had become the place they went to sleep. Partly he felt inhibited having sex in his brother's house – almost as if Robert had taken on the role of parent – but also, his relationship with Justine was changing in ways he didn't understand. Whatever the reason, during that long weekend, there was no attempt at love-making until the final night.

Beth had just rung to confirm that she and Robert would be back home late the following morning. She sounded eager to be back, though whether that meant the break had been a failure or a brilliant success wasn't clear. Justine put down the phone and said, 'That's it, then.'

He felt both relieved and sad. The smell of logs burning in the grate brought an autumnal melancholy into the spring evening. They went on talking for a while, but they were both tired. She started getting ready for bed. He stood on the steps for a minute before locking the door, looking up at the clear, brilliant stars, and then, awed and dismayed, scuttled back inside, turned the keys and rattled the chain into place.

She was waiting for him in the bedroom, beside the big double bed, reflected in the mirror on the wall behind her. 'Better close the curtains,' he said, though there was nobody to see except the owls, who seemed to hoot less on these spring nights, that, or the leaves muffled the sound. She went to the window and leant out. He followed, put his arms around her from behind, cradling her breasts in his hands, burying his face in the sweet-smelling hair at the nape of her neck.

A sound made him look up. He stood listening for any sound of movement from Adam's room. This is what it's like to be a parent, he thought. It amazed him there weren't more only children in the world. He couldn't rest until he'd put on his dressing-gown and looked in on Adam, who was curled up under the covers, only the top of his head visible. 'Fast asleep,' he said, coming back into the bedroom, but the mood had been broken. Justine closed the curtains and got into bed. He slipped off the dressing-gown and lay beside her.

Moonlight made a pale oblong on the polished wood

floor. Under the door was a line of yellow from Adam's night light. Somewhere on the roof a bird's feet scratched. Stephen was taking quick, shallow breaths as much from oppression as desire. He put his hand on her firm flat stomach, marvelling at the solidity of her, the warmth. All around them the house sighed and creaked. In the room next door moonlight flooded through the open curtains on to the white-lace counterpane of Robert and Beth's bed, the hollows in the pillows where their heads had rested still visible though they were far away. He was thinking about Nerys, a vague memory of their early marriage when they'd been in love, happy and innocent, though perhaps they'd never been that. It was hard to remember now.

'What's the matter?' Justine asked.

'Nothing.'

'You want this to end, don't you?'

'I'll be glad when they're back.'

'No, I meant this. Us.'

'No, that's not true. I suppose I want to stop being in limbo. I want something to happen.'

'What?' A cool, almost hostile tone. She was looking deep into the pupil of one eye, the lover's gaze, but there was nothing intimate in her expression. She looked like an entomologist who's just found the wrong number of spots on an insect's backside.

'I don't know. Anyway, it's too soon to think about it. I haven't finished the book yet.'

He didn't want to talk about this or to talk at all. He reached up and touched the side of her face, then pulled her head down towards him. Her nipples brushed his chest, and –

Adam stood in the door. 'I want a drink of water.'

Justine lay back, trying not to laugh. 'Go and get one, then. I'll come and see you when you're in bed.'

She was gone five minutes. When she returned, Stephen said, 'Is he asleep?'

'Is he hell.'

After a while she closed her eyes. He continued to lie as before, listening to her breathing until he was sure from its depth and steadiness that she must be asleep. He lay, tumescent and sleepless, feeling a stab of nostalgia for the cottage, which he missed, though it was only 200 yards away.

He'd just managed to erase the last sexual fantasy from his brain and was settling down to sleep, when, with an enormous whale-like heave of the bedclothes, Justine changed position and, still sleeping, thrust her cool, lordotic arse into his groin.

Oh, Justine. Justine. He turned, cautiously, the other way, thrusting his aching pole into space. Only after an uncomfortable hour spent clinging to the edge of the mattress, fantasies of riotous, Adam-free sex seething and bubbling in his brain, did he finally manage to get off to sleep.

Twenty-four

Monday morning. In six hours Robert and Beth would be back home. Waking, Stephen threw his arm across the empty space and was ambushed by a sense of loss. He thought about Kate waking every morning without Ben beside her. There was no possible comparison, of course, between his momentary missing of Justine's warmth and Kate's loss. He was startled that he'd even made the comparison.

Justine was in the kitchen, fully dressed, frying bacon. Adam, in school uniform, sat slumped at the table, white-faced, bent over, complaining of tummy ache. Justine put a bacon sandwich, normally his favourite food, in front of him.

'I'm a vegetarian,' he said, pushing it away.

'Since when?' Justine demanded.

'Since now.'

'Why now?'

'Why not now?'

'C'mon, Adam, eat up,' Stephen said.

Adam was clutching his stomach. 'I've got tummy ache.'

'He does look very white,' Stephen said.

'He's like this every Monday.'

Stephen sat down beside him. 'Adam, why don't you want to go to school?'

A shrug.

'There must be a reason.'

'Everybody thinks I'm weird.'

'Now why do you think they think that?'

'Because I am weird.'

Stephen was left wondering whether insight was really such a good thing. 'Is there anything else you'd like to eat?'

An exaggerated wet-dog shake of the head.

Justine cleared his plate away without comment. 'Mum and Dad'll be here when you get back, think of that.'

Adam trailed after her to the car and climbed – slow-motion – into the back seat.

'Fasten your seat belt, Adam,' Justine said.

'I can't. It hurts my tummy.'

'The car won't start till you fasten the belt.'

A bit of an empty threat, that, Stephen thought, since Adam didn't want the car to start.

'Adam,' he said, bending into the car. 'If you go to school without making a fuss I'll take you to fly Archie this Friday after school. How's that?'

Justine mouthed at him over the roof of the car. 'I can't believe you did that.'

'What?'

'Bribed him.'

'Promise?' Adam called from the back seat.

'Cross my heart and hope to die.' He caught Justine's

eye as she got into the driver's seat. 'I'm allowed to be irresponsible. I'm only an uncle.'

She smiled. 'Are you staying here?'

'No, I thought I'd go back to the cottage and get some work done. What about you?'

'I've got some shopping to do for Beth.'

'Right, then, see you later.'

It was a matter-of-fact leave-taking, he thought, as he went back into the farmhouse. They might have been married for years.

Quickly, he tidied up the spare bedroom, put the sheets into the laundry basket, did a quick check to make sure he hadn't left any personal belongings behind and then let himself out of the farmhouse and walked quickly down the lane to the cottage. Inside, it smelled cold and musty, even after an absence of only three nights. He lit the fire, switched on the computer and tried to work.

On Friday he'd broken off in the middle of a discussion about the bombardment of Baghdad in 1991 – the first war to appear on TV screens as a kind of *son et lumière* display, the first where the bombardment of enemy forces acquired the bloodless precision of a video game. He'd found it disconcerting at the time, and still did. What happens to public opinion in democracies – traditionally reluctant to wage war – when the human cost of battle is invisible? Of course there was nothing new in strict wartime censorship: it had been imposed in both world wars. But, in the first, nothing could hide the arrival of the telegrams nor, in the second, the explosion of bombs. What had been new about Baghdad and later Belgrade was the combination of censorship with massive, one-sided aerial bombardment so that allied casualties were minimal or non-existent and 'collateral damage' couldn't be shown. These were wars designed to ensure that fear and pain never came home.

But he was finding it difficult to get started. Walk. Walk first. A walk would freshen him up. He decided to take his usual route to the top of the hill, though it was a long walk, longer than he really had time for. At first he tried to jog, the grass he ran through flashing fire as his trainers shook off drops of dew. The sky a clear, translucent blue, and far away on the horizon a plane with the sunlight glinting on its wings had left twin vapour trails behind it, spreading out, thinning, fading to nothingness, though, whether from distance or some trick of the landscape, no sound reached him.

He turned to look back at the cottage and the farm-house far below. Very small and square, they looked, like Monopoly houses. A white van had pulled into the farmyard – visible from here, though it couldn't be seen from the lane – and two men were carrying something out of the back door. A television set. He wondered for one brain-dead moment whether Beth had arranged for it to be collected and forgotten to tell him, but how had they got in? No, it was a burglary. And then he saw Justine's little red Metro travelling along the lane. He prayed for it to stop outside the cottage – it was possible she'd call in for a coffee before taking the shopping up to the farmhouse – but no, she drove straight past without slackening speed, and pulled up outside the farmhouse, which to her would look normal. There'd be nothing to see from the lane. He hadn't remembered to set the burglar alarm, so there'd be no flashing or ringing. He saw her get out and lean for a moment on the car roof, looking up at the hill. She was looking straight at him. He waved his arms and yelled, 'Justine!', but she couldn't hear him, any more than he'd heard the car's engine.

He started to run, hurling himself headlong down the hill, tripping over tussocks, catching his feet, and knowing all the time that, even if he ran till his heart and lungs burst, he still wouldn't get there in time.

Justine leant on the car roof, feeling the metal warm under her bare arms and looked up at the hill and the twin vapour trails from a plane dispersing in the blue sky. Then she heaved the carrier bags out from the back seat and set off up the path.

The daffodils were at their peak, though Beth, who for some reason disapproved of yellow flowers, had restricted them to a single clump by the door. *You're vulgar, you are*, she told them as she reached for her key. *You should be silver-grey or white*. And then, rejoicing in the unsubtlety of daffodils, she carried her bags along to the kitchen and dumped them on the table. Coffee, before she unpacked. Looking out of the window, she saw that the vapour trails had almost disappeared.

Then a scurry of footsteps, a blow between her shoulder blades and an arm coiled round her neck.

Stephen, she tried to say. There was a second when she actually believed this was Stephen, not because it was the kind of thing he would do, but because the other explanation was unthinkable. DON'T LOOK, YOU FUCKING STUPID CUNT. The words burst on her ear in a spray of spit. Fingers poked into her eyes. A hand pressed hard into her nose and mouth. Can't breathe. She threw herself back against him, trying to take him by surprise. He grunted and started hitting her, big flat-handed blows, not like a man or even a woman, more like a toddler batting something away, trying to make it *not there*. Now that her mouth was free, she drew in breath with a screech and expelled it in a scream. DON'T TURN ROUND. I'LL KILL YOU, YOU FUCKING STUPID COW. Frustrated, he began banging her head against a cupboard, cutting her forehead and scalp on the sharp edge. She felt a gush of blood down her face and neck. Huge red splashes appeared on her white T-shirt, dropped like rain on to her arms and hands. Plenty more where that came from. The meaningless thought formed and hung suspended in the darkness. Another roar of rage from him – he was angry with her for being hurt. She focused on him so intently she anticipated his every reaction. He had become the world. She was no longer afraid, or not in the way she'd previously understood fear. Her whole being had shrunk to a single diamond-hard point of determination to live. He thrust her forward against the sink till it cut into her stomach. The pain steadied her. She made a rumbling noise behind the hand, trying to

tell him she couldn't breathe. DON'T LOOK AT ME.
SHUT UP. DON'T TURN ROUND. He banged her
against the sink with every word, his anger feeding off
her fear. She went limp, pretending to faint, then,
judging his height from the direction of his voice, drove
her right elbow into his stomach. A grunt of pain. Then
he swung her round and she found herself staring into
two pale blue eyes thickly fringed with lashes that were
almost white. He hit her, hard, and the middle of her
face exploded in pain. There was just time to think, He's
going to kill me, and then she was fainting, crumpling to
the floor. She was aware of being dragged into the
living room, the carpet leaving burn marks on her back
where her T-shirt had ridden up. Two figures now, two
voices, but the new one was careful to stay out of sight.
They picked her up and threw her on to the sofa,
and then she must have blacked out again, but not
completely. She was aware of them talking, trying to
solve the problem. She'd seen one of them. She could
describe him. They couldn't solve it just by running
away. She went on playing dead. Even with her eyes
closed she knew exactly where they were, as if some
part of her mind had split off and was watching what
happened from somewhere else in the room. She could
see herself lying on the sofa, a hand over her face,
snuffling blood and mucus.

Creeping along behind the hedge, Stephen did a bent-
double, lung-bursting run along the path and into the
kitchen garden. From here he could see the house

through a gap in the hedge. The sunlight flashed on the conservatory windows, but there were no figures moving around inside. Adam had shown him where Beth kept the spare key: incredibly for an intelligent woman, she left it under a stone urn outside the conservatory door. Woodlice scrambled away in all directions as he found the small polythene envelope and took the key out. He slid it into the lock, holding his breath as it turned, praying he wouldn't make any noise getting in. Running down the hill, he'd thought he might burst into the house shouting, 'Police', hoping they'd panic and run, but if they didn't he'd have lost the element of surprise. And they might be upstairs in one of the bedrooms. It mightn't be so easy for them to run. But he daren't think about that. Through the door, across the black-and-white tiles, into the hall. On a table there was a bronze statue of an African man, immensely tall and thin. Stephen picked it up, held it round the legs and edged forward again. Voices, though he couldn't catch any of the words. Deep, slow breaths. It hurt his chest to breathe like that, but he did it. Peering round the edge of the door, he saw Justine lying on the sofa, her face a mask of blood, and, only a few feet away, his back to the door, a man wearing a dark blue sweatshirt and jeans. Stephen could see short, ginger hair, the nape of a pink neck. He raised the statue, took two long strides into the room, and brought it crashing down. At the last second somebody shouted, 'Look out' and the man ducked, deflecting the blow on to his shoulder. Stephen felt the jar of bone breaking travel up his own arm, and then, howling, the man turned and ran.

Kneeling by the sofa, he tried to estimate the damage to Justine. Forehead cut and bruised, nose swollen, but the most worrying injuries were the cuts to her head, though she seemed comparatively unaware of them and was simply holding a hand over her eyes and nose to shield them. He tried to take her in his arms, but she was stiff and unyielding, staring round her as if she expected them to come back at any minute. He dialled 999 and asked for police and an ambulance. While he was phoning, he looked round the room. Television gone. DVD player, music centre. The mantelpiece had been swept clean, but he couldn't remember what had been on it.

'They'll be here in about twenty minutes.'

'Lock the door.'

He was about to argue that they certainly wouldn't come back, but then he saw her expression – the staring hyper-wakeful eyes – and did as she asked. In the utility room his feet crunched on broken glass, and he saw that the small window was shattered. Then back to the living room. He found it hard to look at her face. 'Did you lose consciousness?'

'I think so. Or perhaps I just fainted. I don't know.'

At least, he thought, they weren't rapists. Of course, if they'd been watching the house – Beth had mentioned getting silent calls – they'd know it was normally empty at this time of day, so Justine walking in on them like that would have been a helluva shock.

A whoop and scream of sirens, a hammering on the front door, and suddenly the room was full of men in uniform. He saw Justine shrink back into the sofa cushions, but she seemed more dazed than frightened.

The cut-off part of Justine watched from the hall, as a girl with a cut and bruised face was examined by paramedics. There was nothing unreal about this division. She felt the harsh texture of the hall carpet under her feet.

A face leant close to hers. 'You'd better come along to the hospital, Miss. You'll need a few stitches in that.'

She could tell from the way he said 'a few' that he meant 'a lot'. 'I'm all right.'

'Better be on the safe side.'

On the way out she remembered the frozen food thawing in carrier bags on the kitchen table and turned to ask Stephen to put it in the fridge, but the thought sank back into the darkness before she could speak. Standing there, wrapped in a red blanket, she groped about in her mind trying to recover it, before admitting it was gone.

Only at the last minute, climbing up the steps into the ambulance, did she remember what really mattered. 'Ring Dad,' she called to Stephen.

He nodded, then spoke to the driver. 'Where are you taking her?'

'The RVI.'

'I'll come as soon as I can.'

He blew a kiss. Then the doors banged shut behind her, shutting out the bright day.

After ringing Alec, who sounded winded by the news, but said he'd go to the hospital at once, Stephen settled down to be interviewed by the police. It took about an hour. He was careful to emphasize that there were two burglars, that they'd attacked Justine, that for all he knew they were armed. The broken collarbone – whatever it was – had to be accounted for. He didn't think he was likely to be charged with assault, but he was playing safe. Stranger things had happened.

Long before the interview was over, the house was full of white-suited scene-of-crime officers, dusting grey powder everywhere. And then, in the middle of all this, Robert rang from Orly Airport and had to be told the news. 'Is Justine all right?' he asked.

Full marks, Robert, Stephen thought. He hadn't even asked what was missing.

Stephen was given an incident number to pass on to Robert, the phone number of a glazier who did emergency calls, and was told to expect a visit from Victim Support. Then the young policeman snapped the elastic round his notebook and stood up. He didn't hold out much hope of recovering anything, he said, as Stephen accompanied him to the front door, but this was aggravated burglary and they'd give it their best shot.

Shortly afterwards the chief scene-of-crime officer, a pretty, red-haired girl with a Scottish accent, popped her head round the door to say she was going too.

So he was alone, in a house he couldn't leave till the glazier had come and fixed the window.

He went back over the story he'd told the police, and then the other story: the one he hadn't needed to tell them because – thank God – it wasn't relevant. Locked in his brain, though, was the truth. All the way down the hillside he'd had flashbulbs exploding in his head. So many raped and tortured girls – he needed no imagination to picture what might be happening to Justine. It would not have surprised him to find her lying like a broken doll at the foot of the stairs, her skirt bunched up around her waist, her eyes staring. Years of impacted rage had gone into the blow he'd aimed at the back of the burglar's head. He'd meant it to kill.

He looked around him. One pool of blood in the kitchen, another in the living room, and everywhere, on every window, every door, every piece of furniture, clustering thickly round doorknobs and latches, grey fingerprints, handprints, thumbprints, everywhere, as if the house were suffering from an infestation of ghosts.

Twenty-five

Justine had a fleeting impression of the casualty department as the ambulance men hurried her through it – a row of people sitting on a bench. Because the police were with her, she was taken immediately to a treatment room at the far end of the corridor. The policewoman withdrew. Justine was asked to undress on to paper on the floor and given a scratchy hospital robe to wear. Her clothes and the paper were scooped up and carried away. A young man came and sat beside her, asked if she'd scratched her attacker, examined her fingers and took scrapings from underneath the nails. She couldn't remember scratching him. She looked at her hands, imagined them being bagged up as evidence and taken away.

She couldn't breathe normally, but snuffled through mucus or breathed through her mouth. Audible breaths frightened her – if she'd been able to breathe silently she'd have calmed down much quicker – but mouth breathing made her thirsty. She kept swallowing, running her tongue round her mouth, flexing her lips. At last she got up, walked the few steps to the sink in the corner, took a polystyrene cup, filled it to the brim with water and drank the lot. Then she filled the cup and drank again. It was the first decision she'd made, the first action she'd taken, since they threw her on the sofa and yelled at her to shut up. And it had a curious effect – she started to shake.

There was nothing in the room but this sink, a trolley covered with white paper, and two plastic chairs, mushroom-coloured. She sat on one of the chairs and looked at the other. The separate part of herself wandered round the edges of the room, glancing at her now and then, observing, she supposed, deciding whether that body over there was a safe place to be. She shouldn't be as frightened as this now. She was safe – a police-woman down the corridor waiting to interview her – nobody could get at her here. Even the sounds – they were horrible, but at least she knew what they were. A man on a ventilator whom she'd glimpsed in the room next to hers breathed through his mask with a sizzling wheeze – he sounded like the ice warriors in *Doctor Who* – and then across the corridor there was somebody yelping. Not groaning or screaming – yelping. That door was shut and they were in there with him. Listening to those yelps, she felt a complete fraud. She had nothing worse than a headache and soreness in the middle of her face. It was a different matter when she tried to touch it, then she was biting back yelps of her own. But she was alone now with what had happened, and might have happened.

The cut-off part of herself was moving further away. At one point she saw herself slumped on the chair. Loser, she thought, seeing how the blood had made black spikes in her hair.

Did not see the spikes. Not see them. Only felt and imagined. She tried shutting her eyes and saying I, I, I . . . over and over again. *I* am looking at the sink. *I* am sitting on a chair. See Justine sitting on the chair. Like a child's reading book, she thought. See Justine. See Peter. Peter has a ball. See the ball. See the dog. See the dog run.

No daylight in the room, no window. The strip lighting above her head buzzed, and that buzzing became the sound of pain. And then she heard a familiar voice, hurrying footsteps and her father burst through the swing doors, stopped dead, looked at her, made as if to embrace her and then visibly held back. Why? she wondered. She wanted to be hugged, she wanted him to hold her, and he did, but it was a second, just one second, too late. He thought she'd been raped. He thought she wouldn't be able to bear being touched even by him. Why did this make her hate him? But then she looked at his face and saw he was frightened. And so she made herself talk about the attack, domesticating it, not for herself but for him. And when she spat it all out like that, it really didn't sound too bad. I walked in on a burglary. One of them panicked and started hitting me. I know I look a mess, but I'm all right, honestly, don't worry about me, I'm all right. No worse than being mugged on the street, and a lot better than . . . She forced the words out. A lot better than being raped.

It helped, making this effort – she could see herself in a few years' time telling the story like this with a slight, self-deprecating laugh, and that was good because to imagine that she had to imagine herself surviving. But there was something else behind this bald account, something she daren't articulate – I woke up, it was a normal morning, I did the shopping, I drove Adam to school. It was a lovely day, I was happy, I leant on the car roof, I felt the sun on my back . . . And then that meaningless, brutal, random eruption of violence. Meaningless to her at any rate. The men might have been planning it for months. A criminal psychologist might look at their lives and find the burglary predictable, the violence predictable. Perhaps everything in their lives had led them to that point, but then that was true of her too. And it was no help.

She might feel happy again, but she would never again feel safe.

An hour later she was sitting on the trolley, dressed in clothes Angela had brought in for her. She'd been interviewed, had given the fullest description of the burglars she could manage. At first she'd thought she wouldn't be able to say anything useful, her memories were so chaotic, but the face of the one who'd hit her had imprinted itself on her memory. She only had to summon up the image and describe what she saw. About the other she could say almost nothing – he'd been so careful not to let her see him – but the police kept nodding their heads. She felt they knew who'd done it.

Now shaved, stitched, scanned, taped, she was going home. She'd seen herself in the mirror and it was a fairly horrifying sight, but she didn't care about that. She just wanted to be out. Home. In her own bed.

She walked down the corridor on her father's arm, like an old woman, she thought, though if she was an old woman he'd be dead. It was early afternoon, still a beautiful day. The sun flashed on rows of cars. A bird sang. This shocked her so much she had to stand in the entrance where the ambulances drew up, and stare at the bright light, at the sky. It didn't seem possible.

They'd given her some tranquillizers. Not many, not enough to get addicted, just enough to see her through the next few days. That's why she felt she was seeing the world at one remove, padded in cotton wool. She had an appointment to go back and see a plastic surgeon about her nose – they thought it might need surgery – but that was in the future. At least there was a future. She remembered the shouting, the terror in his voice. He could have killed her. Not because he wanted to, not even because he was violent, but because he didn't know what else to do.

She took a long deep breath. Her father wanted to bring the car to her, but she wasn't having that. She wasn't ready to be left on her own, not even in this public place with people coming and going, so they walked across the car park together. A long way.

Just as they got to the car her mobile rang. Stephen. It was the first time he'd been able to reach her because inside the hospital you had to keep your mobile switched off.

'Where are you?' he asked.

'On my way home. Where are you?'

'Stuck here. I can't leave till the glazier's been.'

'Has Robert rung?'

'Yes – they'll be back in an hour.'

'Will you come round to the vicarage?'

'Yes.'

'Don't forget Adam. He's gets panicky if you're late.'

So many details, she thought. Probably just as well, probably that's what helped people keep their heads together, collecting a child from school, giving him his tea. She rang off. Her father was looking at her.

'Stephen,' she said.

'I thought it was.'

It was a big moment, that. Acknowledging Stephen's claim. His right to ring.

Robert and Beth arrived home earlier than Stephen had expected, only a few minutes after he spoke to Justine.

He saw them walking up the path, Beth trundling their weekend bag, Robert striding ahead, grim-faced, and went to the door to meet them.

Robert touched his shoulder, and brushed past him into the living room, where he scanned the vacant spaces, then puffing his mouth out with relief said, 'Oh, well, it's not too bad. What about upstairs?'

'I don't think they had time.'

Beth went upstairs to check on her jewellery, and came down saying there were one or two things missing, but only pieces she'd left lying on top of the dressing table. Anything valuable she kept in a shoebox in the wardrobe. It wouldn't have taken them long to find that, Stephen thought, but then he remembered they hadn't found the key under the urn.

She sat down heavily on the sofa, staring round her like somebody unsure of her welcome in a stranger's house. 'It's the shock,' she said, 'more than anything.'

'The police want a list of what's missing, as soon as you can. I couldn't remember.'

'I'm not sure I can.' She was staring blankly at the empty mantelpiece.

'I'll put the kettle on,' Stephen said.

Robert followed him into the kitchen.

'Justine seems to be all right,' Stephen said, with a slight edge.

'I know. Beth rang Angela from the airport.' He sat down at the table, looking round at the thickly clustering fingerprints. 'God, what a mess.'

Stephen looked round too, at a patch of dried blood on the work surface near the sink. The air seemed to hold a suspension of fear and pain.

Robert asked, 'How did they get in?'

'Utility-room window. The glazier's coming round to fix it.' A pause. 'The alarm wasn't on. That's my fault, not Justine's. I was the last out.'

Robert shrugged. 'I don't suppose it would have made much difference. It's connected to a security firm, but they're forty minutes' drive away. You can clear a house in half that time.'

'Beth seems very calm. I thought she'd be more upset.'

'Shock.'

Stephen didn't think it was shock. 'This is your incident number,' he said, handing over the slip of paper. 'And now, if you don't mind, I think I'll leave you to it, unless you want me to collect Adam?'

'Would you mind?' Beth said.

'No, of course I –'

'It's just I don't think I can rest until I've got things straight again.'

Robert followed him to the door and out on to the path.

'I'm sorry, Robert.'

'Not your fault. We've all been careless. It could just as well have happened another day when I hadn't set the alarm.'

A brief embrace, and Stephen was walking down the path to his car, thinking how much he liked his brother. That was new. And Beth's toughness – he'd started to sense that quality in her, but the last few minutes had confirmed it.

He glanced at his watch. He'd be in time for Adam, though only just.

Children were spilling out into the playground as he parked the car and opened the window. A knot of people, mainly women, were waiting outside the gates, some of them – he realized as the first children arrived – collecting children of ten or eleven. He and Robert had been walking home alone by the time they were eight. Where children were concerned, everything had changed, and not, he thought, for the better. The kids were red-faced, running, shouting, waving pictures, all over the place. If you saw an adult moving like this, you'd know they had St Vitus's dance. C'mon, Adam. He was tapping the flat of his hands on the dashboard, tempted to ring Justine's mobile again. But she might have gone to sleep.

At last Adam appeared, also carrying a painting, but walking along at a sedate, professorial pace, and alone. He didn't show any surprise when he saw Stephen, though, as he climbed into the back seat, he asked, 'Are Mum and Dad back?'

'Yes. They're at home.'

He looked in the rear-view mirror at Adam's round unhappy face. 'How was it?'

'Bloody awful.'

'It doesn't last for ever.'

But the trouble is, he thought, waiting for a gap in the traffic, it does – virtually – at that age. We daren't let ourselves imagine children's lives. Anybody as trapped in a job as they are in school would go mad. He wondered if he should tell Adam about the burglary, and decided it might be as well to warn him. Adam listened, but showed no particular concern. 'One of them hit Justine, so she won't be looking after you tomorrow.'

'Does that mean I won't have to go to school?'

Egotism was natural in children, but he found it slightly surprising when Adam made no further reference to Justine, though he did ask if they'd stolen his

Playstation and whether he would still be able to fly Archie on Friday after school.

'Justine's back home now,' Stephen said. 'She had to go to hospital to get some stitches put in, but then the doctor said she could go home.'

No comment. Stephen gave up, though he was beginning to think it quite odd. Back at the house, he said, 'I won't come in. But don't worry, Mum's –'

Adam was already out of the car. At the last moment he thrust his painting into Stephen's hands. 'Give her this.'

Stephen looked down. It was the scene every child paints: a house with a smoking chimney, curtains at the windows, a tree in the garden, Mum, Dad, child, dog standing on the lawn, and behind them all, filling the whole sky, an enormous, round, golden sun.

He'd never been to the vicarage, never seen it except on the one occasion when Beth had asked him to drive Justine home from work. Then it had been too dark to see clearly, though he'd had the impression of a large gloomy house set back from the road behind tall trees.

Why not cut them down? he wondered, as he parked the car. They must make the front rooms intolerably dark, but then some people can't bring themselves to cut down any tree, however ancient or badly positioned. A pair of wood pigeons broke cover as he walked up the drive, startling him with the clap of their wings. He rang the bell, heard it clang deep inside the house, and stood there waiting, feeling a fool with his bunch of daffodils.

Alec opened the door. Angela stood behind him, peering over his shoulder. He thought for a moment they might not let him in, but then Alec stood to one side. Stephen had stopped the burglars doing whatever they were thinking of doing next. Which was probably to run away, but you could never be sure. People with limited intelligence and low impulse control come up with some pretty disastrous solutions to problems. Alec had known a great many such people, presumably, over the years, and he could have no illusions about the danger Justine had been in.

'She's in bed,' Angela said.

'They gave her a sedative,' Alec said. 'She's very drowsy.'

'I won't stay long. I just want to give her these.'

They stood together in the hall, reflected, all three of them, in a small bevelled mirror on the wall.

Justine's voice from upstairs called, 'Stephen?'

'Coming.'

They parted in front of him, and he went up the stairs which had a threadbare strip of carpet in the centre of the treads held in place by stair-rods. He'd thought stair-rods were a thing of the past, along with floral pinnies and stottie cakes and bombers' moons. Apparently not.

Justine's bedroom was huge. Angela followed him in and hovered as he walked across the floor to the bed, which was small and single, lost in the vast space. Two tall uncurtained windows let in a fretwork of shadows, moving and shifting perpetually, as a breeze, not perceptible at ground level, ruffled the leaves.

He got a chair and sat down by the bed, wanting to kiss her, but aware of Angela behind him. Aware too that most of Justine's face looked as if a kiss would hurt. Her nose was in plaster. It looked rather like Norman armour and, incredibly, suited her, bringing out something in her that he'd only dimly sensed before. The skin round her eyes was beginning to turn black. She had two bald patches in her hair, each with a ridge of suture lines like black spiky caterpillars crawling across her white skin.

He put the daffodils and Adam's painting down on the bedspread. 'How are you?'

'Not bad.'

She had some colour in her cheeks, but her eyes flickered round the room in a way he didn't like.

Alec was in the doorway too now.

'Angela, do you think you could put these in water?' Justine asked sweetly, picking up the daffodils that had left a small damp patch on the white cotton.

They took it as a hint to leave. He bent down and kissed her on the forehead and they stayed like that, hearing each other breathe, not wanting to move, but then she sat back, raised her knees, and smiled. She was wearing a white nightshirt with a Snoopy design and looked every day of fifteen. His sympathies at that moment were all with Alec. I'd throw me out, he thought.

'How are you really?'

'Not good. Angela's driving me mad. "Poor mother-less child."'

'Have you spoken to your mother?'

'No, we don't know where she is. I'm OK. Or I will be when I can get up and about. I wish I hadn't taken that bloody sedative.'

'It might be a good idea to get some sleep.'

'Not if it means waking up at three o'clock in the morning.'

'Have you got some painkillers?'

'Oh, yeah. Real knock-out stuff.' She held up a bottle of pink pills from the table beside the bed. 'I want to get up.'

'Better not. You've had a shock.'

'So have you.'

He shrugged. 'Oh, I'm bomb happy.'

'What were you going to do with that statue?'

'Kill him.'

'You'd have got five years.'

'Not if they'd seen a photograph of you.'

'Oh, well. It didn't happen.'

She touched her scalp, prodding the line of stitches as he suspected she did twenty times an hour. 'You must have lost quite a bit of blood.'

'It looked a lot. I'm not sure it was.' A pause while she prodded her scalp again. 'How's Beth taking it?'

'Quite well. Tough as an old boot.'

'She's going to need to be, because I don't think I can go back.'

'No, I don't think you should.'

'It scuppers her completely.'

'That's her problem.'

'Perhaps I could have Adam here.'

'Oh, for God's sake, if it comes to that, I'll mind him. What you should think about is going away for a holiday in the sun.'

'Who with?'

'Me, of course.'

'What about the book?'

'Fuck the book.'

'I've never heard you say that before.'

'Then you haven't been listening, because I say that at least once a day.'

Angela came in with the daffodils in a vase and put it down on the table. 'Have you taken your pill, Justine?'

'Not yet. I will.'

'You need a good night's sleep.'

'I'll take it at bedtime.'

Angela withdrew.

'Can't you go downstairs and watch television?'

She shook her head. 'I wish I could go out.'

'Tomorrow.'

He was looking round the room, thinking how much of a young girl's room it was. Posters, photographs, make-up, a red rosette pinned up on a cork board, the relic of some pony-club triumph of the past. Her shoes were lined up neatly in one corner next to the dressing table.

'Do you think we could go somewhere?' she asked.

'Anywhere you like. If you're sure you'll be well enough?'

'I don't see why not. It's a broken nose, for heaven's sake, not a broken neck.'

'All right. Where would you like to go?'

'Don't know.'

He touched her leg through the bedspread. 'You be thinking about it. I'll come and get you about ten.'

He thought, as he went downstairs and was let out of the house by Angela – Alec seemed to be avoiding him – that it had been an extraordinary day. We live our whole lives one step away from clarity, he thought. That moment, careering down the steep hillside, knowing that however hard he ran he wouldn't get there in time, had taught him more about his feelings for Justine than months of introspection could have done. All along in the back of his mind he'd been aware of his priorities in life rearranging themselves without any conscious effort on his part. You thought you cared about that? Don't be silly. The girl. She's what matters.

Poor Justine. What a helluva year she'd had – breaking up with Peter, glandular fever, the disappointment over not going to Cambridge – and now this. But she was strong. She'd come through it. Changed, though. And the changed Justine might have no use for him.

Twenty-six

Left alone, Justine lay for a time quietly watching the play of shadows on the bedspread. Then, just as she decided to get out of bed and go downstairs, she drifted off to sleep. She dreamt she was far out, a long way from land on a frozen lake. She'd been walking for hours, her boots squeaking on the ice, a cold wind flattening her skirt against the backs of her legs. Probably she ought to stop and turn back towards the line of lights behind her, but when she turns round the wind slashes tears from her eyes. Her face is burning. Don't look, a voice whispers in her mind. Don't turn round. She's too far out already. It's dark now and getting colder by the minute. Stop. Turn. Look down. The ice at her feet is thick and marbled, like frozen phlegm. It had borne her weight while she was walking away from the shore, but when she tries to go back it starts to creak alarmingly. She feels rather than hears the sound, a protest, almost a groan. Down there beneath her feet is icy water a mile deep. She tries to set off at another angle and again the ice creaks. It comes to her that there's only one path back to the shore, and that she doesn't know where it is. Ahead there is only the trackless waste of ice, catching a dull gleam from the stars.

She woke up, shivering, instantly alert. A glance at

her watch told her she'd been asleep less than twenty minutes, though she felt as if she'd been walking across the ice all night. The fear of the dream was still on her. She snuggled down under the covers, reassuring herself that she was warm and dry. Safe at home.

Slowly her thoughts ranged back over the day. Even this brief interlude of sleep had given her a sense of distance from the attack. The interview with the detectives in the hospital kept coming back to her. 'Your father,' they said at one point. A few minutes later, they were talking about 'your attacker'. *My* attacker? she'd wanted to say. But he's nothing to do with me.

It still worried her. 'Your' attacker seemed to imply a continuing relationship. If she'd tripped on a kerb and broken her nose, nobody would have been talking about 'your' kerb. They were such harmless little words: 'your', 'my', but they opened the door on to a small dark room, a space so cramped it could hold only two people, herself and her attacker. Don't look. Don't turn round. She sat up and looked, slowly and carefully, at every object in the room, turned, and did the same for the wall behind her. She wasn't going to let the attack define her. Who are you? I'm a woman who got beaten up by a burglar. Oh, no. There was quite a bit more to her than that.

Dad came upstairs and sat with her. He looked so lost and helpless sitting there, she started to feel responsible for him. 'Where's Angela?'

'Gone home. She thought we'd like some time together.'

'That was nice of her. I am pleased, you know. About . . .'

He nodded. 'It might mean leaving the parish.'

'Because you're divorced?'

'Yes.'

'Perhaps it's time to move on anyway.'

'Yes. I'll miss it, though.'

'Yeah, me too.'

They sat in silence for a while. She wanted to get up and have a bath, but she knew he needed to sit there, keeping guard over his little girl. Only I'm not his little girl, she thought.

'Dad, do you think I could have a lock on my door?'

'Yes, of course.' He brightened at once. It was something for him to do. 'I'll put one on tomorrow. Unless you'd rather I got one now?'

'No, tomorrow's fine.' She didn't want to be left in the house on her own. She'd have to face it sooner or later, but not yet. 'Stephen's taking me out tomorrow.'

He thought for a moment, then nodded. 'Good.'

She got up, had a bath, intending to get dressed after it and resume normal life, but the hot water knocked her out. She was barely able to crawl back upstairs and into bed. I'm just resting, she told herself, but fell asleep immediately and slept for two hours, dreamlessly this time.

As soon as he was sure Justine was asleep, Alec went into his study and sat down at the desk, closing his eyes to block out the stale, overfamiliar room. He started to pray, using the Jesus Prayer: *Lord Jesus Christ, Son of God, have mercy on me, a sinner*, repeating the words over and over again, pushing all extraneous thoughts gently aside, trying, with every repetition, to sink deeper into the awareness of God. Sometimes – but he had little hope that it would happen today – he was rewarded, after twenty minutes or so, by a sense of unity with all other living things. This brought with it a joy that illuminated the whole day. Now, the most he could hope for was surface calm, and a reminder that what separated him from God and from other human beings was his own sin.

On the phone this morning Stephen had given no details of the attack, saying only that Justine had been injured and was on her way to hospital. Alec's ignorance was a black hole dragging him in. Rape. Stephen hadn't said that, but Alec couldn't get the possibility out of his mind. Images appeared, unsummoned, spawning other images. Rigid with fury, he beat his clenched fist on the steering wheel. No room now for Christian forgiveness. If he'd had the bastard tied up, he'd happily have taken a blowtorch to his balls.

He'd never been a peaceful man, though over the years he'd fought hard to control his anger. And sometimes all that repressed aggression had paid dividends, enabling him to forge bonds with young men newly released from prison, many of them violent. They sensed a hidden kinship, perhaps, where on the surface there was only difference.

Victoria had known. On their second wedding

anniversary, she'd bought him a print of one of Edward Hicks's Peaceable Kingdom series. 'There,' she'd said, pointing to a lion in the foreground. 'That's you.'

The print hung on the wall of his study now, the only memento of his marriage he had left, apart from Justine. Abandoning the attempt to pray, he went to look at it. The lion is surrounded by lambs, sheep, cows. They aren't afraid of him – though one or two look wary – and he isn't attacking them. God's reign has begun. Only the lion's eyes are full of anguish, the strain of denying his own nature, reinventing himself, second by second: an act of pure will. And the balance is precarious. He remembers the taste of blood. He's afraid of himself. The pupils are huge, black, dilated with pain. On the left of the picture, William Penn is concluding his treaty with the Indians, sealed without an oath and never broken, but the struggle against violence has simply moved back into the individual human mind, and those eyes tell you that victory is far from certain.

'That's you,' she'd said, and kissed him.

The fantasies of revenge hadn't gone. They clung like bats to the inner walls of his skull, and no amount of prayer would dislodge them. His first sight of Justine, slumped in the chair like a broken and abandoned doll, had only reinforced them. He couldn't bring himself to touch her, afraid that, if she had been raped, any man's touch, even his, would fill her with disgust.

'Are you all right?' he asked, knowing the question was idiotic.

'Yes,' she said, after a pause. Everything she said had this pause in front of it. It was like dropping stones into a well.

'Did you see him?'

A blank gaze. 'Yes.'

'It wasn't somebody you knew?'

'No.'

She sounded surprised and he breathed again. But then she said there'd been two men and she hadn't seen the second. Then nothing – not the Jesus Prayer, not a lifetime of discipline and faith – had been able to stop him giving the second man a face.

My fault, he'd thought. I brought this into the house. He'd been so sure of himself, of his own righteousness, his power to do good – *his*, not God's – when he should have been protecting his daughter. Sometimes, when the attempt to be 'good' backfires, you end up being nothing, not even a healthy animal. Any mammal knows to protect its own young, and he'd failed to do even that.

Lord Jesus Christ, Son of God, have mercy on me, a sinner . . .

Back at his desk, he closed his eyes, repeating the familiar words until he'd achieved a degree of calm.

When he opened them again, he saw the last thing he expected to see: a white van parked outside the gates with Peter Wingrave getting out, carrying a bunch of flowers.

Justine mustn't see him. Praying for her not to wake, Alec went to the door and opened it. Peter, who'd been looking down the drive, turned and smiled.

It can't be true, Alec thought. If Peter had been the second man, he'd never have dared come here carrying roses. They were roses. Now that he was close, Alec could see the red buds clustering inside the cone of white paper.

'I heard the news,' Peter said. 'How is she?'

'Asleep, at the moment.'

'Not badly injured?'

'Broken nose. Bruising. Two cuts to her head.'

A pause. They looked at each other, then, wearily, Alec stepped aside. A bit late now to keep him out. He felt Peter shadowing him down the corridor to the living room, almost treading on his heels. So much power this man had, and yet he seemed to have no identity, cling-filming himself round other people in order to acquire a shape. Anybody who impressed him got the treatment; once, not so many years ago, it had been Alec's turn. He'd witnessed Peter's taking on of his mannerisms, his way of speaking, even his religion – though perhaps that was genuine. He had no right to question the reality of another person's faith – certainly not today, when he was doubting the foundations of his own. 'Sit down,' he said. 'Would you like a cup of tea? Coffee?'

'No, thanks. I'm all right.'

'I'll put those in water.'

In the kitchen Alec ran a bucket of water, dumped the roses into it, still wrapped, and got back to the living room as fast as he could. He didn't know why he was hurrying – he wasn't worried about Peter stealing anything, he trusted him absolutely in that respect. No

– what worried him was that Justine might wake up and come down.

'Do they know who did it?' Peter asked.

'No, but they seem to be quite optimistic – she gave a very good description of one of them.' He steadied his voice. 'The one who hit her.'

'Oh, so there were two of them?'

'Yes. She didn't really see the other one.' Alec was looking at Peter's clothes. He was wearing a suit with a polo shirt underneath. 'Not working today?'

'No, I've been to London. I had lunch with Stephen Sharkey's agent. You know Stephen?'

'I've met him.'

'I thought he and Justine were . . . ?'

'She's nineteen. She does what she likes.' He would have to have caught an early train to be in London for lunch. If he was telling the truth – and he was too clever to tell a lie that could be so easily detected – he couldn't have been anywhere near the farmhouse this morning. 'Which train did you catch?'

'I went down last evening. I can give you the number of the person I stayed with, if you like. *Alec*.' The tone was almost caressing. 'You surely don't think I had anything to do with it?'

Alec was compulsively honest. 'It crossed my mind.'

'Oh, for God's sake.'

'I'm sorry.'

'So you bloody should be. What's going on?'

'I think perhaps we'd better not talk at the moment.'

'Alec, I haven't done anything. All I did was go to

London. You were perfectly happy to have me mowing the churchyard a few weeks back. You weren't worried about Justine then.' He waited for a response. 'So why now? I wouldn't do anything to hurt Justine. You know that. I loved her.'

'I wish I could believe that.'

'I went out with her for six months. What did you think it was about?'

'Making me jump. You were always good at that.'

'Oh, I *see*. It was about *you*? Now why aren't I surprised?'

'You should've told her. You had a clear moral and legal responsibility –'

'So why didn't you report me? Why don't you?'

Alec touched his forehead. 'This isn't doing any good.'

'It certainly isn't. You don't actually believe any of the things you claim to believe. Do you?'

Alec didn't bother to reply.

Justine woke to the sound of voices. Dad and Angela, she thought. Angela must have come back. But then after a while she realized both voices were male and that the second sounded familiar. She got up and looked out of the window. Just visible between the trees was a white van.

She wrapped her dressing-gown round her and went out on to the landing, thinking it might not be Peter. She could have been mistaken in the voice, and thousands of people have white vans. Whoever it was, they were in the living room. She knelt on the landing, looking down through the banisters, reluctant to go downstairs and face them, but unable to go back to bed. Like a child, she thought, spying on adult life.

The voices went on. She couldn't catch individual words or even judge the tone. Once she thought she heard her father almost shouting, but mainly it was a low rumble. Then it became louder. The door opened, letting a wedge of light on to the hall floor. She shrank back against the wall, furious with herself for wanting to hide the bruises. Incredibly, she felt ashamed, as if it had been her fault. Ashamed, or vulnerable. Perhaps she simply preferred not to risk a meeting with Peter when she was hurt.

It was Peter. She could see him now.

They were in the hall, walking towards the door. Peter was smartly dressed, suntanned, his hair longer than she remembered. At the door, he turned. 'Well, give her my love.'

Dad said nothing. They were facing each other. For a moment she thought they were going to shake hands, then Peter leant across and kissed him. Dad neither returned the kiss nor pulled away. He just stood there and took it; it might as well have been a blow. Peter stood back, smiling. She knew that look, amused, mocking, confident of his power to attract. 'Oh, I almost forgot,' he said. 'Congratulations on your engagement. You are engaged, aren't you?'

Dad opened the door and Peter went out into the night.

After he'd gone, Dad didn't go back to the living room, but instead pressed his face into the door, hands spread out on either side of his head. He stood there, not moving.

'Dad?'

He turned. 'Oh, you're awake.' He came to the foot of the stairs, obviously delighted to see her up and about. She might have hallucinated the last few minutes. He didn't even look like the same man.

'Yes, I'm feeling a lot better.' It might be true. She was too bewildered by the scene she'd just witnessed to know.

'Come and have some supper.'

There was a covered plate of chicken sandwiches on the sideboard in the living room, ready for when she would feel hungry and come down. They ate them over the fire. Chewing wasn't easy, because the movement of her jaw made her nose hurt, but she forced herself to finish one sandwich before pushing the plate aside.

'That was Peter.'

'Oh, I thought I heard voices.' She didn't want him to know she'd seen the kiss. 'What did he want?'

'He'd heard about the . . . er . . .'

'Burglary.'

'He just wanted to know how you were.' He waited for a response. 'He sends his love.'

She could have done without this.

'He was upset,' Dad went on, 'because what happened to you reminded him of what he did.'

'You mean why he went to prison?'

'Yes. He was in a house stealing money and the old lady whose house it was came back unexpectedly and . . .'

'He beat her up?'

'Worse than that. He killed her.'

It should have been a shock, but it wasn't.

Dad said, 'He was very young.'

So was the little bastard who hit me, she thought. 'I'm very young. I don't go round murdering old ladies.'

'No, very young. Adam's age.'

For a moment she couldn't take it in. 'Christ.' She just couldn't get her head round it. 'Sorry,' she said, a second later, knowing her use of the word would offend him.

When she tried to examine her feelings, she found only turmoil. Not even compassion for the old lady, if she was honest, just a shrinking away from a horror she couldn't bear to imagine. 'Why are you telling me this now?'

'Because I should have told you before.'

'Yeah, I think you should have.'

'I begged him to tell you.'

'He finished with me instead.'

'I'm afraid I was rather pleased.'

'Yeah, me too. Eventually.'

'Would it have made a difference?'

'I don't know. It's easy to say no, isn't it? But I don't know. It might.' A short silence. 'Still doesn't answer the question, though. Why tell me now?'

'Because of . . . Today. The man who did that.' He

risked a glance at her face. 'I know it doesn't make sense, but . . . There is a connection. I keep having these terrible thoughts, but they're not just thoughts, they're more like waking nightmares. No, I shouldn't burden you –'

'No, go on.'

'I imagine I've got him tied up and I . . .'

Unexpectedly she giggled. 'Break his nose?'

He tried to laugh. 'That sort of thing. I didn't think I had this much hatred in me.'

Justine started to speak, stopped and tried again. 'I'm going to get over this, Dad. I've no intention of wallowing in it. *And neither should you.*'

'No, well, I'll try.'

He seemed surprised. Perhaps she'd sounded tougher than he gave her credit for, or perhaps he'd sensed her resentment. Because he had burdened her. The onus was on her to get better quickly, so he wouldn't have to go on feeling bad about himself. Was it fair to say that? Perhaps not. She was too tired to work it out.

'Peter brought you some roses. They're out there. I've put them in water. Shall I bring them in?'

'No, let's leave them, shall we?'

And why choose today to tell her about Peter? Now, when it was too late to do any good? It simply focused her attention back on to him and *his* relationship with Peter. What kind of tropism for the limelight was going on here? And yet he meant well. He loved her. She made herself get up, go to the sofa and sit beside him. He put his arm round her shoulders and she snuggled into his side. It wouldn't hurt to go on being his little girl for a few more hours. One last time. The world would catch up with them soon enough.

Twenty-seven

They were going to the Farnes. Justine couldn't wait to leave, sitting forward in her seat, waiting impatiently for Stephen to start the car.

She was like a kid on the first day of the holidays, he thought, eager for the first glimpse of the sea.

'Are you sure you feel up to it?'

'Yes.' Dad had been asking her that ever since she got out of bed. She felt fine. Only when she looked in the mirror did she understand the reason for the question. Overnight, the bruises had developed. She looked much worse now than she had immediately after the attack. But she felt better. 'I'm all right.'

Almost at once the mist closed in, becoming thicker the closer they got to the coast. Once they were on the way, Justine forgot the burglary, the shouting and banging, the fetid smell of fear. All her childhood she'd gone to the Farnes at Easter, and to be setting out like this made her feel young again. She knew if she said this to Stephen he'd laugh, but age wasn't a simple matter of chronology. In the hospital watching the cut-off part of her self pace round the walls she'd felt ancient.

Stephen nodded at the mist. 'Are you sure they'll take a boat out in this?'

'It mightn't be like this when we get there. It clears very quickly.'

He switched the radio on, found some acceptable music and concentrated on his driving. They were inching forward, the headlights revealing nothing but a wall of mist. Even on the higher ground, where it thinned and became wraith-like, skeins drifting across the road, it was not possible to pick up speed, because the road dipped almost immediately into the next hollow, and there the dense, damp whiteness became impenetrable again. Justine wondered once or twice whether they should turn back, but she couldn't bear the idea. Talking was impossible. Stephen crouched over the wheel, peering into the blankness ahead. She opened her window and there was the sound of the wheels hissing on the wet road, less disturbing to her than the music. Any loud noise felt like a threat. She looked at the rear window, where drops of rain or distilled mist were trapped, pulsing round the edges of the glass. She was aware of Stephen, the bulk of him, but she didn't look in his direction. The atmosphere in the car was tense, and she hoped the tension came from the driving rather than from something she'd done or said. Everything today felt fragile.

At last they turned on to the motorway, and she felt him relax, settle back in his seat, because at least the road was flat, there were no sudden white-outs in the hollows, though the hazard warning-lights were flashing and the traffic crawling along.

'We'll be lucky to get there at this rate,' he said.

But then, as quickly as the mist had closed in, it began to clear, and Stephen found himself driving through a landscape that reminded him of Ben's photographs. Border country. That's why Ben had loved it and photographed it so obsessively, Stephen thought, because he came back from whatever war he'd been covering to a place where every blade of grass had been fought over, time and time again, for centuries, and now the shouts and cries, the clash of swords on shields had faded into silence, leaving only sunlight heaving on acres of grass, and a curlew crying. He thought now that he understood Ben's ties to this place; he was beginning to fall in love with it himself. On impulse he reached out and squeezed Justine's hand.

'Not long now,' she said.

Kate put her eye to the spy-hole in the front door and there was Angela, gaping like a fish in a small bowl.

'Did you hear about the burglary?' she asked, almost falling into the hall.

'Yes, Beth rang. Justine wasn't too badly hurt, was she?'

'No, she's back home. We thought they'd keep her in, but they didn't. In fact, she's gone out.'

Angela sounded breathless. Almost frenetic. 'Have some coffee,' Kate said, resigning herself to a late start. She was so nearly there, it was torture to be kept away from the studio, and yet she dreaded this final effort and would grab any excuse to put it off.

'Everybody keeps asking if she was raped.'

'She wasn't?' Kate asked.

'No, thank God.' She took a mug of coffee and gulped the first few mouthfuls down. 'That's what Alec thought. When he got to the hospital, they'd taken all her clothes away, but apparently they were just looking for hairs on her sweater – things like that. Or perhaps *they* thought she'd been raped. Anyway, there she was and Alec couldn't bring himself to ask her. He couldn't say the word. He's been in quite a state. He says he keeps imagining what he'd do to them if he had them tied up or something, helpless. And he feels dreadful about himself. He says it's like a waking nightmare and the worst part of it is he's such a gentle man. He's not like that at all.'

The trouble was, Kate thought, Alec had always thought of himself as a good man. That made him sound smug and horrible, which he wasn't, but he did tend to assume that in the great war of good and evil he'd always be on the right side, whereas Kate couldn't help thinking real adult life starts when you admit the other possibility. 'We're all a *bit* like that, aren't we?'

'But he's worked all his life with young criminals like those two, trying to give them a fresh start.'

'Yes,' Kate said drily. 'We fell out about it a couple of weeks ago. You remember?'

'Oh. Yes, I'd forgotten that.' An awkward pause. 'He came to see her last night.'

'Peter? What did he have to say?'

'I don't know. I'd gone home.'

Kate offered her a second cup of coffee, but she

waved it aside. 'No, better not. It just makes me jumpier than I am already. *You* must be nervous.'

'You can't spend your entire life cowering behind locked doors. If you do that, the bastards have won anyway.' She poured herself another cup, intending to take it across to the studio with her. 'Did you say Justine had gone out?'

'Yes. They've gone to the Farnes.'

'She's with Alec?'

'No. With Stephen.' Angela said grudgingly, 'I must say he's been very good.'

'He'll take care of her.'

A few minutes later Angela left and Kate walked across to the studio, pausing by the pond to look up at the misty hillside. She hoped it cleared for the crossing. So many times she and Ben had set out to go to the Farnes and nearly always at this time of year. Her heart felt full. A distinct, entirely physical sensation. *Possess, as I possessed a season, the countries I resign . . .*

They parked by the seawall and walked down to the quayside booths, where he bought the tickets.

'You know what we've forgotten to bring?' Justine said. 'Hats.'

'Why do we need hats? I don't mind getting wet.'

She smiled. 'Wait and see.'

It was a rough crossing. The waves were steely-grey with a fine mist of spray flying off them. Their hair and clothes were wet before they left the harbour, but neither wanted to go into the covered cabin, with its fug of human bodies and damp wool. The boat rocked and dipped, wallowing in the hollow of the deeper waves before rising to face the challenge of the next. All the while the black hulking cliffs, the houses and the harbour dwindled into the mist. Ahead there was as yet no sign of the Farnes, no sight of Holy Island either, though by now both should have been visible. The boat had become its own world, in which they turned to face each other, Justine's hair blown across her mouth, drops of spray clinging like grey pearls to the surface of her skin.

'Are you a good sailor?' she yelled above the noise of the engines.

He opened his mouth to reply and gagged as the next sheet of water hit him in the face. 'Not bad,' he yelled when he could speak again.

The boat stopped bumping from wave to wave as they edged into the calmer water between cliffs that rose up out of the mist on either side, grey-black walls of wet granite, streaked white with bird lime. Birds lined all the ledges, lifting off, squabbling, resettling. One of them passed over the boat so low he flinched and could have sworn he heard its wings creak. At the top of the cliffs he could see cormorants, with their serpentine necks and crested royal heads, spreading their black wings out to dry.

The boat moved smoothly on between the cliffs until they came to a landing stage. The two sailors – both very young men, fresh-faced, freckled, blue-eyed, obviously brothers, descendants of the Vikings who'd plundered and pillaged and raped all along the coast, and not, emphatically not, of the monks who'd done none of these things – leapt on to the shore, tied up the boat to the staithes and handed the passengers out. An elderly man slipped on the green-slimed stones and would have fallen if it hadn't been for the supporting hand. Gradually, in twos and threes, they streamed up the hill to the cluster of buildings at the top.

Stephen and Justine had waited for everybody else to get off, before jumping on to dry land. On either side of the path there were terns' nests on the bare earth, some with chicks, speckled like the surrounding sand and shingle, huddled against the cold. Stephen bent down to look more closely, then straightened up. Immediately, they were above him, the adult terns, white wings angled back, beaks gaping red, claws outstretched as they swooped on to his head. Somehow he didn't believe they would touch him. They'd just dive-bomb him and go past. But then he felt their claws and beaks jabbing his scalp. He put his hand up and brought his fingers away, smeared with blood. 'Christ.'

Justine was laughing. 'C'mon, let's get away from the chicks.'

They marched at a brisk pace up the hill, Stephen flailing his arms around in a vain attempt to keep off the terns.

They followed the paths around the island. He was startled to see an eider duck sitting on her eggs immediately beside the path, and all the while the terns attacked, hovering inches above his head. A small child, screaming with fear, walked past with her father holding a folded newspaper over her head. 'It's not a good idea to bring small children,' Justine said, which struck him as an understatement. And then they left the terns' nests behind, and the screeches faded into silence, to be replaced by the squabbling of kittiwakes in their tenement slums.

Gradually the mist thinned and the sun shone more strongly, though their shadows were never more than smudges on the grass. They lay on the edge of a cliff, looking down on the grey and white backs of seagulls to where, far below – he daren't think how far – the wrinkled sea fretted at the rocks. He was trying to recall a phrase from *Ulysses*, something about the snot-green, scrotum-tightening sea. Snot green, yes, but also blue, purple, grey, brackish brown, flecked here and there with white, the sleek dark heads of seals rising and falling with the waves. He rolled over and lay on his back, sucking a stem of grass. Justine was staring out to sea, not looking at him, not appearing to be aware that he existed even, and he wondered if she were back in the farmhouse, terrified and alone.

He reached out and touched her arm. She smiled, but went on looking out to sea.

She was thinking about Peter and the bloody roses. When finally she'd gone into the kitchen to look at them, she'd found half a dozen red, tightly furled blooms, each with a length of thin wire wound round the stem and through the bud itself, pinning the petals closed. No matter how much air, light, water, food you gave them, they would never open, but wither and die in the bud. She'd seen roses presented like this before, and had always disliked them, so it was irrational to associate them exclusively with Peter. But she did.

Peter's ideal woman would be a doll, she thought, a puppet that would stay in any position you put it in, without life or volition of its own.

Completely the opposite of Stephen, who was so scrupulously careful not to constrain her in any way that he sometimes gave the impression of indifference. Go, he always seemed to be saying. Any time you like. Go.

Though he was looking anxious enough at the moment.

'Come on,' she said, getting him by the hand and pulling him to his feet. 'Let's go and see the puffins.'

Kate had worked till her neck ached from holding the same position too long, but when, finally, she stopped, the thought crossed her mind that she might have finished. You couldn't always tell. There was a long period sometimes when you had to inch forward, knowing that one more unnecessary chip of the plaster could set you back three weeks.

Somehow or other she had to recover freshness of vision, to look at this as if she were seeing it for the first time. The secret was to put the critical intelligence to sleep, peel off the hard outer rind and work from the core. If she could have read a detective story, or played a game of chess, and carved simultaneously, that would have done the trick – anything to distract the top layer of the mind – but unfortunately she needed her hands.

She stepped back. It had looked like a fish at one point, on dry land, flapping, mouth open to gasp in the murderous air. Now it was more like a pupa starting to hatch, grave cloths peeling away to reveal new skin. What it didn't look like, close to at any rate, was a man.

She climbed down from the scaffold, her thighs wobbly underneath her as she reached the floor, as if she'd been on a long voyage and hadn't got her land legs back. Fearfully, she raised her head. Oh, God. Didn't look human even from here. Strong, though. She felt its strength. Christ in a nightie it was not.

She went out of the studio, breathed deeply, suffered one of her infrequent cravings for a cigarette, and walked slowly down to the pond. Branches of willow shadowed the mist. A moorhen picked her way delicately through the tall thin reeds at the water's edge and behind her three chicks, venturing out of the nest perhaps for the first time. Kate watched them, and thought of nothing, only the pleasure of seeing them.

When she turned round, Peter Wingrave was standing directly behind her. She hadn't heard him arrive, and the shock made her jump.

'I was just passing,' he said. 'I thought I'd look in and see how you were getting on.'

Time had weakened the resentment she'd felt at witnessing his parody, or whatever it was, of her working methods, his attempted invasion of her territory, and she found it perfectly possible to smile and say hello.

'Come in,' she said. 'I was just having a break.'

He followed her into the kitchen and watched as she made coffee. Inside the house, with the door closed, she remembered the burglary, but she'd never been nervous with Peter, except for that one night. And anyway she didn't for a moment suppose he was planning to bash her over the head and steal her credit cards. If he was dangerous, it was in more subtle ways than that.

'Did you hear about Justine?' he asked.

'Yes. Beth told me.'

'I went to see her last night.'

'How was she?'

'I don't know. They'd given her a sedative, she was asleep.' As he spoke, he clenched his knotted fingers, the knuckles pink, bunched together, like baby rats in a nest. 'She walked in on them, apparently.'

'Dangerous situation,' Kate said, 'cornering a burglar.'

'Yes.'

'I wonder if they'll catch them?'

'They might. Alec seemed to think so.'

There was no sound in the room except for the faint hum of the fridge. She had the feeling that whatever she wanted to know now he would tell her. Why he'd gone to prison – everything. So the only question was: did she want to know? No. She didn't want the distraction from her work. And she felt too that any emotional involvement with Peter would simply give him scope for manipulation. She tapped the edge of her cup. 'How's the gardening?'

'Busy. Always busy this time of year.'

She felt his disappointment. He'd been looking for another host.

'Oh, I had one stroke of luck – thanks to Stephen – his agent's taken me on.'

'Good.'

'He seems to be quite hopeful about placing the book.'

'That is good news.'

He was less green about the gills than he'd been a few minutes ago. Looking at him, she came to a decision.

'Would you like to see it?' She jerked her head in the direction of the studio.

'Love to.' He was already on his feet.

'I think it's finished.'

'Think?'

'I need to stand back a bit.'

They walked across to the studio, Kate remembering the last time they'd been there together and reminding herself that he didn't know she'd seen him. He stood in front of the figure for a long time, taking it in. He barely reached the top of its thighs. 'Do you mind if I move the scaffold?'

'No, go ahead.'

He pushed it away. Stood back again. 'My God.'

She smiled. 'If everybody says that, I've succeeded.'

No reply. She realized she'd sounded too flippant. It was always a problem at this point to remember the impact the finished work had on other people, because by this stage she felt nothing. Except tiredness, exasperation, the overwhelming desire to be shot of it.

She stepped right back, pretending to tidy up the tools she'd left lying on the trestle table by the door. Now that Peter was back, it felt as if he'd never left. Perhaps in a way he never had. Certainly she'd gone on thinking about him, had sensed him sometimes in the darkness between the white figures, the dark one, the shadow on the X-ray, who could never be counted no matter how often you looked. He'd insinuated himself so thoroughly into this process that she felt the figure was partly his. She hated thinking that, but inside there, buried as deep as bones in flesh, was the armature that he'd made. The carving was hers, but the shape was his.

Peter turned to her. 'He hasn't forgotten anything, has he? Betrayal, torture. Murder. And none of it matters.'

He thought it was about memory. That was interesting, but she didn't want to talk about it. She didn't even want to look at the figure with him standing there, in case his response contaminated hers.

At last he turned away.

'So what happens now?' he asked, as they walked out to his van.

'It goes to the foundry. I'll work on it a bit more after it's cast, and then it's off to the cathedral.'

'It'll leave an awfully big gap. What'll you do?'

'*Live.*'

They shook hands and she watched him walk away. Big hungry strides crunching the gravel, then the familiar cough and sputter of the engine starting up.

From all over the island now little groups of people were making their way back to the landing stage via the tourist information point at the top of the hill, where they bought postcards and film for their cameras. No experience is valid without the accompanying image, Stephen thought, though he bought a postcard of the puffins too.

Then they walked down the hill, enduring further attacks from the terns at every step of the way, and found places in the bow of the boat. The mist was rolling in again, darkening the sea, muffling sounds, like a pad soaked in chloroform pressed down suddenly over nose and mouth. They had to wait for the final passengers. By the time they arrived, breathless, apologetic, holding newspapers over their heads to shield themselves from dive-bombing terns, the mist was thicker than it had been on the journey out. As the boat cast off from the jetty and turned towards land, there was no longer the sensation of steering between high black cliffs, but instead of being alone, wrapped about with clammy white draperies of mist, on the cold, heaving, relentless sea.

At some point Stephen became aware that the two freckly Vikings who owned the boat were worried. He didn't know how many of the other passengers had noticed, but certainly something was wrong. One of the brothers was on the radio speaking to somebody on the mainland, and after he'd finished there was a muffled, earnest conversation between them. On Stephen's right were the parents of the little girl who'd been frightened by the terns. Lowering his voice so they couldn't hear, he said, 'They're in trouble.'

Justine smiled faintly and, also whispering, replied, 'Yes, I know.'

A few hundred yards further on, the ghostly chromatic cry of a black-backed gull startled them as it appeared from the sky, flashed briefly white above their heads, and vanished into the mist. A second later there was a shuddering of the whole boat and a scraping sound as its keel hit submerged rocks. Everybody looked round with startled stares, for the moment half amused rather than frightened, but then the jar and shudder came again and a sense of something being badly wrong spread round the boat. A small woman with dry chestnut hair clutched her husband's arm. A group of young men further along seemed more inclined to treat it as a joke.

'Can you swim?' he asked Justine.

Keeping her voice light, she said, 'Like a fish, but there are seven kids, and some of them probably can't.'

The water would be cold. He doubted if even a strong swimmer would last long. Oh, but it was ridiculous. People don't die on days out at the seaside, they die in wars, terrorist attacks, all the bloody stupid inane events he'd spent his life covering. He met the gaze of the little girl's father and they exchanged a flaring of eyebrows. The mother had gone very white, but the little girl prattled on, playing with a plastic pony with a purple mane. This is a wake-up call, he thought. Or a go-to-sleep call, his brain replied, indifferent. He recognized that indifference, the feeling of his life balanced like a feather on the palm of his hand. But then he looked at Justine and thought, no. Not yet.

For a third time the boat scraped across submerged rocks. The brothers made another call to land, and the boat changed direction. Five minutes later, the arm of the harbour became visible as a band of deeper grey in the all-encompassing mist. A hundred yards further on, they could see a huddle of houses, all with their lights on, as the little town gathered around its firesides and contended with the early dark.

Slowly, people started to talk. 'Sea fret,' somebody said. 'Have you noticed they've started calling it "the haar" on the telly?' A rumble of contempt. Just what a cartload of southern poofs would call it. Apparently, sea-fret was a north-east coast speciality, and now it wasn't actually threatening to kill them they were becoming fond of it again.

Once on dry land, the passengers dispersed rapidly, a group of people momentarily united by danger indifferent to each other again, strangers.

'That was a bit too eventful for my liking,' Stephen said, as they walked away from the boat.

'What, after Bosnia? I don't believe you.'

'I'm afraid of drowning.'

It was true. From childhood he'd had a horror of inchoate depths, full of things that nibble off toes and eyelids. He could even remember what had sparked the fear: the wreck of a boat near Slaughden Quay in Aldeburgh, where they'd gone for their half-term holidays. In fine weather the boat's greying wood was a familiar landmark, but, coming home from a walk one dark and stormy afternoon, he'd seen it in a different light, cold and slimy, with the river water rising remorselessly over its rotting timbers. Something about it terrified him, and he'd run all the way back to their rented cottage. How old would he have been? Seven, eight? Couldn't have been more than that.

'I could do with a drink,' Justine said. 'What about you?'

They found a hotel with a public bar and settled down with glasses of whisky over a log fire. They had the bar almost to themselves, except for a noisy crowd of golfers at the other end, who'd abandoned the attempt to play and were drinking determinedly instead. Apart from them, the hotel seemed to be empty. Stephen was glad of the noise because under cover of that boisterous and extroverted chatter he and Justine could talk casually, or not talk at all and just stare into the flames.

'You know we needn't go back,' he said after a while. He had nothing on till Friday, when he was having lunch with Kate and taking Adam to the Bird of Prey Centre after school. 'I could ask if they've got a room.'

'All right. Yes,' she said, downing the last of her whisky. 'Good idea.'

They had a double room. He checked in, then went to get their stuff from the car. Not that they had much, except coats and spare sweaters. They went up to the room together, and while the landlady chattered on, Justine sat on the bed, testing it. It was a big, old-fashioned bed with head and foot boards, creaky springs and goose-down pillows piled high.

Their windows overlooked the harbour, where a dozen or more small boats rode at anchor, their rigging producing a constant clicking and thrumming. A disturbing noise. It was the sound he'd heard when he'd found the half-submerged boat, and perhaps that was why he associated it with fear. But he was anxious – as he had not been anxious on the first night they'd spent together. Justine sat on the window-seat, looking down on the boats. Stephen rested a hand on the nape of her neck and then, afraid the gesture might feel too proprietorial, stepped back and caught the tail end of a smile on her lips.

'Do you feel hungry?' he asked.

'Not really. I think I'd like to go for a walk first.'

'OK. It's not raining?'

'No, look at the water.'

Stephen moved away. Justine turned to look at him, her eyes that sullied, bewildered blue that moved him so deeply. They stared at each other, aware of the bed waiting for them, tempted. But he didn't want to do that, he wanted there to be a long, slow careful approach. In a way, courtship, though it was an odd word to use when they'd been sleeping together for months.

They walked for miles along the beach, buffeted by the wind that blew the last vestiges of mist away. The waves roared up the sand, spread out in great arcs of foaming lace, then withdrew quietly, with a long slow dragging sigh. They played at being chased by the waves, and once, overconfident, he did get caught and splashed out with his trousers soaked to the knee. Like children, he thought, the pair of them, but with something that was not childlike there as a constant undertow, pulling them towards the moment of fulfilment in that bed. Sex was in every glance, every shout of laughter, but only once, struggling up the sand dunes to where they'd left the car, did they hold hands.

The bar was full of locals when they got back, and under cover of the noise they talked, leaning back into the high settle by the fire. The whisky winked and glinted in his glass, and the heat from the flames made his lips feel big and bloated, fish lips. Stop drinking, he told himself. Then suddenly the bar started to empty, and they were alone with each other and the fire.

Justine was feeling along her right cheekbone.

'Is it still sore?'

'Only when I press it.' She forced a smile. 'I think you're very brave, going round with me at the moment. Everybody's probably looking at you and thinking, what a bastard.'

'Bloody stupid woman, keeps walking into doors.'

But it wasn't funny. After a while she said, 'It was a steep learning curve. When Dad was letting out our flat to the Fresh Start Initiative, quite a few of the people who stayed in it were battered wives who'd finally managed to get away, sometimes after years and years of abuse, and I used to look at them and think, You're young, you're healthy, you can earn your own living, why the bloody hell did you put up with *that* for years? But as soon as it happens to you, you realize how easy it is to be cowed. The shock. It's almost like an animal, a mouse or something, playing dead.'

'Playing dead isn't a bad strategy if you're not strong enough to fight back. Physically.'

'I'm disgusted with myself.'

'You shouldn't be. You did the right things.'

'I thought I was a fighter.'

'You can't fight two great big beefy blokes.'

'But they weren't. Big beefy blokes.'

'They were stronger than *you*.'

What is it about her? he thought, as she continued to stare into the fire. Some quality in her that he didn't think he'd ever encountered before, and was almost unable to name. The word that kept coming to mind was 'gallant', an old-fashioned word even applied to men, and it had never, even in its heyday, been applied to women. And yet that was the word, or as close as he could get. 'Come on,' he said, standing up. 'Let's go to bed.'

Kate had kept herself busy all afternoon with jobs around the house, but all the while the figure went on changing inside her head. She daren't let herself think directly about it, and so ended up by splashing corrosive cleaning fluids around the inside of the oven with such abandon she was left with thin red burn lines above the rubber gloves.

Housework was much more reliably satisfying than art, she thought, wiping her hand across her forehead as she finished. Scrub these surfaces long and hard enough and you could scarcely avoid ending up with a clean kitchen. Break your neck on the risen Christ, and there's no guarantee you'll be left with anything except a broken neck.

Daren't drink. Daren't phone anybody. It would be disastrous to talk about it now and impossible not to. The answering machine clicked and whirred, but she shut the door on the voices.

Then, at the last possible moment, she went across to the studio, locking the house door carefully behind her as, only two days ago, she might not have bothered to do – and let herself into the studio.

Moonlight. A white floor. The white silent figure pinning down its own shadow. She stood in front of the plinth. The figure seemed different, though really it was her way of seeing it that had changed. Partly because of Peter. Because somebody else had seen it. The resemblance to a fish, or a pupa starting to hatch, was still there, but no longer dominated. He was a man now. All this time he'd been alone with the clouds and the moonlight and the shadows forming and dissolving on the floor, and in that time he'd become a thing apart.

There was a life here now that no longer depended on her.

For a long time they stood and stared at each other. Well, there you are. She framed the words silently in her mind, dropping each one into a deep well. Finished.

Then she bobbed her head and slipped out quickly into a night of stars and shadows.

The load fell from her shoulders as she walked across the yard and let herself into the house. Who could she tell? Nobody – it was too late to ring anybody now.

She went into the living room to find Ben, though it was not Ben, only a thing made of bronze.

Better, really, to remember him as he'd been that first weekend they spent together in Northumberland, when they went into Chillingham Church and found, around a corner, unexpectedly, Lord and Lady Grey lying together on their tomb, in a peace that five hundred years of turmoil had done nothing to disrupt. Unconsciously she felt for Ben's amulet. Two couples, one flesh and blood, one alabaster. Now only one couple left. She pressed her lips to the cold bronze of Ben's forehead and went slowly upstairs to bed.

Moonlight shining in through the uncurtained windows lit up the high white bed. The wind and tide were rising, scouring the little town as if it were a barnacle they were trying to scrape off a rock. Stephen opened the window and streams of cold air passed over his face and chest. The thrumming of rigging against the masts had become a frenzy.

'I hope we'll be able to sleep,' he said.

'Oh? I was rather hoping we wouldn't.'

She'd come out of the bathroom, naked, and was standing beside the plump bed. He started pulling off his clothes. She pulled back the bedspread and slipped between the sheets, where she lay watching him, her pupils so dilated that her eyes looked black.

In a way that sometimes happens, once or twice in a lifetime perhaps, he knew he would remember this moment till the day he died. Naked, he went across to the bed and pulled back the covers.

She said, 'Do you love me?'

'Yes.'

'Good. I love you.'

He climbed in beside her and for a moment they said and did nothing, lying side by side, fingers intertwined. The moonlight found the whites of her eyes. For a moment he saw the girl in the stairwell in Sarajevo, but she'd lost her power. This moment in this bed banished her, not for ever, perhaps, but for long enough. He rolled over and took Justine in his arms.

Twenty-eight

It seemed a shame to wake her, so he slid out of bed in the grey dawn light, found the clothes he'd scattered over the floor last night in his haste to get them off and crept with them into the bathroom. He dressed, then tiptoed out of the room.

Downstairs there was a smell of bacon frying. The relentless hotel trade which dictates that the working day should end after midnight and start again before dawn. Mouth filling with saliva, he crossed the bar, which was full of the smells of cigarette smoke and stale beer. Even the red plush banquettes seemed to exhale a stale sat-upon smell, as if still warm from last night's backsides.

He was afraid he might find the door locked and have to ask somebody to come from the kitchen to let him out, but no, it was open. He stepped out into the chilly dawn air and stood staring up and down the street. Deserted – until a trolley with chinking milk bottles came into sight further up the hill and stopped long enough for the girl driver, muffled up against the chill, to get down and deliver several bottles. He turned his collar up and set off in the opposite direction.

As he came out from between the houses, he saw the sea. He started to walk on the beach in deep fine, unpolluted sand, until he came to a row of 'dragons' teeth': gigantic blocks of concrete scattered along the edge of the dunes in a rough line like a child's bricks. Tank traps – the detritus of the last war. They were covered with graffiti: NFC RULES, SUNDERLAND ARE WANKERS. Ben would have loved them. They reminded Stephen a little of his last photograph: the abandoned Russian armoured cars in Afghanistan, filling almost the whole frame. No room for anything else except a strip of sky and that small, white, moribund sun.

A minute after he took that photograph he was dead.

Stephen had been travelling in a convoy behind him. They were flagged down, warned not to go any further. Ahead, in a gulley by the side of the road, was what looked like a heap of rugs. He'd known before he was told that it was Ben. Nobody could be sure that he was dead, only that he'd been seen lying in a bomb crater by the side of the road. Stephen had known with absolute certainty that he wouldn't be able to live with himself if he didn't go to find out. Ben might be wounded or unconscious: it was just barely possible that he could be saved.

And so he ran, bent double – as if that would have made the slightest difference – to the armoured car. He told himself to go back, and went on running. He ran round the side of the vehicle, saw nothing, and then, at the bottom of the pocked and scarred hole, he saw him, lying on his back, his camera only a few feet away.

Stephen dislodged stones and pebbles as he scrambled

down the slope, briefly hopeful because Ben looked untouched. But he didn't stir. His open eyes stared into the white sun without wincing. There was an ants' trail of blood coming down from the left temple. He looked surprised. Stephen expected to be shot himself at any moment – obviously a sniper had the road covered. His teeth were chattering. Oh, so they do that, he thought, calm enough, shocked enough, to be interested. He started to unfasten the chain from round Ben's neck, but his hands were shaking too much, so he caught a loop of it between his fingers and wrenched it off. The catch had lasted longer than his luck. Then the camera. He must have come down here to take a photograph, lining up his camera for the shot, while somewhere out of sight another man lined up his gun. Nothing here but stones and rocks. But then Stephen looked up and saw them, the wrecked tanks. He'd been driven past them twenty times perhaps, but he hadn't spotted what Ben saw. From the bottom of the crater they looked like a wave breaking. A sun so white it might have been the moon hung in the sky behind them. All the time, he was talking to Ben, saying, 'You fucking idiot. You stupid, fucking fool. Your life – *for that?*'

Clutching the camera to his chest, he turned and ran back, his boots loud on the gritty road, expecting at any moment that final explosion of pain in head or chest, but he reached the armoured car intact. Somebody tried to speak to him, but he pushed them aside. He was shaking with rage and grief. He wanted to huddle down somewhere private and cry, but when he got into the backseat and turned his face away the tears wouldn't come. He felt totally dry – no spit, no sweat, no tears. Like one of those trussed up, desiccated bundles you see in a spider's web.

He still hadn't cried for Ben. Missed the funeral. Hadn't managed to squeeze out a single tear. But at least Kate had the amulet. That mattered. And he'd brought the last photographs back.

He walked down to the sea – calm today, creaming over on the sand, each wave withdrawing with a small rasping sound, like a tiger's purr. Here the sand was partly shingle. He started searching about, looking for flat pebbles to skim, and had found five or six really good ones, when he heard a shout and turned to see Justine coming down the dunes towards him. Her hand went up and felt the padding round her nose, then to her scalp to check that the two barbed-wire fences were in place. Last night had been extraordinary – the sex passionate and yet interspersed with tender, almost sexless kisses. He had been so afraid of hurting her.

She came straight into his arms and kissed him.

'Can you do that on the sea?' she said, looking at the stones. 'I thought it had to be calm water.'

'It is calm. Look at it.'

She started searching for her own pebbles. Instant competition. That's my girl.

'No, too big. Here, have this,' he said, giving her his best one.

They were intent, childlike, silly, innocent, though it

306

was sex that had brought them to this state. His back hurt. Justine's lips, breasts, thighs burned from contact with his chin.

She threw the first pebble. 'Two.'

'One and a bit.'

'You're a hard man, mister.'

He threw his first pebble, which sank, ignominiously, with a detumescent plop. Justine started giggling. 'Just you wait.'

This time he got the flick of his wrist exactly right. He knew, before the stone left his hand, that this one would walk, miraculously, across the water, each point of contact setting off concentric rings that would meet and overlap, creating little eddies of turbulence, but always, always spreading out, so that the ripples reached the shore, before, finally, it sank.

'There,' he said. 'You see?'

Then he put his arm around her shoulders and they walked on, half in the water, half on land, while behind them the sun rose above the dunes, casting fine blue shadows of marram grass on to the white sand.

Author's Note

My thanks go to Neil Darbyshire of the *Daily Telegraph* for enabling me to attend the opening of the Milosevic trial at the International Criminal Tribunal for the former Yugoslavia at The Hague, and to Neil Tweedie, foreign correspondent of the *Daily Telegraph*, for helping to make my visit a pleasant experience.

I am grateful to Gillon Aitken and everybody at Gillon Aitken Associates for their continuing support, and to Simon Prosser and everybody at Hamish Hamilton for their enthusiastic publishing.

A special acknowledgement must go to Donna Poppy: the most tactful, conscientious and meticulous of editors.

No words can express what I owe to my husband.

Among the books I found thought-provoking and useful in the writing of this novel are Martin Bell's *In Harm's Way*, Julia Blackburn's *Old Man Goya*, Fergal Keane's *Season of Blood*, Don McCullin's *Unreasonable Behaviour*, John Simpson's *Strange Places, Questionable People*, Susan Sontag's *Regarding the Pain of Others* and Janis Tomlinson's *Goya*.

The mistakes and shortcomings are, as always, mine.